THE CAGE FIGHTER

PAUL GREENBAUM

Book layout by www.ebooklaunch.com

ONE

It was a night of mixed martial arts. Morales and I were the featured bout. Coach banged on the door and poked his head into the dressing room: my boxing trainer, Tom Kelly, who went by the strange nickname of Phantom.

"You got about five minutes. Ready?"

I nodded. He left.

I went to the urinal for the third time in fifteen minutes and squeezed out the last drop. Again, *bam-bam-bam* on the steel door. This time Coach came in.

"It's time, Lazio. Let's go."

I walked down the aisle into the noisy auditorium like a gladiator entering the Coliseum.

It doesn't change. A man takes stock of himself each and every time he walks toward a one-on-one battle with an unpredictable outcome. Some nervousness is good. *Keeps me sharp. Even the gladiators must have been nervous.*

The disheveled crowd milled about, thousands crowded into an old stadium rented for this bout. All sorts were in the audience: other fighters checking out the competition, out-of-shape men and their women at the food stands, a scraggle of twittering teenagers. In the front row, erect as a young tree, my karate teacher Sensei Miamoto Omura and his wife and daughter.

It was an honor to have my teacher there. Many of the traditional karate masters didn't approve of these fights, yet Sensei, one of the finest instructors in New York, had come to all of mine like a father attending his son's school plays. As I stepped into the caged fighting arena, I bowed low from the waist. Sensei returned the bow—barely a nod, as was customary.

Morales was already in the cage. We stood on opposite ends, a good distance apart. He caught my eye and sent me a slight nod.

Some call it clairvoyance, but Sensei taught that every man possesses another, subtler set of senses: inner eyes, ears, smell, and touch that make it possible to read a situation before it happens. He encouraged us to feel a room before we opened the door, to smell danger before we walked unthinking into it. In a fight these senses enable you to feel your opponent, to read a man's spirit.

Coach, also acting as corner man, stood next to me massaging my shoulders.

"You gotta fight your fight, just like we practiced. You can take him, Johnny."

The announcer shouted in the artificially hyped voice universally adopted at fights and circuses.

"Ladies and gentlemen, the main event of the evening, sanctioned by the New Jersey athletic commission—a lightweight bout!" A sweeping gesture to me. "JOHNNY LAZIO ... is currently undefeated. This mixed martial artist's professional career has twelve wins, no losses, and no draws." He waited for the loud applause to die down. "ANTONIO MORALES ... is also undefeated with twelve wins, no losses, and one draw." More big applause. *Neither of us appears to be the favorite.* "Of these undefeated warriors, who will go home the winner?"

To prepare for this moment, Phantom and I had immersed ourselves in Morales's career. We'd sat in the audience for most of his fights, gone over each of the videos in slow motion. The guy was fluid, his reflexes uncanny, fists too fast to see, and his blows came from who-knows-where. He'd take you out with either hand, and the only words that fit the way he was in the ring were ones like *ruthless* and *brutal.* All but a couple of his fights had ended by knockout. My record was similar. I'd never been badly hurt or even knocked down. The media had touted this bout as the toughest test of our respective careers.

Phantom, primarily a boxing coach but savvy enough to coach any style of fighting, said Morales was the superior boxer. In grappling and submissions we were equally matched. We both weighed 156 pounds.

At five eleven, Morales was taller, thinner, more graceful, and had a four-inch advantage in reach. I was five seven with thickly muscled chest, shoulders, and arms, less well-proportioned. My spindly legs didn't match my upper body, but I could whip them with blinding speed. Most of my knockouts were from kicks and the crowd loved it.

As the referee motioned us to the center of the cage, Coach slapped me hard on the back of the head and made the sign of the cross.

"Go to work, son."

We stood inches from each other, toe to toe. Morales's dark eyes were calm as he touched his gloves to mine.

"Good to see you, Johnny. Best of luck tonight." He nodded again in a slight bow, his eyes smiling. I tipped my head.

What you see on television can't compare to looking into a man's eyes, smelling his breath, and feeling his energy. Staring into each other's eyes may not seem like much, but the eyes can intimidate, strike fear, and activate deep unconscious doubt. Once a fighter is psyched, he's beat before the first punch is thrown.

Each fighter finds his own way in this ritual. I didn't bore my eyes into an opponent like a crazy man, but I'd been told that my gentle, no-nonsense approach was more disarming than the snarling face and evil eye. I smiled and briefly scanned Morales. He smiled and bowed politely for the third time, his white teeth brilliant against his smooth, dark skin. *He's confident!*

The referee looked both of us in the eyes.

"Men, you will obey my commands at all times. I want to see a clean fight. Are you ready?"

We both nodded.

"Okay, fight!"

Morales threw three hard lefts followed by a right. I backpedaled just out of reach and sprang in with a single jab that tagged him square on the point of the chin. It wasn't a hard punch but perfectly timed: it caught him just as he was coming in. His legs buckled slightly and he stumbled back. In a fight, confidence can be as fickle as a spring day, and his flew from his face like a cat that slips while walking on a fence.

I pushed off the ball of my right foot and shot the heel of my left foot into his ribs. It knocked him back against the fence of his own corner.

I moved in with a quick combination to the body. He lowered his hands to defend. *There it is.* Kicking fast and high with my right leg, I landed a hard blow. It was nearly perfect, except Morales managed to get his arm up to block. The kick, however, was powerful enough that the force transferred right through his glove into the side of his neck. He buckled and hit the canvas like a felled tree. I could feel the thunder of the astonished crowd vibrate through my feet as I jumped on top into full mount and started raining down punches, trying to finish. Morales blocked my right and underhooked my arm. In less than a split second, he bridged up forcefully, shrimped out, and placed his right leg under my left in a single butterfly hook. He elevated me with his leg and flipped me with a beautiful sweep. During the tumble I wrapped both my legs around him in closed guard, but he exploded out and jerked to his feet. Still dazed, he touched his neck where the kick had landed and muttered under his breath. He flashed his gleaming teeth and danced around a little, nodding his head in appreciation.

"Excellent, Johnny, excellent!"

I smiled. Fighters often do this when hurt: he was trying to cover up that he was badly shaken. A split second quicker and the fight would have been over in the first round.

My friend, I'd have gone home without being touched.

The ref pointed at us: "Fight!"

Morales pranced around seriously, carefully, tried to jab and dart. I shot a straight kick to his gut, which he partially deflected with his arms. He clinched, trying to bide some time to clear his head. I pushed him away, but with great effort he grabbed my leg and bulled me down to the canvas. I immediately snaked my arm under his chin and connected my hands around his throat. The guillotine, one of his— and my—favorite moves. It's a windpipe choke and the pressure it puts on the neck is awesome. A man can't last more than a few seconds if this hold is applied securely. I've ended many a fight with the guillotine-style chokehold, but I didn't have a good enough position with my legs. Morales pulled his head out of my grip and stood up.

Damn! Morales is a beast on the ground. I can't keep him down!

I stayed outside his punching range and fired round kicks to the back of his leg. Every time he moved, there was my right foot attacking his left leg—powerful kicks that made the muscles spasm, crippled the nerves, and sapped his strength. It almost seems like cheating to attack the legs, but it's absolutely fair in these bouts. If you can take the sap out of a man's legs, you've got him. Those sitting in front groaned every time my leg struck home. You could hear it landing with a thudding slap, flesh striking sharply against flesh, with the weight of the bone behind it. No fighter could stand this for long, and the pain I saw in Antonio's eyes was so bad I could almost feel it.

I had him entrained into my movement, a trick of the game: get a man used to a certain pattern, and when he thinks it's coming do something different. Just when Morales expected a round kick to his leg, I fired a straight kick to the stomach, spun around, and nailed him with a brutal back kick. Before he could recover, I hit him with a left and a hard right that twisted his head. He crumpled into the fence.

Now he was in trouble. Briefly I saw Sensei's face, smiling and nodding. I charged in, hit Morales with a straight left and missed with the right. I twisted my body and put my full weight into a left hook that sent his mouthpiece careening across the stained canvas like a leaf jerked off a tree in a wind gust. Morales hit the canvas hard, hurt bad. I briefly hesitated, hovering over him. This wasn't right. Why wasn't the ref stopping it? His upkick slammed into the point of my chin. An electric shock went through my brain. The ring got blurry, and everything turned upside down.

Morales jumped shakily to his feet. He sensed I was in real peril. Strength surged quickly into his body, his eyes instantly focused. He hit me twice with his left and followed with a hard right. I would have gone down had I not overhooked his arm and tucked my head into his shoulder, trying to buy a few precious seconds to clear my head. Mercifully, the horn sounded and I stumbled to my chair. Coach guided me as I sat down heavily. An ice bag plopped down on the back of my head and water splashed on my face. He opened a bottle under my nose.

"Don't talk," he said. "Take some deep breaths." Phantom was massaging the muscles of my upper back and neck, up high near the brainstem. "You gotta keep away from him until your head clears. Johnny! Just stay away from him!" All I heard was the fear in his voice.

The horn sounded. I danced around and threw a few tentative jabs. Morales brushed them aside and pressed forward like a tank. A wicked left sent me into my own corner, right where the Omura family was sitting; I caught a quick glimpse of Sensei's face: unbelievably intense, a mixture of disbelief and embarrassment. My back was against the cage. I covered up and managed to slip and duck a few punches out of instinct. I didn't see the straight right that smashed my nose, shattering the cartilage with a sickening crunch. A flare of bright light erupted in my head.

I hit the canvas heavily, fought to get up, and lifted my head slightly. Morales dropped his weight and hit me on the ground, with a powerful blow again to my nose that smashed the back of my head into the canvas. The ref got between us, stopped Morales from hitting me again. My senses failed like the final fizzling of a light bulb.

• • •

I woke in bed, my muscles clenched, drenched with sweat. Coach was by my side. His hat was in his hands, which were crunching it up.

"Johnny! You okay?"

"I think so, where am I?

"Hospital."

"What happened?"

"You remember anything?"

"Not much."

"After you passed out, you lay like a dead man except the muscles of your legs were twitching. The doctor came into the ring, three minutes later you're still out. The doctor did the right thing, he called the ambulance. I followed it here."

"How long have I been out?"

"Almost an hour."

To be rendered unconscious by being struck in the face by a man's fist is, in itself, dangerous. The brain is jolted, moves unnaturally quickly in its cerebral-spinal soup. Little tears disturb the delicate vessels. But to be knocked unconscious for an hour is extraordinarily dangerous—and rare.

"An *hour?* No!"

Coach nodded.

The nurse came in. "How are you feeling, young man?"

"My head's felt better, but I think I'm all right."

"Can you tell me your name?"

"John Lazio."

"Do you know where you are?"

"Hospital."

"What day is it?"

I hesitated. "Saturday night or Sunday morning. That would make it either September twenty-eighth or twenty-ninth."

"It's early Sunday morning," the nurse said. "You have a fairly serious concussion, and your nose has been badly fractured. We're going to keep you as a guest to make sure there isn't any cerebral hemorrhaging. If all's well, you can go home tomorrow."

The nurse left. I was quiet for a few minutes.

Finally I said, "I blew it, Coach."

"You lost. Sooner or later every fighter loses."

"Not me. Not to Morales."

"You had him."

"Almost doesn't count."

Coach looked at the floor. "Well, Lazio, since you're up and around I'd better get going. Take a good long rest and when you're feeling up to it, I'll see you in the gym, okay?"

"Yeah, I'll see you. Thanks for all your help and thanks for coming to see me."

I didn't watch him walk out of the room. I closed my eyes and leaned heavily back on the bed. *Everyone loses, sure, sure they do. Everyone has a bad night.* I could say it a hundred times, but the pit of my stomach didn't buy it. I put the covers over my head and turned out the light.

TWO

At eight the next morning I woke feeling like a truck had hit me. I rubbed my eyes, groaned, and mumbled a few curses before looking up to see Evangeline, Sensei's daughter, sitting in the chair smiling big and shaking her head.

"You look like refried shit."

"Thanks. What are you doing here, Lena?"

"Watching you sleep."

"How long have you been watching?"

"About an hour."

"Why didn't you wake me?"

"Did you know you snore?"

"With a busted nose what do you expect? Is Sensei here?"

"What crack's your head been stuck in? Of course he's not here."

On the surface, to other people, Lena was a polite, reserved Japanese girl who'd never say anything like that to her parents. I tried for a wry smile.

"After the fight he was in a perfect rage. He stormed out of the building and we practically had to run to keep up with him. He drove home without a word and went straight to his study."

I expected as much.

• • •

Less than seventy-two hours ago I'd been riding the high road of my life.

I'd knocked at the door of my karate teacher's home. Lena let me in.

Sensei knew the sound of my walk. Before my knuckles touched the door of his study, he called for me to come in. He always faced the door, so as I entered, I came directly into his presence. His aura so powerful I could feel it even though he was kneeling on an Oriental rug in front of a low table made of dark, lacquered wood. The only other furniture offsetting the stark walls was a small bookshelf. I tipped my head in a low bow. Sensei nodded.

Though I had seen him nearly every day for the last twelve years, the sight of my teacher never failed to impress me. Sensei was sixty-two, small and slender, at first glance not at all imposing. Yet if you noted the erectness of his bearing and the thick cords of muscle on his neck, you could sense the dynamic power of an athlete at rest. If your eyes happened upon the first two knuckles of his hands—five times the size of normal knuckles and perfectly rounded like a ball-peen hammer—you might suspect something extraordinary. Such weapons had been forged through many years of breaking wood and bricks. A direct look into his black eyes was startling. They were the fathomless eyes of a tiger, a tiger that could rip off your head if he had the mind.

With a slight movement of his head, Sensei motioned for me to sit. I knelt on the floor next to him. On the low table was a glass of rice wine. When Asian people say "wine," it's likely to be ninety-eight proof and take the finish off anything it spills on. It was Sensei's habit to drink a single glass before dinner. Also on the table was an old Japanese book, opened. I glanced at the yellowed pages. A tiny, wizened man dressed in an immaculate white gi and black belt stared back. He sat in a chair, some two dozen students behind him.

Sensei cleared his throat. "As you know, this is my father. He taught me karate." I nodded. I'd heard about his father many times, and a large portrait of him hung prominently on one of the dojo's walls.

"I would like to have met him," I said.

"Don't be so sure," Sensei said with a slight frown. "He was a hard man, a difficult teacher. But he was a great martial artist. In his day he defeated many men in combat."

He turned the pages back to another picture: an even smaller, severe-looking man with the absolute no-nonsense bearing of a warrior. His black belt was so worn it was just a string of dirty threads like a weathered clothesline.

"My grandfather was my father's teacher."

Again I nodded.

"It was my honor that Grandfather taught me when I was young." Sensei smiled as if remembering something not entirely pleasant. "In his life Grandfather was never defeated in combat."

I knew both their stories well. Sensei had repeated them many times, and Grandfather's picture hung right next to his father's.

Sensei sighed. "In Japan fighters didn't brag about how good they were. Our matches were never for sport or money. We fought for the honor of karate, we fought for the honor of our school and our lineage."

Lena knocked quietly at the door, then placed dishes of fish and vegetables and a pot of white rice on the low table, bowed, and went out into the hall. But just before the door closed, she looked at me and stuck her finger down her throat. I did my part and swallowed a smile. When Sensei wasn't looking she'd often swing her hips and walk like a model. I wasn't sure if she was trying to make me laugh—it was hard not to—or show rebellion.

Sensei, who spent much of his time here meditating or reading, usually dined alone. We ate in silence, fully focused on the act of eating. Lena returned to remove the dishes and wipe the table, giving me an exaggerated wink. Sensei, seemingly oblivious to it all, picked up the book, still open to the picture of his grandfather. He tapped it three times with his forefinger.

"My family comes from a long line of Samurai warriors."

I nodded. He'd said that, too, many times, but the words seemed charged with emotion. Whatever he felt was hidden behind his stoic black eyes.

"You know I have no son. My only child is Evangeline."

"Lena's a great kid."

"Yes, but she is a woman, so I have not taught her karate. She cannot continue the lineage. But you, John? When we first met you were a child. Now you are my top student. You are ... like a son. I know you will bring honor to the family Saturday evening."

To say I was his top student was an unbelievable honor, but to imply I was part of Sensei's family was an honor so great it can't be adequately explained. Nor had it been given to any of the other students in the dojo, although there were many who'd put in more years.

"I'll do my very best, Sensei."

"It makes me cringe when you Americans say that. Trying your best is a loser's excuse. To a warrior there are no silver medals."

There was no way to face Sensei now. I couldn't even bring myself to call.

• • •

Lena said her goodbyes when the doctor came to examine me. Soon afterward the nurse kicked me out with instructions to rest and relax.

"It's not simply a broken nose," she said. "Your sinus has been damaged, the entire bony structure of your face has to mend." Working out, climbing into a ring—even to spar—was strictly forbidden for at least six weeks.

On the drive home I adjusted the rearview mirror to survey the damage. *Refried shit?* Lena wasn't joking. A bandage covered a small but deep cut on the bridge of my nose that had been closed with six stitches. A patch of dried blood showed through the gauze. I gingerly touched my nose. Not only was it hideously swollen but it felt like hot, raw mush, and I found it difficult to breathe through the nostrils. Add two huge black eyes, and I looked more or less like a grotesque raccoon.

I pushed back the mirror and sighed. So much time, energy, and hype had been put out. Not only by me but also Coach, Sensei, and others—and in six minutes it was finished, over, with nothing to show for it but a busted face. I'd spent countless hours working with my team and at the boxing gym, countless more thinking and planning the outcome. Now there was a vacuum, a gaping hole. I didn't know what to do with myself.

Coach sent me the DVD of the fight. I saw it right away. It was like he said: I'd had him beat but made one fatal mistake. For the briefest instant my concentration had lapsed, I hesitated, and in a fight, that's all it takes. For the ten thousandth time I asked myself why. *Why didn't I finish him when I had the chance?* Actually, I'd had two chances. When I knocked Morales down the first time, I could have jumped on top and hit him on the ground before the ref stepped in. *I blew it twice!* It was sickening to see myself smashed in the face, falling to the canvas. People stood around gawking while my legs twitched like a dog running in a dream. When the doctor came into the ring someone switched off the camera.

I became morbidly obsessed with watching the fight. I viewed it at least two hundred times, spent hours watching it in slow motion and freezing the action at certain spots. I watched like a detective, carefully looking for a clue as to why I'd made such a blunder. But there were no external clues. The "why" was inside me.

I tried to work out but quickly found the nurse had cautioned me for good reason. Even the slightest exertion gave me terrible headaches. About all I could handle were gentle walks through my neighborhood. The fall weather was perfect: cool nights and warm days. But the turning leaves, gold and red against the clear open sky, made little impression in my misery.

In mid-November I showed up at the boxing gym eager to get going. I shadowboxed and hit the heavy bag for a few rounds while Coach glanced over my shoulder. When it came time for sparring, he shook his head.

"You're not ready. It's too soon."

"The doctor said I could work out after six weeks."

"I don't care what the doctor said. You need to calm down, let yourself heal. Why don't you take a vacation or something, go somewhere with your girlfriend?"

"I don't have a girlfriend and I don't want to rest. If I'm going to be champ I've got to get back in the saddle. Why the hell—"

"We'll start training when you get your head straight."

"What kind of answer is that? Never heard a coach tell a fighter *not* to train."

He shot me a look, started to say something, then shook his head slightly as if deciding against it.

"To be champion, you're gonna need more than just training."

Phantom sometimes got like this, threw up a wall that wasn't going to budge. I shrugged my shoulders and walked out.

It was funny calling a guy his age Phantom. It sounded like a name from a comic book. But Tom "The Phantom" Kelly was the name he went by as a fighter, and he still liked it. Story goes he earned that name. He'd sneak like smoke under his opponent's guard, nail him quick, and slip out without being hit. Phantom trained me without charge—he loved boxing and wanted to keep his hand in— but I paid him what a good coach is worth, slipped him an envelope filled with cash after every fight. He was sixty-something, Irish, white-haired, short, and solid. He carried forty extra pounds, most of it in the belly. You could smell last night's alcohol on his breath and coming out in the sweat that made huge wet spots under his armpits. But he was one of the best coaches in the business and still had knockout power in both hands. Mostly, I trusted his judgment and experience.

Sensei was pissed and Phantom had given me a mandatory hiatus. That was okay. I didn't need a dojo or gym to practice, or even a teacher. I still had my team, a group of about twenty mixed martial artists. Several were world-class contenders, and all of them were seasoned fighters. We met as often as five times a week. It was a gathering of hard-core fanatics: all of these guys were crazy, and we'd push each other to the absolute limit. If we survived the level of training we put ourselves through we'd likely fare well in the cage.

My whole team had been at the fight, I hadn't seen them since. As I walked through the doors of the gym, they greeted me like I was a long-lost brother. Then we got right down to business. First we went through an hour of stand-up fighting, one man against the other, all weight classes, without resting. Next came groundwork: wrestling and Brazilian Jiu Jitsu, usually the most grueling part of all. I paired with Will Johnson, the youngest and least experienced member of our team. He had yet to fight his first professional bout.

We started standing, as we would in a real fight. I threw a high left round kick and feigned a straight right. With his guard focused high, I charged in for a single leg takedown. He was ridiculously wide open so I grabbed both legs, picked him up, and dumped him hard. Will got his legs around my waist in a closed guard. In a flash he pulled my right arm straight, shot his legs over my head, and used his hips as a fulcrum underneath my elbow joint. He had me in a wicked arm bar. I quickly pulled out my arm and he switched into the triangle choke. For thirty seconds we barely moved. If it were a real fight the ref might have stood us up. Fans prefer to see continuous action. But a lot of Jiu Jitsu players get pissed off when the ref prematurely stops the groundwork. In these seeming stalemates is the real fight, where the heart of the fighter emerges. During our team practices we rarely separated the fighters. We let it go, sometimes long after the five-minute time was up.

Will slowly inched his body forward until he had positioned himself precisely where he wanted. He cinched the triangle tighter by pulling his hamstring against my carotid artery, which cut off the blood to my brain. A fraction more and he would put me to sleep. The urge to submit welled up; I was on the verge of tapping out but tried to relax. It seems almost impossible to fight and relax at the same time, but tension was my most dangerous enemy. I needed to let go, at least inwardly. We strained against each other for what seemed like eternity. And then, for just an instant, his strength faltered, he couldn't keep the pressure. As he tried to readjust his legs, I managed to "posture up": muscle my head out of his grip and roll out.

"Yeah!" someone said. "You almost put the hurt on the big man himself!"

It was more a shot at me than a compliment to Will.

An undefeated fighter possesses an aura like the sun: you can feel it wherever you go. But lose and the glow fades fast. You're tarnished. I wasn't the big anything anymore, just another contender. There's more psychology in winning than anyone who's not a fighter realizes. It's more than self-confidence. It's also the other man's confidence. Losing changes what's possible. Soon after the first man broke the four-minute mile—once believed unattainable—many were able to do it. Once a man's lost, it's easier for him to lose again, simply because others know he can.

Even worse, so does he.

THREE

The next morning I woke determined to get back in the groove and forced myself through the routine I'd practiced for over a decade: an hour of meditation, an hour of yoga, then tai chi. Only after that would I take breakfast: a strong cup of espresso with lots of cream, no sugar, a large glass of freshly squeezed carrot juice, and an English muffin. Following a short rest, I exercised intensely much of the day. In the evening I practiced with the team. Still, I found it hard to get motivated.

I didn't feel right. I had no inkling what depressed was any more than I knew what it was to be a cripple, but icy fingers gripped my normally carefree life. Phantom had said it was going to take more than just working out. And there's the saying that insanity is repeating the same thing over and over and expecting a different result—more like stupidity. *But that's exactly what I'm doing.* There was something deep inside that needed attention, but I didn't know what it was and I sure didn't have the tools to make it right. Intense workouts and meditation were all I knew. Up till now they'd worked just fine.

• • •

Sensei believed each individual seeks his or her own nirvana. To a monk enlightenment is peace, compassion, and equanimity. A businessman's enlightenment is the clarity with which he runs his business and his acumen in attaining wealth. A martial artist's development is mirrored not only in the way he lives his life but especially in the way he fights. Karate, Sensei said, hasn't evolved much from the old days. A thousand years ago you had to be skilled or else you'd have ended quickly in a puddle of blood. It was only *after* it was no longer necessary to wear a sword on your hip that the fighting arts began to emphasize humility, compassion, and wisdom. Yet despite the more recent path of self-development, the mind of the martial artist was still measured by his combat skills. The bottom line: if a man wishes to call himself a martial artist, how good is he with his hands?

Sensei was in a league of his own. He never used force against force; he believed force to be the lowest level of skill. When he fought he stood relaxed, seemingly in a trance. He moved spontaneously, as if by magic, to find his opponent's weakest spot. As a teenager I was certain he was a sort of wizard. I'd seen him fight many challengers. Never once was he bested.

Like that time in Chinatown, at what was supposed to be a dinner promoting the *brotherhood* of karate. A good half-dozen schools, over a hundred people, were sitting down to lunch in a huge restaurant. A younger, larger Japanese man came over to our table, the master of another school. "I've heard that your karate is the best, Omura Sensei," he said softly. "Perhaps someday you will honor me with a lesson?" Sensei's eyes got very bright. Next thing I knew, the tables were being pushed aside. The two men were in the center while the rest of us stood watching. Sensei moved so quickly I didn't see what happened. It seemed that he barely touched him, but the other master fell to the ground gasping like a stuck fish. The fight lasted about five seconds. Later I asked in awe: "How do you learn to fight like that?"

"Karate seeks the same spontaneity as the Zen masters. To find it you must stop the movement of the mind. The moment you think, you get hit. When a master fights he doesn't think of losing face, of being defeated, not even of death. He has no expectation. There is *nothing* to impede free movement. In karate we call this *no mind*."

Barely breathing, my entire being focused on his every word, I asked: "How can I find it?"

Sensei looked at me, practically bursting out of my skin, and chuckled softly.

"Not like that! Don't hunger for a goal—begin the practice for its own sake. Learn to be still inside. Quiet your mind and sit in absolute silence."

What he said about goals made little impression. There and then I vowed to attain no mind, even if I had to practice eight hours a day and sit in meditation until my legs went numb and useless—for the rest of my life, if that's what it took.

• • •

Standing in line at the local market, I was completely absorbed. A sharp punch on the shoulder startled me. I quickly raised my hands and eyes—Len Takuchi! Embarrassed I'd been caught so off guard, I smiled and nodded my head in a slight bow. The first man to earn a black belt from Sensei over thirty years ago in Japan, Len had moved his family to America to help him set up our school. Len was Sensei's senior instructor and next to Sensei himself had been the most influential in my training.

"You had him, Johnny, what the heck happened?"

"Anything can happen in a fight."

Len's eyes narrowed. "*Really?*"

I kept silent. It would be disrespectful to argue or answer back.

Len waited until I'd mastered my reaction, then said, "What're you doing tonight?"

I motioned to my groceries. "Making dinner. Why?"

"Every once in a while I go to a little place downtown. There's a young lady I see." Len was married and had three boys, the eldest only two years younger than me.

"What young lady—what are you talking about?"

He looked at me like I was an idiot.

"I'm talking about getting laid. The girls are clean and young. Listen, John, clearing your head will be good for you."

I couldn't dispute the necessity of clearing my head.

"Every karate master knows you can't think straight when your pipes are blocked! Come on, you'll have the time of your life."

• • •

We drove to Chinatown, left the car in a parking garage, and walked down Canal Street. Len stopped, motioned with his eyes, and opened a heavy steel door. We climbed three flights of stairs and entered through an equally heavy steel door at the top of the stairs. The walls of the waiting room were pastel rose with gold trim. Cracked old leather chairs sat on polished hardwood floors, offset by an inexpensive Oriental rug. Someone here loved to grow things: a variety of plants were thriving. The overall effect was tasteful if low-grade luxury. A few middle-aged men were reading newspapers.

A short, thickset Chinese woman in her sixties sat at a desk facing the door. Her complexion was an unhealthy yellow, and the skin around her mouth and eyes had little wrinkles that, underneath her makeup, looked like cracks in old china. Her hair was a uniform jet black, probably dyed. There was an unmistakable strength in her face, and though she hid it well there was also anguish and trepidation in her sharp, streetwise eyes. Apparently she knew Len well. She beamed at him, got to her feet, and bowed slightly.

"Miss Sugi will be right with you, sir."

Within seconds a stunningly beautiful Japanese woman in her early twenties appeared, wrapped her arm around Len's, and led him into the interior of Asia House. As they disappeared through the red curtains he turned and winked. I stood there with my jaw hanging. The mama-san closely watched my face; then she smiled.

"Who do you want to see?"

"I don't know."

She spoke into a small microphone. "Miss Kim—gentleman waiting."

In seconds, a heavily made-up, slightly overweight Korean woman in her late thirties came out to meet me. Miss Kim took my arm, then led me through the red curtains and into a luxuriously tiled bathroom.

"Take off clothes." She pointed to a locker.

I took them off and pushed them into the locker without folding them. I looked at Kim. She smiled and gave me a tiny silver key with an elastic band, like the ones you get in a health club.

"First we take shower."

"We?"

She giggled. "Yes, I wash back for you."

Kim washed my back with a long-handled brush, eyeing my physique as she scrubbed.

"You very strong man," she said.

"Thanks."

"What happen to your nose?"

"Don't ask."

"Okay, honey, does the brush feel good?"

I nodded. It did feel good. No one had scrubbed my back since I was a child. It had been so long I couldn't even remember the sensation—and she cleaned more than just my back. It was a surprise but made good sense. Who could blame her for wanting to make sure the customer was clean?

"You want Jacuzzi or sauna?"

I began with the whirlpool then opted for the sauna as well.

"Don't stay in too long," she said. "Too much heat make you tired. But you are young." This she added with a suggestive raise of her eyebrows. "Nothing make you tired, huh?"

The sweat dripped from my legs and onto the floor of the sauna. Kim didn't attract me. At twenty-seven I considered her an old lady. *She'll do for the night.* The sweat beaded on my arms and forehead. I sighed heavily. We were raised Catholic. Although religion wasn't a huge part of our lives, it lived and breathed under the surface of my mind. I could still hear Father Haggerty's voice: "Good boys don't do these things. It's a sin. It's a sin in the eyes of God and man." *Good boys? Where does this crap come from?* I tried to imagine all guilt and conflicting thoughts leaving my body along with the dripping sweat.

Kim returned, led me back to the shower, and dried me with a warm, microwaved towel. She wrapped the towel around my waist and led me up the stairs. We went down a long hall and into a room so tiny the single bed took up nearly the entire space. A small lamp sitting on an old wooden nightstand cast a circle of dim yellow light. A picture hanging over the bed of a red lotus sitting in a pool of still water was the only decoration. Kim motioned for me to sit on the bed and sat next to me.

"What do you want to drink?"

"Nothing, thanks."

"No drink?" she said with a look and tone of such astonishment it seemed as if I'd violated a sacred ritual.

"I guess I'll have a beer."

Her broad smile told me I'd redeemed myself.

"Be right back, sweetie," she said as she left the room.

I sat on her bed and waited.

With a quiet knock at her own door Kim returned. On a silver tray she carried a bottle of Budweiser and a clean glass. She opened and poured the beer for me. I drank about half and put it down.

"You finished?"

I nodded.

She motioned with a smile and a wave of her hand. "Lay down."

"How do you want me?"

Kim laughed brightly. "You new at this?"

"I've never been here before."

"Never come to place like this?"

"No."

"Relax honey, I don't bite!" Kim giggled at her own joke. "First I give you massage. Lay on your stomach."

I lay face down on Kim's bed. She knelt on my backside and pressed acupuncture points along my spine. "You like, eh?"

"It feels great, but can you go deeper?"

With an almost imperceptible sigh of displeasure, Kim pressed deeper. After ten minutes she stopped.

"Okay, massage over."

"Are you finished already? I could go for more."

"If you want massage, there's a woman who does only that. I call her for you if you like. But I thought you were here for something else?"

"Yes."

Her smile was back. "Okay then, massage over."

The next thing I knew, Kim's mouth was on my genitals. With a move so rapid I wasn't sure exactly how she did it, a condom was over my penis. But try as she might—and massage wasn't her only skill—I was limp as a strand of overcooked pasta. Frustration was written all over her face.

"Hey what's wrong? You go someplace else before you come here? Maybe you just tired—huh, strongman? I told you not to stay too long in the sauna. What's the matter? Maybe you want younger woman?"

"No," I said. "You're a fine lady, Kim, but I think you're right. Maybe I'm just tired. Sorry."

The frustration vanished from her face, replaced by a happy smile.

"No, honey, I sorry for you, no fun tonight."

"It's okay, Kim, don't you worry about me. I shouldn't have stayed so long in the sauna."

Actually, another woman *was* a good idea, but I lied to save Kim's face. How many times had Sensei told me: "You Americans blurt out whatever thought crosses your mind, regardless of its effect on others." When I said Americans pride themselves on being direct, he told me that in Japan, being too direct is considered the mark of a simpleton. "It's far wiser to do whatever is necessary to save face."

"I don't like to lie," I said.

"Consider it strategy," Sensei said. "The strategy one uses to save face is the same skill it takes to be a good fighter. But saving face can be more complex than a fight, which is fast and direct. With saving face you must think and plan ahead, sometimes for years. You never know when you'll need an ally, and the person you shame today may harm your family generations later. Saving face is an important art to practice."

For me, saving face was a hazy line. I didn't like it. If people never said what they meant, how could you trust that anything was real? On the other hand, the truth would have hurt Kim, and this little white lie sure made her happy.

I put my clothes on and sat in the waiting area. Len came out on Sugi's arm looking elated and a bit worn around the edges. He saw me, grinned broadly, and punched me on the shoulder again.

"Didn't I tell you you'd have the time of your life?"

FOUR

It was half past midnight and I'd been lying in bed for over an hour. I should've been exhausted: I'd gone to the boxing gym and done fifteen rounds on the heavy bag, ten on the speed bag, and ten skipping rope. Phantom still refused to let me in the ring. *He's made his point, what's his trip?* In a fit of annoyance I threw on my clothes, got into my car, and steeled myself for the nearly two-hour drive.

On my eighteenth birthday, I'd moved from Queens to Northern Duchess County. The sole reason for leaving the city was to be within walking distance of Sensei. Even if it snowed three feet, I could still make it to karate class. Some city boys would have found the abrupt change overwhelming. I liked it. My rustic, six-hundred-square-foot cabin was nestled between a lake and thousands of acres of forest. My body attuned itself to the cycles of nature, and the quiet and peace of the land seeped into my soul. I had a couple of cats to take care of the mice that always find a way into a cabin, and my old pointer Ernesto's wordless devotion eased any pangs of loneliness.

I didn't work a regular job, didn't have to. With the winnings from my fights I added to a small nest egg saved from a job I'd had as a teenager. Strange that mixed martial artists make a lot less than boxers. Especially since mixed martial arts is far more popular. The champs of each division do well enough, making damn good money for a fight. Still a far cry from the millions you could make in a championship boxing match. Contenders like me fared more poorly, but even at my level it was always supply and demand. If a contender was popular and people liked to watch him fight, his manager could negotiate a better purse. The ten thousand I got for the Morales fight was on the high side for a fighter of my ranking, but my flashy kicks sold tickets. No way was I rich, but it was enough. The cabin was paid for and my lifestyle was simple.

I pulled into Chinatown around two. At that hour it was easy to find a spot on the street. *There's the place.* I glanced around to make sure no one was watching, pulled open the heavy steel door, and headed up the three long flights of stairs. My eyes took a second to adjust to the gloom. The stairwell was lit only by an exposed light bulb glaring from the top of the landing. By the time I climbed the first flight of stairs, the steel door closed behind me with a loud click that made me flinch.

As I got to the third floor my heart was beating fast, more from nervousness than exertion. I opened the door and walked into the waiting room. As if she hadn't moved a muscle since last evening, Mama-san sat at her desk, scanning my face with the expertise of one who's had many years practice in reading men. I didn't take her scrutiny as an affront. In a city like New York anyone could walk in off the street. A glint of recognition in her eyes led to a smile.

"You're back already?" she cackled. "Aren't you the eager beaver? Do you want Miss Kim again?"

I shook my head. "Do you remember when I was here yesterday with my friend?" She nodded. "I'd like to see the woman he was with."

Without missing a beat she spoke into the microphone. "Miss Sugi—gentleman waiting."

I watched Sugi intensely as we walked together to the locker room. She was one of the loveliest women I'd ever laid eyes on. She was tall for an Asian woman, at least five seven, and with four-inch stiletto heels she towered over me. Jet-black hair fell to her waist in slight waves. A few curls had been dyed honey-brown. She wore skintight shorts that displayed perfect legs. Her upper thighs blended into a tiny, incredibly firm backside. Compared to most American women she was twig slender, yet her hips were curvaceous.

"This way," Sugi said as she led me to a room at the end of the hall. Apparently each woman had her own personal space, used for customers and also for sleep. "Here." She slapped me sharply on the backside as she guided me through the door. Lingerie, bras, stockings, and clothes were piled on top of a tall dresser. Near the door was a tray with a glass left from a recent customer. On the floor were various articles of clothing, on the bed a black miniskirt and red panties she'd probably just peeled out of and now tossed on her dresser. They threatened to topple the prodigious pile, but she pushed it back against the wall with a deft shove.

"Oh, I've *got* to straighten up this mess," she said with an adorable pout. "But I'm busy busy busy." She looked at me cunningly. "Maybe you help Sugi put clothes away?" Her voice was so sweet and her manner so polite, it was hard to say no.

"Where?"

"Put the dirty clothes on the floor, make a pile. For the clean stuff ... skirts third drawer from the bottom, shirts second. My underwear goes in the top drawer."

I folded her shirts and miniskirts as neatly as possible for a neophyte in this department. To determine if her panties had been worn, I resisted the urge to smell and instead opened them wide and looked at the crotch. Stained panties—the secretions of women! I handled them with awe and embarrassment. As to her bras, I had no idea how to fold bras and simply placed them in the top drawer.

"Sit down." An airy wave at the bed. I sat.

With a stage-like flourish, Sugi took off her shirt. I watched with a lump in my throat.

"Help me with the clasp."

She sashayed over to the bed, every shift of her body exaggerated. Her bra was tightly cinched but I finally got it loose; it fell away revealing perfectly shaped breasts slightly larger than tennis balls, her nipples the color of milk chocolate. The corners of her lips curled into a slight smile.

"You like?"

All I could manage was a nod.

"Sugi has a present for you."

"What?"

"This." She unbuckled her belt, and her miniskirt fell to her ankles. She rolled her panties down, slowly, and flung them away from her. She was shaved clean except for a patch of hair shaped like a diamond. She looked at me intently, obviously enjoying my discomfort, seeing her sexual power reflected in my eyes. She laughed at the shocked look on my face. I felt thirteen.

"Lay down." She said it in a tone somewhere between command and tedium. "I give you massage." She put considerably less time and effort into it than Ms. Kim had. After a few minutes she said, more brightly, "Okay, massage over. Turn over, please."

I was barely breathing as Sugi moved to get on top of me. She put her naked body on mine and just lay there. I felt the warmth of her skin and her breasts pressing against my chest. Her thigh pushed at my groin. God, how good it felt to be with a woman. It had been a long time, *far too long*. The scent from her skin and her perfume overwhelmed my senses. I inhaled her into my body. Her face was only inches away, a wisp of her raven hair resting on my cheek, her mouth so close I felt her breath and could even smell her scarlet lipstick.

Sugi lifted up slightly, took my hands in hers and put them on her breasts. "Squeeze," she said. I cupped them and squeezed. "Harder!" I took her nipples between my fingers. She moved so that we were groin to groin and pressed against me, holding for a while then relaxing. Perhaps, since I was barely moving, this was her way of stimulating herself. "Harder," she said in a tight voice. I pinched harder. "That's it. That's the way I like." She looked into my eyes. "Okay! You want to be inside Sugi?" I nodded. She opened her mouth and slowly and exaggeratedly stuck out her tongue, as if she were going to lick my face. Little drops of saliva dripped off her tongue and trickled on my cheek. She shifted to massage the saliva into my skin with her fingers. Her hips put direct pressure on me. It was too much, and I came before we even started. From start to finish the whole thing lasted about five minutes.

Sugi's eyes widened in surprise, and she frowned. "You come too quick," she said sharply. But then her voice changed right back to sweetness. "You make another appointment, honey. Maybe you do better next time?"

My heart was still racing as we returned to the locker room. Sugi stood next to me, applying fresh lipstick, while I sat on the wooden bench quickly pulling on my clothes. After I was dressed she put her hand into mine, slipped her other arm around my waist, and leaned her head on my shoulder. With the brightness of a fresh, supple flower, she paraded her fantastic lover past the row of giggling women and the mama-san. When we reached the door, she gave me a two-hundred-watt smile and winked, puckered her full red lips and blew a kiss.

"I'll be waiting for you, honey." Only after she turned and disappeared behind the red curtains did I open the steel door.

I slunk down the stairs with the scent of Sugi still clinging to my skin. The cold air hit my face, reminding me I was no longer in the never-never land of Asia House but back on the streets of New York City. The asphalt was black and shiny in the light rain and the misty air seemed yellow from the lights of the stores and lampposts. The roar of the city had settled into a lower-pitched hum.

The late-night crowds were heading back to their apartments, rubbing their eyes, looking to their beds. And in these wee hours, there was a palpable transition as other breeds of New Yorkers began to emerge from their apartments and enter into the rhythm of the city. Made me think of jungle animals who rest during the day and come out at night.

The usual guys were selling drugs from a doorstep while a gaggle of twenty-dollar hookers aggressively pursued customers on the corner. A woman dressed in rags pushed a shopping cart piled with clothes and strange, tattered possessions. She stumbled, cursed loudly, sat on the curb, rolled up her pants displaying hideous varicosities, and mindlessly rubbed her ankle. In the center of the block a few drunks slept on cardboard boxes covered with filthy blankets and sheets of cardboard. A man walked toward me dressed in dark clothes, his arms swinging. I glanced at him as he passed. He stopped dead in his tracks, in his eyes the terrified look of an animal when it's cornered. I should have seen it coming. Here was someone so fragile that even glancing his way was threatening. "What the hell are *you* looking at?" If I kept looking there'd be only one outcome. I slid my eyes to the ground and kept walking.

Backing down fit my mood perfectly. First Morales, now this! *Pathetic!* A world-class fighter shouldn't have such stage fright around a woman. Phantom might not let me in the ring, but no one was going to keep me from seeing her again.

• • •

In the following week I thought of Sugi a lot. Into my well-ordered, disciplined world, creeping like a worm burrowing through rotten wood, were thoughts of her little room, her scent, her tantalizing mannerisms. Having an ugly woman's saliva on my face would be disgusting, and if a man spits on you it's an insult. But the tongue of a pretty woman is candy. The most disturbing part: these were not hopeless fantasies. I'd always considered a beautiful woman a treasure to be won, but Sugi didn't need to be courted. This Asian goddess was for sale, all of her. It would take just a phone call, a drive to Manhattan, and of course her fee.

Sugi had given me her card, or rather the stock card of Asia House all the girls used. In a large clear hand she had written across it: *love, Sugi*. I picked up the card, held it in my hand; I thought about calling at least a dozen times. Finally one night just before I went to sleep, I did. After several rings Mama-san picked up.

"Asia House, may I help you?"

Did she live there, sleep at her desk with the phone in her hand? Probably.

"Yes, hello. I'd like to make an appointment for tomorrow afternoon."

"Certainly sir. Which lady you like to see?

"Sugi, please."

"She will be waiting. What time please?"

"Four o'clock."

"Very good, thank you so much for calling. Good night sir."

I hung up the phone and wiped my sweaty palms on my pants. I was already nervous.

I left at eleven-thirty, an hour that gave me a fighting chance of avoiding traffic. The plan was to get there early, find parking, do a little shopping, then catch a bus to Asia House. Following my "date" with Sugi, I'd stay in the city and treat myself to a fancy dinner. By eight the traffic would have died down and I'd go home effortlessly.

• • •

The day started out as anticipated: I cruised into the city, did some shopping, then made my way toward Asia House. I was a little early and stopped at a coffee shop to gather myself. I ordered a cup of tea and went to the restroom to wash my hands. Staring back from the mirror was a pasty white apparition with nervous eyes and a nose that looked like the mark of Zorro. Funny, until I looked in a mirror I'd forgotten that the cartilage hadn't mended quite right. Scar tissue in the center of the nose, an inch below the bridge, twisted in two different directions like a misshapen *S*. Damn. I'd worn my favorite clothes, even put on aftershave. Returning to the table, I sipped tea and took stock of myself.

What the hell are you doing? This isn't a date. Who cares what you look like? But I did care.

In this condition, it'll be worse even than last time.

The logic was flawless. I dialed my cell phone.

"Hello Asia House, may I help you?"

"Yes, I have a four o'clock appointment with Sugi. I'm afraid something's come up—I won't be able to make it."

"So sorry please call us again."

"I will, and please give Sugi my apologies."

"Certainly, good night sir."

Instead of celebrating at the fancy Italian place, I grabbed a slice of pizza and headed home. It was claustrophobic in the slow-moving traffic and it took two hours just to make it to the Taconic. It was another hour before I pulled into my driveway. Once home, I slumped, face in my hands, elbows resting on the dining room table. All things considered, I was glad I hadn't gone, hadn't embarrassed myself with Sugi a second time. But I was thoroughly disgusted with myself. *You crawled back home like a beaten dog.* It was the first time in my life I'd let fear keep me from doing something I really wanted to do.

Lying there on the couch it dawned on me: the place in which I now suffered had been foretold ten years earlier.

• • •

At sixteen I began studying meditation with a sixty-year-old Chinese Buddhist named Ting. Every Saturday a small group of students gathered in his apartment in Brooklyn. We sat, cramped, on his living room floor. The winters were cool and drafty; in the brutal heat of a New York summer it was almost unbearable. You could smell the breath and overheated bodies only a few inches away. I watched the sweat bead on my classmates' upper lips and on Ting's forehead. He shaved his head regularly, but thin blue-gray stubble sprouted through the shiny skin of his scalp after a few days.

Unlike Sensei who could knock me down with as much effort as it took to brush his teeth, the meditation master's arms were as thin and undeveloped as a woman's. I figured I probably could have killed him with a single blow. But his frailty was as much a facade as my bulging biceps. He spoke softly and held the strong and fearless stick of kindness in his heart.

When I first met Ting he scanned me from head to foot, then looked carefully into my eyes. He placed his hand on my bicep.

"Very strong man," he said, in a thick Chinese accent. It was hard to understand him. Feeling a little self-conscious but secretly pleased, I shrugged my shoulders in a gesture of false modesty.

"Make muscle," he said.

I obliged by making a fist and tensing my arm. As he squeezed my bicep he motioned to his orange-robed disciple, who was constantly at his side. "Feel his arm, you see how strong?" His disciple dutifully touched my arm, making the appropriate murmurs of approval. Ting's manner seemed so unsophisticated he could be taken for a simpleton, which would be a mistake. Ting held two doctorate degrees: one in psychology, the other in physics.

Master Ting and I were as opposite as two people can be. I'd developed my brawn and trained in methods of hurting and killing. Ting's life had been devoted to promoting peace. I wondered how he was able to show such patience with cocky, strutting know-it-alls like me. Perhaps he was able to see to the part crying out for understanding, or even deeper to the part that was alive and awake, just waiting for the right nutrients so it might unfold like a flower bursting into bloom.

As with Sensei, I was expected to bow in his presence, but unlike the karate bow where I bent at the waist and tipped my head, the Buddhist bow required me to put my palms and fingertips together and drop my head slightly. Ting always returned the bow, but then with a soft hand he clasped me on the bicep. I flexed my arm and he laughed—a real laugh, a laugh that showed glee. At first I thought he was making fun of me, but I came to realize it was his way of showing affection. It became our habitual greeting.

After a few months of study Ting asked, "Why you want to learn meditation?"

Like a talking parrot I regurgitated Sensei's reasons.

"The great warriors were more than just brawlers. They knew the secret of going inside and quieting the mind. I want to achieve 'no mind' so I can be a great fighter. Meditation will help."

He cocked his head, the way a dog sometimes will when trying to understand someone speaking to him.

"Ah ha," he said—and so my education began.

I was endowed with great reserves of energy. Karate came naturally; sitting and attempting to harness the wild bucking bronco of my mind was far more challenging. Yet meditation and martial arts shared a basic tenet—discipline—and discipline I understood. I trained hard, practiced every day, sometimes twice a day, and I followed the directives of the master to the letter. Well, almost to the letter. Buddhists were vegetarian; they didn't believe in harming the life of any being. Nor was a good Buddhist supposed to drink alcohol. I devoured anything in front of me and occasionally had a drink.

After a couple of years Ting considered me a serious student. At least he could see that I tried hard. And though it was clear my motives were merely to become a more proficient fighter, he took an interest in my progress. Although Sensei was by far the more major influence, I grew to deeply admire Master Ting. In time I learned to love and respect meditation as an art unto itself.

After long years of practice, I could easily sit for an hour or more, barely moving a muscle. When the mad stream of thoughts eased down to a trickle, there was peace, a rest from the ever-busy mind. It was delicious, indescribable. Words couldn't do it justice. And answers to deep questions did come. It was as if I dipped into a reservoir of information, mysteriously, without even trying. In fact the less I tried, the more the answers came. Ting called this receiving, not from the head but the heart.

• • •

It had been a decade, nearly to the day, when I arrived at Master Ting's for the usual Saturday meditation. But the atmosphere at Ting's was anything but usual. There was a visitor, an old Chinese woman named Shu, said to be a famous master of divination. Shu had begun training at the age of five and honed and practiced her craft over a lifetime. Supposedly, she could predict the future and read a person's life like an open book. Since she'd arrived a few days earlier, she'd stayed alone in her quarters. None of the students had so much as set eyes on her. Ting made it clear no one was to pester her or ask for help. She didn't use her skills for fortune-telling; she would not, he said, be doing readings for anyone. That was fine by me. Practitioners of divination were interesting, but I didn't want anyone telling me about my own life.

I'd been sitting in meditation but fatigue had set in. I was getting close to falling asleep, so I got up and walked into the kitchen to prepare a cup of tea. In the hall I came face to face with Ting and the old lady. Usually I felt comfortable in Ting's presence, but a twinge of fear crept up my belly and into my throat. He motioned to the old woman standing at his side.

"John, this is master Shu."

The tiny, thin woman's gnarled face had been deeply touched by the sun. Her skin was the color of a beat-up oak desk. She stood quietly and looked into my eyes for a long moment, an intense gaze that made me nervous. I looked away, but curiosity compelled me to lock eyes with her again. She slowly shook her head and let out a long whistle. In the few years since I'd known Ting, his English had improved tremendously, but old Shu spoke with a heavy accent.

"Your life will not be easy." Shu laughed, but her laughter had a strange tinge of sadness. "I wish I could tell you different."

I was more than surprised that she seemed to be doing a reading on me, the very thing that wasn't supposed to happen under any circumstances. And I certainly hadn't asked for it. Ting looked about as shocked as I'd ever seen him, his black eyes—his whole face—alight with interest.

Shu shook her head slowly. "You have an eager soul, yours will be a busy life. There will be little time for you to rest. It will be one death after another, a series of little deaths, for the entire length of your life."

"Excuse me, what do you mean by *death*?"

Her eyes gleamed, but she looked at Ting to answer. Apparently, he was *her* student.

Ting nodded reflectively. "When I was a young man starting out in meditation, younger even than you, my teacher took me aside. 'I will offer you two things,' he said. 'The first is enlightenment beyond your wildest dreams.'

"I blurted out: 'I'll take the enlightenment.' My teacher laughed as if I'd told the funniest joke. 'For great enlightenment you would need to pass through much pain. But what if you could have a life of peace and contentment—not much pain, yet less enlightenment. Which would you choose?'

"I began to answer right away that I'd do anything to find truth, but my teacher stopped me with a wave of his hand. 'Think on it and tell me in a week.' And in a week my teacher came to me and asked, 'So what will it be?'

"'I'll take the pain,' I said.

"This time my teacher didn't laugh, but looked at me carefully, almost sadly. 'Only the most eager will take the fast path,' he said. 'But to walk so quickly, everything you do not need in your life will be taken from you.' Then he smiled and said, 'This is the little death: you shed your skin like a snake.'

"But I still didn't get it." Ting said.

Neither did I.

Shu's eyes sparkled. She paused and thoughtfully stroked her short white hair while looking slightly over my shoulder with unfocused eyes.

"Hmmm, in twenty-five or six years ... there may be a leveling out, you may find what you came here to do, and perhaps even have peace. But you might also die quite young, depending on which course you take."

"Twenty-five years? You've got to be joking," I said, in an attempt at a lightness I didn't feel. "I'll be an old man by then. That is if I'm not dead, right?" Ting smiled at the implication that I'd be old in my early fifties and waited for Shu to continue.

"In ten years what you think you are will be challenged. Your belief in yourself. There will be a fork in the road. Around this time you will meet someone who will help to navigate."

"Like my teacher here?" I patted Master Ting's arm.

"It will be different. This one will be able to touch you more deeply than any man or woman who came before—and you will be ready to be touched."

FIVE

I'd called Ed, my manager, to talk about a fight, and just speaking with him had been a cold, hard slap. I had to get back in the groove—and I needed Phantom's help. *Taking a break from the whorehouse is probably a good idea.* I showed up at the boxing gym, worked out hard, no backtalk, and I didn't push him about sparring. After ten straight days, Phantom invited me back into the ring.

I climbed between the loose-fitting ropes of the practice ring onto the canvas stained with decades of use and smelling slightly of mildew. My sparring partner was a kid I'd never seen before. Tall and lanky, with a build similar to Morales, Jeff was eager to show how tough he was. He fought fast, hard, and reckless, and was just unpredictable enough to be dangerous. He grazed my jaw with a wild right that startled me. I moved inside and jammed his arms, slammed a left into his ribs, and stunned him with a sharp right uppercut. My left hook connected, his eyes went back, his legs buckled, then he was out on his feet. Phantom was between us in an instant, moving mighty fast for a man his age.

"Jumping Jack Jesus," he yelled in his raspy Brooklyn accent. "This isn't a fight! Don't take his fucking head off. That's enough for tonight." As I lifted the rope and climbed out of the ring, he gave me the stink eye and threw me a towel. "Hit the fucking showers, Lazio."

When Coach was angry or excited it seemed every third word out of his mouth was an obscenity.

He looked carefully into Jeff's eyes. "You okay, kid?"

"Yeah, I'm okay," Jeff said.

"Then what the hell's wrong with you? You got fucking rocks in your head?" He waved a finger and shook his head. "You got tagged because you let John fight his fight. With your height you should've kept him outside and hit him with so many jabs he'd think twice about coming in." As wobbly as Jeff was, Coach made him throw a few punches before letting him out of the ring. "That's it, jab, one, two, three—again!" Jeff went through the motions until Phantom uttered the words that formally ended these sessions: "Okay, shower up."

The hot water washed over my tired muscles, and even after rinsing with pure cold I was still perspiring. Phantom met me as I was about to leave.

"I spoke to Ed yesterday," I said. "I'd like to talk to you about it."

"Any time," Phantom said.

"How about now?"

"I'm on my way to the Bronx to get a bite to eat. Want to come?"

The boxing gym was in Brooklyn and it was a long drive home.

"I don't feel like going all the way to the Bronx."

"You ever been to Vito's?" he said. I shook my head. "Worth the drive. It's probably the best Italian place in the city."

"Okay, Coach, let's go."

I turned to leave, but Phantom's meaty forearm barred the way.

"Hold on! It's cold outside, keep yourself covered after a workout. You got a hat?"

"Yeah." I fumbled it out of my pocket.

"Then why the fuck isn't it on your head, you nincompoop?" Phantom yanked my ski cap out of my hand and placed it on my head. He zipped my jacket up all the way, like a mom with a toddler, and slapped me hard on the back of the head.

"All right, now let's get the fuck out of here."

We took his beat-up white Ford, the shocks like mush. Phantom lead-footed it over the bridge, bouncing over potholes.

"Hey, Coach, I thought people were supposed to slow down when they got older."

Phantom grinned. "Driving fast keeps me young."

"You might die young."

"Already too late for that."

I smiled and settled back in my seat. With Sensei, I always worried about putting my foot in my mouth. With Coach I didn't have to.

We parked on the street and walked under elevated subway tracks to a dark, hole-in-the-wall kind of place.

"This is the best Italian place in the city?"

"It don't look like much but don't say anything until after you taste it."

"Fair enough."

A waitress seated us at a booth with a spotlessly white starched tablecloth. In a minute she returned with a menu for me and a large carafe of red wine for Coach.

"So," Phantom said, "what did Ed have to say?"

"He says there are two possible fights." In mixed martial arts the organization decides which fighters will put on a good show and draw a big crowd. Afterward it's turned over to the fighters.

"Who?"

"Nuñoz."

"That doesn't surprise me. You and Nuñoz both lost to Morales, now everyone wants to see you get together."

In November, Morales had fought Fernando Nuñoz, one-time champ of the lightweight division. Antonio made quick work of Nuñoz, choking him into submission after beating him near senseless three minutes into the first round.

"Who else?"

"Haines."

"Everyone wants a piece of you, but Haines? He won his last three fights. I like that kid, he's fast and strong."

"Ed doesn't think it makes sense to fight Haines just yet."

"He's right! If you beat Nuñoz, potentially you get a rematch with Morales. Haines is also less of a paycheck. Worse, Haines's a big risk, a dangerous man to face on a comeback. If he won, you'd be in no-man's-land as far as a title shot. What're you thinking?"

"Not so long ago I would've been thrilled to fight either of them. But now I just don't know."

Coach pushed away his plate and looked at me carefully.

"We got to have a serious talk about your fighting."

"What?"

"This afternoon with Jeff? It all looked good on the outside—one more punch you'd've knocked him down. What *really* happened? You got hit, lost your head, and overreacted. There wasn't any reason to be all over an inexperienced kid like that."

"I thought fighting was about knocking people down."

"Don't get smart with me, Lazio."

Phantom barely seemed to watch, but he saw everything.

"You're right, Coach."

"If you ever want to get out of the peewee league, you've got to keep your cool. Are you still even remotely entertaining the idea of winning the title?"

"I still want it."

"Then I'm hoping you can get to the next level."

"Any suggestions?"

"Sure, if you can handle the truth."

"I'll try."

He looked at me like he wasn't sure I could. I tried my best bring-it-on expression.

"You're a talented fighter, but you're not a mature fighter," he said finally. "Every fighter's immature, until he grows up."

"How do I do that?"

"By facing yourself."

"How?"

"That last fight with Morales is a hell of a start. It's not just losing. You took a wicked blow to the head. Some fighters are never the same after they get hit like that, they don't come back. Something's gone, like it's been taken from them. It's more than just confidence, they lose their spirit, and once that's gone they're finished as a fighter. It's time to quit."

I swallowed hard. My eyes slid from Phantom's and rested, unfocused, on the table littered with the remains of our food.

"Why are you telling me this, Phantom?"

"To be champ you've got to get through Morales."

I squirmed.

"To beat Morales you're going to have to face yourself, which means finding what you're made of. There isn't anything harder than pulling this out of your guts."

"Don't you think I know that?"

"I don't know, son. *Do* you?"

No point in lying, Phantom saw right through me. "I *don't* any more. It wasn't chance or a lucky punch why I lost. I choked. I'm not sure I have what it takes."

"You think a man becomes champ with luck? Not *one* of them had a cakewalk, even the greats like Ali. What do you think he had to go through to beat Foreman? Age, years of inactivity, every one of his losses, every weak point had to be examined, scrutinized, held up to the fire. Even your martial arts guys, Bruce Lee—all those "sum dum fucks"—had their demons. Fighting's not unique, either, you have to face yourself to get to the top of *any* game. That's the maturing process. But let me tell you, it takes guts. Everyone's got the flaws but few have what it takes to look at them."

We got up and walked to the car. "Meet me at the gym tomorrow, an hour early," Phantom said, "and every day from now on. I'll try to come up with some ways to help you train for this."

Driving down the street, almost as if he were talking to himself, he said, "What we've got to do is work on your psychological game. I don't mean strategy, more the *emotional* side. Fighting is a lot like poker. If you want to play for high stakes you're going to have to learn to keep cool."

SIX

At two o'clock I was the only one at the boxing gym.

"From now on we're doing things my way," Phantom said.

"When have we *not* done things your way? What's going to be different?"

"I want you to learn how to box, real good."

"Coach, I *know* how to box!"

"You box like a karate guy and all you karate guys *think* you can box, but if you didn't have your kicks and grappling, I'd never put you in the ring with a pro."

"I practice with boxers all the time, right here at the gym."

"Only a couple of these guys are pros, and you've never been in the ring with any of them. Nobody here is even ranked. You've never fought anyone top-notch. Stop arguing and listen—your hands are your weakest link. Take it from me, the better you are with your hands the less you'll get rattled in the ring."

So began a new regimen. Phantom treated me as if I were a novice just off the street. I raised my eyebrows when he explained the four weapons of boxing: the jab, straight punch, hook, uppercut. Compared to martial arts, boxing is downright simple. But within boxing's streamlined elegance lies its stunning effectiveness. *Coach was right!* There were fine points I'd never learned. I'd thought I knew what a jab and a hook were, but Phantom showed me how to put speed and body weight into my jab, and how footwork helps to shift every ounce of weight into a hook.

"Good job, Lazio. Everything's looking better. You're hitting harder than ever."

"Thanks, I *am* hitting harder. At home I got a device that measures the force of my punch, so I know it for sure."

"This is just the beginning. Soon you'll be so good with your hands nothing will fluster you."

Phantom had his ways to work on my emotional game and I had mine.

• • •

Mama-san was busy helping another customer. I hadn't noticed the brown bags under her eyes, so deep makeup couldn't hide them. She got the other man squared away and turned to me.

"It's been a while. Where have you been?"

I shrugged my shoulders.

"You went to another house?" Mama-san asked, her eyes serious as a snake's.

The question caught me by surprise. I laughed uneasily.

"No, no, I've just been busy—you know how it is?"

"Okay." She smiled. "Who do you want to see?"

"Sugi, please."

"I'm sorry, she's busy now with a customer. If you want to see a special lady, it's better to make an appointment."

I frowned slightly. In my anxiety, I'd forgotten that all-important detail. Mama-san sensed the gears turning in my head and peered into my eyes with a knowing smile.

"How about you pick from the girls that aren't with customers?" She walked me over to the row of women sitting against the back wall. Thankfully, Miss Kim wasn't there. "Pick the one you like," she said, as if I were choosing off a menu.

I looked them over. Some looked down, others stared brazenly, checking me out—which of course was exactly what I was doing to them. I felt my face flush and my legs go a bit wobbly, but there wasn't one that struck me.

Mama-san smiled. "I have one lady I think you like, very pretty, she's not in the line. Please have a seat and wait a minute. I'll see if she's busy." She spoke softly to one of the women, who quickly got up and skipped down the hall. I sat on one of the cracked leather chairs and waited. A bald elderly man in the chair next to me smiled. I smiled back, feeling conspicuously awkward.

• • •

It isn't like going to a whorehouse had never crossed my mind. I didn't act on it because of training. Sex and training didn't mix, or so I'd been told. In the boxing gym, a few days before my first professional fight, the workout finished, Phantom was giving me a few last-minute pointers. Paolo Santomero, a tiny seventy-five-year-old Italian who owned the gym, shuffled up to us. Once Santomero had held the world bantamweight title. Now he looked like a shriveled prune with unsteady legs, shaking hands, and a voice that sounded like something out of *The Godfather*. He grabbed my shoulder and pinched my deltoid between his fingers, his head tipped slightly. He looked like he was judging the ripeness of a melon.

"Yeah, Phantom … Johnny looks good."

"He's ready," Coach said. "*If* he fights the way he did tonight."

"Thanks, Mr. Santomero," I said as I turned to leave.

"Lazio!" Coach said. "Take it easy the next couple of days. Don't work out much. If you run, make it slow, not more than a mile a day—and whatever you do, don't stick your dick in anything before the fight." Santomero punched Phantom on the shoulder and guffawed. I turned, surprised, to see both men laughing it up like a couple of old braying donkeys. I'd heard coaches talking like this—as if it were some kind of superstition.

"Why?" I asked.

"Ruins the will to win," Santomero said. "A fighter never wants to get laid before a fight."

"Okay, I'll stay away from women." Not a big sacrifice, since I wasn't seeing any.

"You don't want to play with yourself either," Santomero added.

"Don't lose any sleep over it," I called as I headed out the door.

• • •

Maybe it's for the best that Sugi's busy. If this Cindy's half-decent I'll practice with her. I smiled. Ting often said, "Your entire life, anything that passes before your eyes, is training, mulch for your garden." *But what kind of training is this? Ha!* I snorted out loud, causing the old fellow next to me to glance up from his paper and give me the fish eye.

Cindy walked up proud and erect, in that well-grounded, slightly shuffling way common to Asians. She was barely five feet tall, young and fresh-looking. I guessed her to be somewhere between eighteen and twenty-two. Her hair, so shiny it could have been oiled, was fashioned into a loose braid that hung midway down her back. Even in the dead of winter her skin was a rich, golden tan. She had a full face and high cheekbones. Not much makeup, just a little gloss on her full lips and a trace of mascara and silver eye shadow. Her eyes—innocent, slightly amused, and bright liquid-black—reminded me of a child's. *Beautiful!* Not in the seductive movie-star style of Sugi, but strikingly lovely. She looked at me, smiled warmly as she shook my hand, weaved her arm into mine, and led me through the red curtains into the bathing area. I already liked her.

Chatting like a happy bird, Cindy washed my back, wrapped my waist in a warm towel, and led me up the stairs. We stopped at the second floor. A woman escorting a man, also wearing just a towel, continued climbing.

"Are there more rooms upstairs?" I asked.

Cindy nodded.

"How many floors does Asia House occupy?"

"Three floor. The waiting room and bath are on first floor. The second and third floor are bedroom."

"How many women work here?"

"Twenty-five girls are regular. We sleep here and the woman at front desk—she the owner, her name Mrs. Li—she also sleep here. There are ten extra girl who work as free agent, they not live at house. The owner hire them when it very busy or if regular girl is sick or on vacation."

Cindy had a pronounced accent, but my years of hanging around the dojo had taught me to decipher even the thickest. The trick is simply to slow down and concentrate. Cindy's voice was soft and sweet. Really she spoke quite well if you listened closely.

We strolled together down the long, dimly lit hall to her room. On this, my third time at Asia House, I had the presence of mind to look around a little. Shallow tables hugged the wall at carefully placed intervals. Above the tables were mirrors with ornately carved frames.

A few prints of famous artists were placed strategically. The idea was to give this old, rather dilapidated space a touch of elegance. But even the dim light couldn't conceal the warped stairs and balconies, peeling paint, or cheap carpet. Asia House, however, made the most of what it had.

As we walked, I caught my half-naked reflection in the mirror. What an interesting place, this dimly lit beehive with its long halls and little rooms. Coming off the streets of New York you were transported into the timeless world of the East. The slightly perfumed air of Asia House, warmed from hissing cast-iron radiators, seemed to exude femininity.

Cindy walked slightly behind me and patted my shoulder to signal that the room just ahead to the right was hers. I pushed open the door and walked in. Each of the three tiny cubicles had been similar, yet different. Kim's room was stark and bare, Sugi's a lingerie explosion. Cindy's room was neat but not obsessively. A small wooden dresser, an old nightstand, and a single bed consumed nearly the entire space. A candle burning on the night table cast flickering shadows on two framed pictures of an Asian man and woman hanging on the wall. A small shrine sat on a corner of her dresser: a brass incense burner, a bowl of fruit, and a vase of fresh flowers—an offering, I assumed, to whatever gods she believed in. Chinese restaurants have statues of Guang Gung, the god of war. Why not a shrine in a whorehouse?

Cindy offered me a drink and I readily accepted. I was already feeling a little anxious and was happy to drink a few sips of beer and lie down for the massage. Her occasional small talk broke the silence.

"You very well built. You lift weights to keep in shape?"

"I use weights, but mostly I do martial arts."

"Hi-ya!" She pretended to hit me in the back. I turned and blocked her punch. She giggled and tried to put my arm in a wrestling hold. I smiled. It was fun being teased this way by a beautiful woman.

"What do you do for work?

"Actually, fighting *is* my work."

"Really! So that's how you face get that way?"

I nodded.

"What *do* you do then, when you not fight?"

I turned and looked her carefully in the eyes, fully expecting her not to understand.

"My life is mostly about training and fighting."

"I had uncle who famous boxer in Thailand. When we young we not believe the things he do. He kick trees with his shin, he take punch anywhere in body, he say to punch him hard as we can but it just hurt our hand. He even let us hit him with club."

"Thai boxers are tough customers," I said. "I have great respect for them."

Cindy seemed to understand and even respect my devotion to the martial arts.

"Massage finished. Turn over please."

I turned over and looked into her dark, smiling eyes. A wave of uneasiness tightened my solar plexus. I almost wished we could end our session right here. I had the distinct urge to flee. Maybe we could just talk for the rest of our time? *Right! You go to a whorehouse to make chitchat with the ladies.* Cindy took out a condom. I don't know how or why the words came out of my mouth.

"I don't like condoms. Is there any way we can do without it?"

A shadow of fear flickered across her face.

"Look, I'm clean. I have no sexual—or for that matter any other— disease. I swear it!"

"You not worry about me?"

"Should I?"

"Not really," she said. "I take very good care and we checked by doctor all the time." She put the condom down. She came closer and looked deeply into my eyes. She seemed to be reading me, searching for the best way to make an entry. More than anything, I wanted to have sex with this woman, but I knew it in my bones: I was too uptight.

Cindy stopped, got up off the bed, and retrieved my half-empty glass of beer. She handed it to me and sat back down on the bed next to me.

"Here you drink."

I drained the glass in a few gulps and handed it back to her. She put the glass on the nightstand. Then something very strange happened.

Cindy pushed me down on the bed and held me in her arms for a long moment. She lifted her face slowly to mine and kissed me. It was the very last thing I expected. I'd heard prostitutes might perform every act of sex but never, ever, would they kiss you on the mouth—this they saved for their boyfriends or lovers. Kissing was considered to be the most intimate form of contact. Why would Cindy want to kiss a complete stranger?

More puzzling, this was not the kiss of someone providing a service. It was a real embrace with soft lips and tongue, infinitely sweet. I hadn't had a kiss like that for a long time. Her arms held me softly. The taste of her lips, her tongue, and the shape of her mouth seemed slightly different from white women. For a moment, I forgot my nervousness. Without any foreplay she helped me enter her. It lasted only a few minutes and couldn't possibly have been satisfying for her. But after not having sex for so long, I was elated. And though by any standards mine was a pitiful performance, I felt more like a man again.

• • •

It was quite late when I hit Canal Street, feeling good, and stopped at a café for a bite to eat. By the time I made it home it was four a.m. Ernesto was relieved I'd finally returned and sniffed me thoroughly, no doubt curious about this weird change in schedule and the different smells I was wearing. After letting him out I went straight to bed.

Just before I fell asleep I remembered Cindy asking me after our session, "You want to take shower?"

"Thank you," I said. "But no."

I wanted to leave her essence on me for a little while longer.

SEVEN

Afetr an intense workout with Phantom, I drove to Chinatown, hoisted open the heavy steel door of Asia House, and all but bounded up the stairs—by the time the door clicked shut I was already at the second floor. Mama-san gave me her smile, followed by a wink.

"Who you want to see? Miss Sugi or Miss Cindy?"

"Didn't I make an appointment with Cindy?"

"I'm joking with you, she's on her way." And no sooner were the words out of her mouth than Cindy walked up to me with a happy smile. She weaved her arm into mine and dropped her head on my shoulder—she seemed as glad to see me as I was to see her. In the locker room I removed several layers of winter clothes. She took me quickly through the bathing ritual and up the stairs to her room, then brought the silver tray and the bottle of Budweiser. We sat on the bed.

"What is you name?" Cindy said.

"Johnny Lazio."

"How old are you?"

"Twenty-seven."

"You married, Johnny?"

"What would I be doing here if I was married?"

"I had feeling you not, but you be surprise. Most men that come to Asia House married. You have girlfriend?"

"No."

"Why not? You young, you handsome man, you not married and most important you have good heart." I wondered if she meant it, but it pleased me all the same.

"Twenty-seven old to be single. If you live in northeast Thailand you have wife and family already."

I grimaced. "You sound a lot like my mother."

"Like you mother?" She laughed and pushed me roughly down on the bed. The massage lasted only about five minutes, and Cindy put almost no effort into it. I turned over and lay on my back, looking up at her. She moved toward me and softly, tenderly brushed my lips with hers. She put herself completely into it. It didn't seem to be an act or out of duty. She moved her head down to my groin—*she's so beautiful, her lips are so warm*—I touched her shoulder to make her stop. It was too exciting. She looked up, questioned with her eyes.

"I don't need any extra stimulation."

Cindy wanted to experiment, to find what would be most successful. First I was on the bottom, then she was on her hands and knees. I got flustered and the sex was shorter even than the first time. Somehow, I'd turned into the world's worst lover.

There was still plenty of time before her next appointment. Cindy dressed and handed back the towel to wrap around my waist. Going by past history with Kim and Sugi, I assumed our session was over and moved toward the door. Cindy's smiling eyes looked into mine and she patted her bed. I shrugged and sat cross-legged with my back against the wall, facing the length of the bed. She sat directly across from me.

"From the way you touch me you been with woman before."

I nodded.

"Tell me about her."

God, she was abrupt! It had been almost ten years since Heidi. I didn't let myself think of her and never spoke her name, not even to the air. And I come from a long line of emotional stoics.

My Irish mother learned to be quiet as a burglar when she was very little, lest she incur the wrath of her father, a violently abusive drunk. Whatever feelings Mom had were secret things, so cloaked in layers of sternness they were impossible to decipher. Dad was second-generation Italian. He'd walk around the house singing, hug and kiss me and try to make me dance with him. Other times he brooded darkly and silently. During those times, no one knew what was bothering him, and he never let us in. My feelings were secret, something to be kept to myself—although why I was so ashamed of them, I didn't know.

Cindy noticed me stiffen.

"Is okay, you don't have to tell."

What the hell? Talking to Cindy was more anonymous than confessing to a priest. She knew none of my circle of friends and family. I was paying her by the hour, who knew how many times we'd see each other? I let out a long sigh and groaned.

"Once I loved a woman—a girl, really. I was sixteen, she was fifteen. We were together for two years. Her name was Heidi."

Cindy grabbed my hands and pulled me up. She took my place against the wall, sat behind me with her arms around my waist, almost like a mother holding a child in her lap. I pulled slightly back but she didn't let go. Her slow breath warmed my cheek. Something inside me began to uncoil, something painful, unfamiliar, like the loosening of a tightly wound spring. To my horror tears came to my eyes. I managed to blink them back and hold my face in the expressionless mask I habitually maintained. Thankfully she couldn't see my eyes.

"Tell me about her," she said.

"There's not much to tell." I tried to steady my voice. "My friend introduced us. She was one of the most beautiful girls in the neighborhood."

I'd always been shy and awkward around females, my previous attempts at relationships short-lived, juvenile affairs that didn't progress beyond a few dates. As for Heidi, sixteen was a pretty freaked-out age for me: I still had remnants of the terrible acne I suffered during puberty and serious doubts about my attractiveness to the opposite sex. My horniness was off the charts—I was certain that if I didn't have sex I'd soon go crazy.

"What you do together?"

"Just high school stuff. Hung out after school, went to movies, went out to dinner every Saturday night."

"It was the first time for you?"

"For me, it was the first time, Heidi had done it before."

My parents had been out late and Heidi told hers she was sleeping at a girlfriend's. We were in bed kissing. She'd been in several relationships, and to her sex was natural. After a long stretch of clumsy fondling, she decided to move things along.

"Don't you want to make love with me?"

"Sure," I said, a little dizzy. "In a couple of minutes."

A thin line of surprise crinkled her fifteen-year-old brow.

"Don't you want to do it? *I* do."

Move, you dope. Who knows how much time passed, my heart pounding, sweat rolling down the small of my back, and I couldn't do a damn thing even though I desperately wanted to.

"I'm hungry," Heidi said. "What do you have to eat?" Half dressed, we raided the refrigerator. How could I ever forget the joy and shock of Heidi sitting in my mother's kitchen chair bare-chested, munching on a sandwich, her nipples erect in the drafty room? Then she took me by the hand and led me into the living room.

She'd finally figured out my problem. She pushed me onto my back on the couch, peeled off her pants, and started kissing and touching me. She pulled off my pants and got on top. No amount of fantasizing had prepared me for the sensation of being inside a girl, feeling the heat and wetness deep in her core—

"You loved her?" Cindy's voice broke into my reverie.

I looked at the bed. My voice cracked. It sounded harsh as it bounced off the walls of her tiny room.

"You know," I said, "we *thought* it was, but in the end it was just puppy love ...

we did some dumb things."

Cindy learned forward, barely breathing.

"I want to hear."

"You've got to remember, we were just kids, still in high school. We lived in our parents' homes."

Cindy nodded.

"Heidi's home was in a rich neighborhood, right in the heart of Queens. It backed up to a park with woods all around. I had a job at a fast-food place. After I finished work, around nine or ten, I drove to her house and parked a couple of blocks away so no one would hear the car door slam. I'd see the candle she kept burning on her windowsill to signal that everything was okay. I climbed up and stood on the fence just under her window. It's a wonder no one called the cops."

"What you do at her house so late?"

"Just saying good night."

We *had* to see each other, couldn't even wait until the next day. I stood on her fence and tapped on the window. She might have fallen asleep, but when she heard me she came to the window. Her breath and lips were sweet and warm with sleep. We pledged our hearts and souls to each other. After kissing good night for the tenth time, I jumped off the fence and ran back to the car. I don't think my feet touched the ground.

Cindy sighed. "It is like fairy tale!"

Some fucking fairy tale!

I'd never talked about Heidi, much less my feelings about her or how it ended. I didn't meet Cindy's eyes but stared at her brown-skinned calf and foot.

Heidi and I had planned the whole marriage thing, right down to how many kids we wanted. She was good with pencils and watercolor and drew beautiful cards for me picturing a couple with babies. They were always signed, "Love, Heidi, the mother of your children."

The card thing became a ritual. I had a whole collection of cards with paintings of families and babies and always, *always* it was the same message: I was the one for her, she wanted to marry me, she'd love me forever. It made me feel good. It got so I longed to hear it, I gorged on it. And when, one day, she didn't say it quite so enthusiastically or as often, I worried.

I'd endured just about as much of this as I could take. I looked up and was, for an instant, surprised to see Cindy staring at me with a pensive look in her eyes. I'd almost forgotten I was here in this little room, or even at Asia House. I was feeling very off-balance but couldn't put a finger on exactly what it was. I stared defiantly back at Cindy.

The drizzle earlier in the evening had progressed into a downpour. The rain was coming sideways, drumming heavily on the room's only window, which overlooked the dirty brick wall of the neighboring building. I leaned my back against the wall and groaned.

A knock on the door interrupted us. It was one of the girls that worked there.

"You better hurry up, Cindy, your customer is waiting. Mrs. Li is mad."

Cindy glanced at her clock.

"Ah, I'm late." She walked me to the locker room and quickly fixed her makeup. She gave me a kiss in front of other girls and their customers, which widened a few eyes. My lips were hard and cold.

"You have to let yourself out," she said. "I've got to go."

It was just after two in the morning as I hit the sobering cold air of Canal Street.

I don't remember driving home. When I got to my cabin I went straight to Ernesto's bed. He yawned, his doggy breath somehow comforting. I sat holding him for nearly an hour.

EIGHT

E d called. "Lazio, you thought about our last conversation?"

"Phantom and I talked it over, we'll go with Nuñoz."

"Smart move. The fight's going to be a holiday special, the second Saturday in January. Less than a month away—you be ready?"

"I'll make sure I am."

"Good, John. Because you know this one's a career maker—or breaker. If you win you've just had one loss, you're still at the top. Lose and you're yesterday."

Before my defeat to Morales, I'd relished the idea of fighting Nuñoz. I figured I'd beat him, not easily but without too much trouble. He was only decent with his hands and feet. What made him exceptional was his grappling and submissions. His body was almost superhumanly flexible; he could throw in an armlock, leglock, or choke so quickly his opponent never knew what hit him. Once trapped in one of Nuñoz's Jiu Jitsu holds, you were dead in the water, the pain so great you had to tap out or go to sleep.

Phantom and I went over every match Nuñoz fought. We viewed the fight with Morales last. We watched it at least five times.

"Jeez, look at that!" Phantom whistled. "Nuñoz don't take a hit so good. He gets frazzled. And when he's frazzled he can't use his Jiu Jitsu. Now look, he's hurt. Do you see, John?"

A part of me didn't want to look. Morales beat the hell out of Nuñoz with powerful lefts and a thunderous right that snapped his head back. Watching gave me a sickening feeling in my gut. *God, his hands are fast.* Nuñoz was out on his feet, and quick as a winged fairy, Morales got his arms around his neck for the kill. Sharp, clean, powerful—an alligator's jaws slamming shut—it was all over. Some part of my psyche remembered: dizzy, hurt, like a wounded deer fighting desperately to find enough strength to escape. But there was no escape.

"There it is! Here's what I was looking for." Phantom put the tape on pause. "Nuñoz can't box worth shit. See how he keeps his head up, he don't protect the jaw. He's just a good high school wrestler and a kick-ass Jiu Jitsu player. He's in fantastic shape, so he'll try to outlast you. When you're tired, he'll shoot for the single leg, but hurt him and he gets confused. He can't stand up with you, John. Set him up with the hands, finish with those kicks of yours, you've got him."

I'd been unconscious—for an hour! Such a length of time, an hour of my life lost. *Where did I go?*

"I'm talking but I don't hear anything coming out of your mouth," Coach said. "Let's try again. Lazio, did you see that?"

"Sorry, Coach," I mumbled. "I saw it."

He looked at my white face carefully. "You okay?"

"Good, good, fine."

Twenty-three days before the fight.

• • •

Maybe I blew the whole thing up in my mind. Maybe Sensei had forgotten it by now; maybe he'd want to help me prepare for the fight with Nuñoz? He believed nothing is as close as the master-disciple relationship, not even your family. Could one fight change that? My car seemed to drive itself to the dojo. How strange it felt to be walking up the steps, little bag holding my workout clothes, as I'd done almost every day since I was fifteen, waves of nostalgia contracting my chest when I opened the huge, hand-carved wooden doors.

Twenty years ago Sensei had bought this old church and ripped pews, pulpit, and carpet from the large room that had once been a place of worship. Now it was an airy open space with polished oak floors. The large, gorgeous stained-glass windows were the only clue to the building's former use, but to me the dojo was, had always been, a sacred place. So much of my life had been spent here. I'd grown up in this building through sweat, agony, and large doses of humble pie. And like a homing pigeon, I was returning to the nest.

I didn't see Sensei, who was probably in his office. He liked to sit at his desk and compose himself before each class. Men I'd worked out with for years greeted me and pounded me on the back, talking and joking. As Sensei walked lightly, purposefully into the room—instant electricity—everyone bowed and silently scrambled to line up. It didn't feel right to take my usual place in the front line, where the more advanced students had the privilege of standing. I stood at the back with the white belts.

Sensei scanned the energy in the room. He expected everyone to be centered and completely focused. If a man had problems with his girlfriend, was thinking about his dinner, or was distracted for any reason, he sensed it. He fined the offender a hundred knuckle push-ups—to be done rapidly on the spot while everyone waited. Most of the time we were compelled to be in the present; no one knew what would happen next.

Sensei bowed and the entire class bowed in unison, as if we were a single entity. The silence of the dojo was broken by his command.

"Horse stance!"

Bare feet squeaked against the oak floor. Stance training is the bread and butter of karate, and you could never practice the basics enough. For beginners Sensei reminded us: "Feet straight, toes relaxed, knees out, spine straight. Drop your weight evenly into both legs as if you were sitting on a chair." With a practiced eye he surveyed our efforts. "Lower!" We dropped our center of gravity a few more inches. When satisfied he left the room, leaving us to suffer. From my old place in the front line I hadn't noticed how strenuous this was to the neophyte. Legs had begun shaking like Jello after thirty seconds, and when Sensei returned after ten minutes, most lower belts had already collapsed in utter fatigue. When they saw him they made a feeble attempt to regain the posture. Sensei, of course, missed nothing. He knew very well who was giving it his all and who was coasting.

"Cat stance," he said.

The cat stance notched the degree of difficulty a little higher, especially since we'd had no rest and our legs were rapidly tiring. You had to put 95 percent of your weight on the rear leg. The toes were slightly curled back emphasizing the ball of the front foot, which rested lightly on the ground. Sensei came up behind a two-hundred-pound guy perspiring profusely and looked him in the eyes. His leg shot out, dumping him to the floor with a splatter of sweat.

"If you had five percent in the front leg," Sensei said, "I couldn't knock you down so easily."

After five minutes he gave the command to switch legs. We'd been holding stances for twenty minutes. Even the most seasoned were nearly finished. My muscles screamed and sweat beaded up, forming little streamlets that rolled down my back and legs and onto the floor, making small puddles around me. To an observer, the postures might seem simple enough. But much as the pot-bellied spectator of a boxing match sits in an easy chair urging the fighter to punch a little harder, unless you've experienced stance training you can't imagine how painful and difficult it is to carry on once fatigue has set into the muscles.

"Box stance!"

This was the hardest of all. Seventy percent of the weight was on the front leg and you had to drop your center of gravity so low your knee nearly touched the ground. Muscles were cramping. Every fiber of our bodies and minds screamed to give up. To the left of me was a yellow belt, a young man named Wes. His legs were grotesquely shaking, lurching back and forth as if he were having a seizure. And yet he was still holding the pose.

Sensei came and stood by his side. He brought his head close, practically whispering in his ear.

"Where's the pain?"

"Ev-everywhere," Wes stammered.

"Concentrate," he said. "Find the exact spot."

"It's in my legs."

"That's not good enough, go further. Where does the pain originate? Focus!"

Exhausted as he was, Wes shut his eyes and went inside. A sigh of astonishment escaped from his throat. Through my own fatigue, I nodded and smiled inwardly. I'd been in his place. If you were able to focus, if you could go into the pain deeply enough, it vanished, simply wasn't there. And sure enough, it happened to Wes.

"I don't know," he said. "I can't find it!"

"Pain comes from the mind," Sensei said. "You can go much further than you think. Good job, Wes."

Wes almost collapsed, more from hearing his name uttered by Sensei than from exertion. Most of us believed, in the beginning, that Sensei didn't know our names. But he did. In fact, he had a photographic memory. He used the stances as a rite of passage, a gate through which a student had to pass. Until a student proved himself, he never called him by name. After this rite of passage had been successfully negotiated, Sensei used his name and took a much greater interest in his progress.

The stance training was merely part of the warm-up. Then came punching and kicking drills, *kata* practice (pre-arranged forms), technique drills, and we always ended with *kumite* (free sparring).

Not once during the entire evening did Sensei glance in my direction.

On my way out I was surprised to see Lena, who rarely came to the dojo since getting her driver's license. As a child she'd loved karate, but Sensei wouldn't teach her. She was allowed only to watch. In her own way she was part of the dojo, sitting off to the side on the floor, focused and still as a stone. Seeing Lena made me think about Cindy for the first time this evening. One of the most amazing things about karate class was that you focused so intensely nothing else existed; it was as if the entire world vanished. Afterward your life slowly trickled back into your consciousness.

"How old are you, Lena?"

"I'm over twenty-one. Why, you want to take me for a drink?"

I shrugged lamely. "No, it's just that ... well, you're all grown up, you're a woman now."

"How nice of you to notice. Shit! After all these years you don't know how old I am?"

I was seventeen when Miwa, Omura's wife, went to Japan to care for her father, who had cancer. It caused her tremendous pain and guilt to leave the care of her household to her ten-year-old daughter. It took him nine months to die, and Lena and I formed a strange partnership. I showed up at their house at four-thirty in the morning and spent a few hours cleaning house and cutting vegetables for lunch and dinner. After breakfast Lena and I went shopping, and she made sure the vegetables and fruit were perfect. "No, Johnny. Sensei would never eat that apple. You see?"

In the late afternoon I'd return. The three of us drove to class together. After class Omura went to his study while Lena and I prepared dinner. She carried a tray to Sensei's study, then the two of us ate in the kitchen. Unlike her mother, who was so quiet she seemed nearly mute, Lena was loquacious as a joyous young bird on the first day of spring. After Omura's bath was drawn, we tackled her homework. I made her read English over and over until she was more competent than most kids her age. I corrected her writing until she could express herself well. With her homework complete, I left quietly through the back door, only to return in what seemed a few short hours. Lena had to handle lunch by herself, but I made sure she had everything she needed. When her mother finally came back—it was the longest nine months of my life—Lena bowed deeply. When she raised her dark eyes, they glistened with tears.

I always thought of Lena as a child, but she was probably about the same age as Cindy. Now she wanted to know where I'd been.

"Are you training, Johnny?"

"Yeah, with the team, and Phantom's sure putting me through the ropes."

"Except for tonight you haven't been to the dojo?"

"No."

"Why not?"

I motioned for her to follow me to the hallway where announcements were posted. It was the furthest point from Omura's office. Though I now realized Sensei couldn't hear and see through closed doors and walls as I'd once suspected, I wasn't taking any chances.

"If it's about that fight, Dad can be awfully old-fashioned," Lena said.

"He wanted me to win and I let him down. I disgraced him by losing." I took a deep breath. I'd thought it a thousand times, but it was the first time the words had touched the air.

Lena said, "My understanding in karate is that one can only disgrace himself?"

I thought it over for a second. "Normally, maybe, but it's not just me. I'm part of a family. I let down the whole lineage: his father and grandfather and all the Samurai that came before."

"Bullshit," Lena said. "They're all dead. They can handle it, and Dad's going to have to get over it."

"Maybe," I said with no conviction whatsoever.

Out of habit my eyes scanned the students who'd been selected to test for the next belt, a higher belt symbolizing a higher understanding and responsibility in karate. To my utter astonishment my name was posted.

"You can't be serious," I said out loud.

"Serious about what?"

"Look at that." I pointed. "My name is posted to test for second-degree black belt!"

"Yep, there it is," Lena said. "And in two weeks! I think Dad misses you. This is probably his hopelessly repressed way of extending the olive branch."

Testing for rank is a common tradition among martial artists. Most schools hold "belt" tests every month like clockwork. Ours did not. Sensei believed the progression of rank from yellow to orange, green, blue, purple, brown, and black belt was an Americanized development that keeps a student hankering after a tangible goal. He thought perfection of the art of karate should be incentive enough. When a student asked how long it took to get a black belt, he shrugged. Or said, "We'll see." Or offered a tiny smile of amusement. Or, more cryptically, "When your belt turns black." Here, Sensei was referring to the old way of Karate. When a student started he was given a white belt as part of the uniform, merely to hold up his pants. After years of hard handling it got dirty. In our school no one knew how long it would take to achieve a black or any belt.

Though I'd wanted a black belt from day one, Sensei had taken me through the ranks slowly. I wore green for six years, as long as it took most others to make black. It was another five years, eleven in total, to earn black. It stung my pride to see others promoted while I, who tried so hard, was left behind. But to have damaged pride was good, Sensei believed. Hurt pride meant a hurt ego, and the ego had to be subdued to achieve humility.

If a bruised ego made you a better person, I should have been a saint by now. Sensei had been harder on me than anyone, constantly correcting any breaches in etiquette. During kumite, he trained me to fight or be knocked down; I earned the nickname "star gazer" in the dojo, because every time I sparred with Sensei I ended up flat on my back looking at the ceiling.

Other schools provided a curriculum that could be memorized and polished for the test. In our dojo you never knew when you'd be called to test or *what* would be asked. You had to be prepared for anything, might have to perform any skill you'd learned, no matter how obscure. Sensei always tested the candidate severely. He liked to continually stretch our perception of limits, until we weren't sure if there were any at all.

There had been a day at the beginning of summer when I was racing through the woods and stepped in a nest of yellow jackets. I had more than a dozen stings on my legs, arms, and chest. I had to be driven to the emergency room. The doctor said I was sensitive to the venom and had a severe reaction. He gave me an antihistamine and told me to drink a lot of water and rest.

We had class every night and Saturday morning, and Sensei's most rigid rule was never to miss. Up till now I hadn't even been late. But the venom had taken a lot out of me. Staying home and relaxing seemed prudent. I called Sensei at home.

"Sensei, I can't make it tonight. A bunch of yellow jackets stung me and my body's all swelled up."

"Hmmm," Sensei grunted.

"The doctor told me to rest."

"When did you get stung?"

"About four hours ago."

"If you have not died by now you will survive. I'll see you tonight."

• • •

The most rigorous portion of the belt test was kumite. A man might have to fight four opponents at the same time. This wasn't pretend—the attackers were hitting for real. Another might have to defend in total darkness. Still another might fight one man after another for hours, without rest or water. A candidate might be asked to break bricks or wood, or fight with real weapons. The tests were always designed for individuals, to make them face their innermost demons and potentially push them over the edge of their self-limiting beliefs. That these tasks were seemingly generated on the spot was part of Sensei's genius.

The evening of the test, I arrived at the dojo a few minutes early.

Before testing, just as before a fight, you must have a completely empty stomach. Mine rumbled uneasily, but it wasn't from lack of food. I was nervous, unsure of my reception. Lena said Sensei missed me. It hardly seemed possible after the way he'd treated me the other night in class. I put on my dress gi, knotted my black belt, and tried not to think.

My bare feet made translucent sticky prints as I walked on the immaculately polished wood floor of the dojo. The entire school, about seventy-five students, was in attendance. All were dressed in spotlessly clean and pressed uniforms. The highest-ranking black belts sat at a long table with Sensei in the center, the position of honor. In a testing situation the occupants of "the table" acted as the jury, with Sensei as the supreme judge. But even the jury members never knew what to expect. They might have to get up and spar with the candidate, if Sensei so deemed. I'd sat at his side many times as part of this jury. The lower-ranking students knelt on the floor.

One hundred and fifty expressionless eyes watched in absolute silence as I bowed to Sensei and the other black belts. As was customary, I stood waiting for instructions. None came. The chair squealed as Sensei got to his feet. He walked out onto the floor and stopped right in front of me. He bowed, his eyes icy cold. No words, but I well understood. Several involuntary gasps and an "Oh, shit!" broke from astounded onlookers. It was the first time any candidate had had to fight Omura Sensei himself.

As was typical with Sensei, he never even got into a fighting stance. Immediately he hit me in the chest, just over the heart.

"Your defense still needs improvement, John," he said as a round kick smashed into my side, stealing my breath. At sixty-two he was still unpredictable; he moved like a ghost and hit like a sledgehammer.

I felt a hot flash of anger. *If that's the way you want it.*

Sensei kicked again. I grabbed his leg and kicked out his supporting leg, knocking him hard to the oak floor. He got up quickly. His eyes had that strange brightness I'd seen at the Chinese restaurant. No student had seen him on the ground. He'd lost face and was mad enough to chew up nails and spit out rust. Every eye was riveted on us as I danced, shooting a fast flurry of punches to his gut, then one to his face. My bare knuckles made a red welt on his cheek.

There must come a time in the cycle of life when the younger man passes the old. Reaching the point of defeating your teacher is a cliché in kung fu movies, but never had I imagined myself able to do it. My guts tightened with the strangeness of it, the love and anger that fueled my desire to break away from parental authority. Maybe it was time to leave the nest—the hard way.

Through long years of sparring with Sensei and watching him I knew his style, probably better than anyone. He was a master of defense, preferring to stand and wait for the attack. With my size and height, I forced him to change his strategy. I stood outside and picked at him. Occasionally a punch or kick got through. He had to move. He advanced, throwing powerful kicks and punches, but my youth gave further advantage. It was relatively easy to dance away from his attacks, and the training hall was so large I could run indefinitely.

Sensei was breathing heavily as he continued the attack. He was a fantastic fighter—were we the same age, I knew I wouldn't have a chance against him. His chest was heaving but he never gave up. He advanced through my flying hands and feet and connected a hard kick to my gut. I chopped a short right to his stomach. He grabbed my right shoulder with his left hand, his right arm around my waist and right hand at my belt, then pivoted and tried to throw me to the ground. But at the last instant I pivoted and got the exact same hold on him. For the second time Sensei crashed to the floor.

My instincts urged me to jump on top, get him in a Jiu Jitsu hold, and finish him. But I hesitated. Didn't my teacher deserve respect? Didn't martial etiquette demand courtesy? Shouldn't I help preserve face instead of burning all bridges?

I extended my hand. He allowed me to lift him up but then continued the momentum toward me—he butted me solidly with his head, right in the bridge of my nose, the same spot where Morales had broken it. The force of the blow and the intense pain brought tears to my eyes. For a second, I couldn't see a thing. Sensei brought his foot up and kicked me hard in the balls. I collapsed to the floor, rolled into a fetal position, nauseous pain rising to my throat.

"Karate is not that flashy stuff you have learned in the ring. It is doing whatever it takes to survive."

Sensei looked down at me on the floor. His face was sweaty, tired, and proud. Hot anger blazed in his eyes. His voice rang through the dojo.

"A man must have the balls to go for the kill. This is something a man either has in his heart or not. It is not a thing I can teach. He is born with it. You *hesitated*, John, the very same way you did against Morales. You lack the guts to be a true warrior. You have failed the test. Get out of my dojo!"

I picked myself up and left. None of the students had moved. Not a sound could be heard but Sensei's rapid breathing.

NINE

U sually things looked better in the morning, but not today. Sensei had taught me that each martial artist has a heritage, a family, and generations of martial artists standing behind him. That's why it's so vitally important to maintain an unblemished bond with your teacher. The teacher is the link, the medium: a channel through which the power of long-deceased masters flows into you and gives strength, direction, stability. Only when you've experienced this can you understand its power. Or how it feels to have that link severed, quickly. I was in a state of shock, a naked animal cub left to fend for itself.

After struggling through my morning workout I drove to Master Ting's. Ting was the last remnant, the only part of my life that remained unchanged. I arrived around one. A Chinese couple in their sixties were at the dining room table, which displayed five intricate vegetarian dishes on a revolving platter. I'd always admired this setup. You didn't have to ask anybody to pass the food; you just rotated the lazy Susan to the dish you wanted. My eyes riveted on the mock duck. To my taste buds, the pressed, seasoned tofu was more flavorful than the real bird. Ting watched my eyes and smiled.

I bowed and said "Excuse me" in Chinese. He started to lift himself from his seat. "Don't get up, Master Ting," I said. "I'm sorry for disturbing your lunch." Ting got up anyway.

"Please, please, no need to excuse. You're welcome here anytime, and let's drop the 'master.' My name's Ting."

This was a little ritual with us. I always called him master because it would be disrespectful not to honor the title he'd earned over a lifetime spent practicing his art. He always insisted.

"This is John Lazio," he said to his guests. "You hear of him? He's a famous fighter—and my student. When he has a fight, he comes here every week to meditate."

It might seem out of place for a monk to hold fighting in such esteem. But the Chinese consider it an accomplishment to excel at any endeavor. Meditation masters appreciate the amount of training, concentration, and focus it takes to win a fighting contest. Some have even been fighters themselves, like the famed monks of the Shaolin Monastery.

A little smile on his face, eyes gleaming, Ting invited me to sit down.

"Have some food with us—some duck, yes?"

"Thanks, Master Ting, but if I get too full I won't want to practice. If it's all right, I'll just go and meditate?"

Ting nodded.

I bowed to the guests, who shook my hand and wished me the best of luck. I thanked them in Chinese.

In the living room was a huge altar. I lit a handful of incense sticks and placed them in the brass burner. Soon aromatic sandalwood wafted through the air. I got down on my hands and knees and placed my forehead on the floor in a gesture of respect. Nine years ago, Ting had given me the Buddhist vows, known as taking refuge in Buddha. I didn't consider myself a Buddhist, didn't know exactly what I was. But I was sincere. That's what Ting recognized in me from the start: a burning desire to find truth. Meditation, more than anything I did, made me feel as if I were touching its boundaries.

I walked down the hall to the tiny cubicle Ting let me use when I meditated here alone. It was a bare room with only a round cushion to sit on. I brought my own blanket to cover myself if I got chilly. Usually I would sit, spine straight, body immobile, for an hour or more.

There was no way what I was doing now could be called meditation; I was merely sitting on the cushion, thoughts racing like cars on the highway.

Sensei's punches and kicks had hurt, but far less than his words. He was mad, I knew, but still. I'd hesitated, lost my focus for a second—but damn it, I knew how to go for the kill. My former knockouts proved it!

Ting's fingertips tapped lightly at the door. Sensitive as a cat, he must have noticed something was off with me.

"Your fight didn't go so well?" he said.

"I lost, but I have another one coming up soon. What's bothering me most is I've had a falling out with my karate teacher."

"Hmmm." Ting nodded solemnly. Being from a long lineage of Chan Buddhist masters, he well understood my concern.

Periodically, each student had some private time with Ting. These interviews served to answer any question that came up in practice. Some found these sessions mysterious or confusing. It was common for meditation masters to use nonsensical, paradoxical, or outrageous statements to shock the mind into enlightenment. With me Ting seemed quite straightforward. In fact, he never really answered my questions at all. Usually, he'd smile and say: "You sit and practice, then you find the answer." But today he shrugged.

"How's the meditation going?"

"I can't seem to get away from my thoughts and feelings."

"What method are you using?"

Ting had taught many methods but I always used the same one: to focus on a spot two inches below the navel and two inches in toward the spine. In Japanese this was known as gathering yourself in the *hara*, called the *dantian* in Chinese. The hara is the very center of the body or being. Concentrating here makes you strong and courageous; when your consciousness is fully centered here, supposedly, a mountain could fall down next to you and not disturb your calm. Sensei believed focusing on the hara to be the ideal meditation for martial artists.

"I still focus on the dantian."

"And how long have you used this method?"

"Over ten years. Since the beginning."

"And you reach a deep state of quiet?"

"Most of the time."

"What do you do when thoughts come?"

"I push them away and keep focusing on my dantian."

Ting sighed and smiled. His eyelids closed slightly, as if he were understanding something for the first time.

"You've developed a very strong mind, John, but I'm going to ask you to try another method."

"Why?"

"You're missing something important."

"I thought meditation was about focusing the mind until there are no thoughts."

"If you push them away ... it's escape."

"Escape!"

"If a burglar breaks into the window of your home, what do you do? Do you run into another room and shut the door? It seems to solve the problem, you appear to be safe in your room, but really, there's still a burglar in your house. That's what you do when you push thoughts away. Confusion goes unobserved, unnoticed, it returns to the unconscious depths it came from."

"Is that bad?"

"What's unseen doesn't go away, and what's repressed comes out in unhealthy ways. Under pressure, it will always return to haunt our lives. We just don't understand why or what happens."

"How can I tell if this is operating in my life?"

"It operates in everyone's life, more or less. You'll know it's there because it activates the nervous system, makes us tense, pulls us from our center. Inside we struggle, lose what's natural. Confusion steals our happiness. How about you, John—are you happy?"

Sometimes.

"How do I deal with this?"

"Don't push anything. Be easy, gentle, let it all be. Watch thoughts as you would waves of the ocean. They come and go, crashing endlessly on the beach. You can't change the waves, they're not good or bad, they aren't even yours. Just watch them, unconcerned."

"What do you mean not mine?"

"The mind is a receiver. It picks up thoughts like radio waves from the entire field of mental energy. People think what goes on in their heads is unique, they believe they hatch original thoughts. This is the main problem: we believe in the authority of our minds, we're so sure the voice in our heads is true and sound. This is the tragedy— identifying with our thoughts. We wake up in the morning, hear the voice in our head, and believe this is who we are. It isn't! The mind tells you lies. It's not to be believed or trusted."

• • •

I resumed my sitting and this time tried to watch everything. But after a few seconds I got completely lost in my mind's ramblings. When after an hour I got up to leave, as unproductive as this session seemed, two things were clear. First, Sensei had been right: I'd hesitated and it had cost me the fight. But inside was a quiet knowing. I wasn't sure how, but I'd come back, with Sensei or without.

Second, I wanted to see Cindy before the fight.

TEN

Anywhere near December, New York City can be both the best and worst place to be. The major avenues are well lit, and even at eleven p.m., throngs of people choke the streets. Store windows display all manner of finery. Strategically positioned bell-shaking Santas encourage pedestrians to feed money into black collection pots that hang from tripods. Sidewalk vendors set up tables on major avenues and hawk cheap imitations of designer clothes, wallets, and watches. Muggers, beggars, and street people lurk in the shadows, always on the lookout for an easy mark. Yet underneath the hype is a strange softness absent most of the year: a feeling of friendliness and tolerance, of what might even be called goodwill toward man.

• • •

Except for a tiny fake tree with a string of colored bulbs that flickered weakly on and off, Christmas hadn't made much of an impression at Asia House. Fine by me. I didn't feel much like celebrating.

Mama-san got to her feet, smiled broadly, and slightly bowed. Out of habit I tipped my own head. She probably gave this extra recognition only to those she considered regulars. *So the latest chapter in my life is that I'm a regular in a whorehouse.* It was my third time in three weeks.

"Hello sir, good evening."

"Good evening, Mrs. Li."

Mrs. Li raised her eyebrows. She seemed surprised I knew her name.

"Miss Cindy will be out in just a few moments. Will you wait, please?"

I sat on one of the leather easy chairs and grabbed a newspaper. I was too distracted to actually read it. I knew the sex I'd experienced at the whorehouse should be a lot better. Cindy didn't intimidate me like Sugi, yet still buttons got pushed, sensitive feelings that had been locked away were exposed. The issue was still fear, and fear was weakness. But tonight had the potential to be different. I'd begun the practice of tantric yoga.

Tantric yoga has a unique angle on sex, holds it in reverence as the only activity that creates life. Sexual energy in both man and woman is not only the source of vitality but also genius. A burst of *kundalini*—traveling from the loins and up the spine to the crown—is the creative juice behind every literary masterpiece, work of art, or great invention.

A man's seed, therefore, is treasured at all costs. For men, ejaculation during intercourse is considered wasteful unless the couple is trying to make a baby. Masturbation—losing the sperm to the air for a few seconds' pleasure—is throwing your life force out the window. One drop of sperm is more potent than a thousand drops of blood. *That's why you can't have sex before a fight. It's not the sex, it's the ejaculation!* Enough ejaculations and the average man gradually depletes his juice until he's a stiff-jointed, weak-willed, dim-eyed bull having only enough drive to make it through work and graze in front of the television.

Where it originally came from I didn't know, but the Indians, Chinese, and Tibetans each added a certain flavor to the practice. Of course, as with all methods of enlightenment, it wasn't tossed to just anyone but prescribed individually, painstakingly matched with the personality of the seeker. If I'd been studying under a master in Tibet, I'd never have been chosen for such a method. Supposedly it was given only to those not all that interested in sex to begin with. But now the choice was mine.

Tantric yoga strives to prolong the sex act. If a man can increase his staying power, he can build up tremendous energy with a woman. Naturally, learning to control ejaculation, decrease penile sensitivity, and develop sexual stamina takes practice. The "practice" isn't boring. It's similar to masturbation—you stimulate yourself until erect—but there's no fantasizing, no tensing the body or facial muscles as men typically do while masturbating. On the contrary, tantric yoga advises approaching sex loosely and lightly. You relax every muscle in your body and breathe slowly and easily through the entire process.

As you became really excited, near climax, you perform a series of pelvic contractions that put the brakes on the urge to ejaculate and at the same time pump sexual energy toward the brain. The circulation of energy is an important piece of the "meditation." The sexual energy travels up the spine to the head, then loops back down to be stored in the hara. This solo practice is prerequisite to practicing the same "meditation" with a woman.

A radiantly smiling Cindy appeared and ushered me straight to the locker room to remove my winter clothes. She led me to the bathroom for a quick shower, and naked except for a towel I walked with her up the stairs and down the hall to her bedroom. From the top of the stairs I saw a man sitting in a folding chair, talking with two of the women. He was about thirty-five, medium height, and maybe thirty pounds overweight. He waved to Cindy.

She waved back and said with pride, "This is the boxer."

He looked me over carefully and nodded his head in curt greeting.

"Who is that guy?" I asked her when we were out of earshot.

Cindy laughed. "He friend of Mrs. Li. He come here and just talk to girls. I don't really know why he come. He not a customer."

"Why did you point me out to him?"

"He always say he big martial arts expert. I tell him about you."

The biggest thing about him seemed to be his belly, but you never know. Sensei always said that with fighters you can never judge a book by its cover. Perhaps he was so good he didn't need to keep in shape?

Cindy wasn't very talkative, and since I was almost always quiet, we didn't speak. The silence wasn't uncomfortable. We'd only spent a few hours together, but it seemed like we'd known each other for much longer. She patted the bed for me to sit, and I watched her as she lit the candle on her nightstand. I'd seen the other girls as they sat together in the lineup or walked in the halls with their customers. Many of them wore tight miniskirts and bikini tops that displayed pretty much all their goods. Cindy wore a short black miniskirt, no doubt required dress for Asia House, but she covered her legs with black tights. On top she liked to wear a white blouse. She looked more like an Asian schoolgirl than a prostitute.

She took off her clothes—absentmindedly, gracefully—and placed them on the dresser. She seemed quite comfortable, even when she noticed me watching her intently. She smiled and sat next to me on the bed. She didn't offer me anything to drink this time, nor was there any massage. She pushed me lightly down on the bed and embraced me. I got hard immediately. *Take action—go for what you want.* I motioned for her to lie down. I spread her legs and brought my face down to her vagina.

"No!" she cried out and pushed me away. Startled, I moved quickly away. "What's the matter?"

"I not clean there, you know, my job, other men—it not right for you."

She drew a line with oral sex. I was flustered, but still excited. I held her in my arms, did a few long pelvic contractions to calm down my erection. Cindy raised her eyebrows.

"You okay?" she asked.

"Yes, why?"

"You face look funny."

Oh. I hadn't yet learned to stop tensing my jaw or smile while performing the contractions. I was still tense as I awkwardly got on top. Quick as a submission hold it was over with, finished. In humiliation I pulled out and dropped my head on her warm, sweet-smelling belly, feeling it rise and fall with her breath.

I sighed deeply. Somewhere, there had to be an old Asian proverb: *man no relax penis not work.* I was utterly disgusted with myself and too embarrassed to say anything. What was I doing here? With each session I was just making myself more of a fool.

Cindy propped herself up on her elbow and looked into my eyes. Her steady gaze was soft yet candid, piercing deeply into me. In some inexplicable way we understood each other at a profound level. I couldn't quit. I wasn't about to run away.

Finally, she broke the silence. "Last time you tell me about Heidi."

"Please, let's not get back into that—besides, there's not much more to tell."

Cindy ignored me and asked the million-dollar question: "How was sex with Heidi?"

"Good. Fantastic, really."

I leaned heavily against the wall. Hard to believe I was once a good lover. It seemed so far away it could have been a different life, certainly a different me. In lovemaking my chief pleasure was seeing that the woman had pleasure. I'd been very attentive to Heidi, learned what she wanted, how to satisfy her. In those days I was able to last a long while, and by the time I came she'd already had multiple orgasms. Satisfying a woman, hearing her little moans, seeing her eyes closed in pleasure, feeling her body shaking out of control—*that's* what had made me feel like a man. What was happening to me?

"You so young, where you do it?" Cindy said.

"At my parent's house. I had a little bedroom not much bigger than this room of yours. It had a fold-out couch, and when the bed was pulled out you could hardly open the door. I ran home from school and waited under the covers, naked, until she got home, took off her clothes, and joined me."

"You do that every day?"

"Yes, well, on school days Monday through Friday. On the weekends we found another place. Those two years were the sweetest in my life," I said. "After lovemaking Heidi curled up next to me, her head on my chest." I could always tell from her quiet breathing and the little twitches in her body that she'd fallen asleep. It was delicious to have her against me, to feel her warmth, smell her hair.

"I tried to stay awake but always drifted off. When we woke up, I walked her home in time for dinner."

More memories loosened and came to the surface. I was happy then as I'd never been happy before. It was an amazing thing to be loved by a woman, but fleeting, like life itself. At sixteen, with Heidi lying beside me, I felt the age-old possessiveness a man can feel for a woman. I wanted to hold her as mine, to keep her love forever. But the love of a woman was something she bestowed. It couldn't be held any more than you can hold the freshness of a rose.

"In Thailand this *never* happen in parent's house. Where were your parents?"

"Mother was sometimes home."

"Your mother *let* you bring teenage girlfriend in your bedroom for *sex* and she at home?"

"Things were pretty wild in New York during the nineties. I think my parents were just happy to know where I was. But of course Mom hated it. She used to say I was violating the rules of decency and the laws of her home, but in the end we did it anyway."

"Where were girl's parents?"

"Heidi told them she was at a girlfriend's or staying at school. Anything but what we were really doing."

Cindy gasped.

"It gets better," I said. "We had sex most every night at *her* parents' house."

"How you do this?"

"I snuck in."

"Into *parents'* house!"

"Yeah, but isn't our time nearly over? Don't you have another customer?"

"Yes."

"Then let's get back to this later."

She nodded. "Wow! This I got to hear," she said, then added, "If I was Heidi's mother I hate you a lot." She was trying to sound cross but there was admiration in her shining eyes. She shook her head and made a little clucking sound with her tongue and lips. "You very romantic man."

"Yeah, I was romantic, and a little crazy. And you know, it's not that I don't like my life now. I'm doing exactly what I want. But I was never happier than those couple of years with Heidi—or for that matter more tired. I'd slip out of her house at four-thirty to catch the bus home. By five I was already falling asleep. Even if all the seats were taken and I was standing up. I don't know how I made it through the day."

"Sex too much, sleep not enough," Cindy said.

Once again I was lost in thought.

"What you think about now?" Cindy said.

"Just that I've got a fight in less than three weeks and I won't be coming to see you until it's over with."

"Yes I understand. Keep away from women and man get very fierce. But in our case not necessary."

"Why not."

"I good for you, good luck girl. I bring luck to you."

Cindy smiled, took me in her arms, and hugged me tight. When I started to pull away she wouldn't let go but brought me tighter into her body. We stayed together for what seemed like a long time, her head tucked into my chest. When I opened my arms her eyes were slightly misty.

"Before the fight you come back to me one time. We have no sex. I give you massage. We just talk. You don't pay me, it be like date, okay?"

"That's very kind of you. Thanks, Cindy."

"So you come?"

I nodded.

ELEVEN

Winter. The snow was too deep, impossible to drive in beyond the entrance of the state forest. *Just like the old days*: on foot, a winter dawn, fresh heavy snowfall, the air washed clean and so cold it hurt in my lungs. All fighters have their rituals, and the forest was mine. As a farmer walks the earth before he sows his seeds, it was necessary to come here first.

Even under a two-foot blanket I found it, could've found it at midnight I'd been here so many times. I made my way along the river, the same river I jumped in to cool myself in the summer heat. Now it whispered under a foot of blue-gray ice. I walked to the top of the steep hill, to the center of a pine forest overlooking the gorge. *My spot.* I surveyed it reverently.

The snow was even deeper off the road, but I worked out anyway, dancing around a tree, shifting my body, pivoting and kicking from all angles, lightly touching the trunk with the ball, heel, or edge of my foot. Despite the cold, dribbles of sweat came out of my pores. After an hour and a half I flattened the snow, sat on my jacket, and covered myself with a blanket. I sat in silence for half an hour, the steam rising off my body into the fresh air.

It was my practice to contemplate an upcoming fight in my imagination. If I could get a clear image, I knew I'd win. Today there were no premonitions of victory, just Sensei popping in and out of my mind like a jack-in-the-box. He was such a presence, ingrained in my very way of being. He had taught me everything I valued; I owed this very spot to him. Over a decade ago he'd told me to find such a place.

"The location is important," he said, "away from noise, pollution, and electromagnetic fields—away from all distraction. Pick a spot that makes you feel good, a place where you want to practice."

I'd hunted for it like an explorer searching for new land. When I found it I knew it was right: high on a hill, deep in the fragrant pines, the sound of a waterfall crashing into a deep pool. I came every day, spent hours punching and kicking countless thousands of times. I learned to drop my weight into my legs and pivot on the balls of my feet. By relaxing my waist and spinning, I could whip my legs with great force. After years of practice, I developed extreme dexterity with my feet. I could dance around a tree and blast it with tremendous power or brush it like a whisper from any angle or position. The ground where I worked was worn from my movements. There was a circle, almost like a crop circle, two inches deep in the earth around the tree. Sometimes I stayed all day. If I got sleepy I lay on the ground and slept. The land became part of me.

One evening, after class was finished, I told Sensei I'd found my spot. He nodded and looked carefully into my eyes.

"Come to my house for dinner," he said. It was the first time I'd eaten with Sensei, alone in his study—a great privilege. When the meal was finished and Lena had taken the dishes, he told me a story.

"Once there was a Korean master who vowed to practice outside for a year." My ears perked up. I knew Sensei didn't waste words. "The winters were brutal but this man resolved to go the full year, and he did, even through hardship and illness. Each day he put a pine needle in a jar to mark the passing of the day. He didn't stop until he'd collected three hundred and sixty-five."

To really learn from a master you had to approach as a woman, not with a male mind full of concepts or the will to attain. The old scriptures didn't even refer to it as teaching or learning but as *transference*, from the teacher to you. Truth was not learned but caught. You had to be receptive and even receptive wasn't enough. You had to be like a fresh, nubile woman, willing to be molded by the touch of her beloved. The love you had for your teacher made you fertile inside, as a woman who longs for a baby. Then, and only then, would the teacher's seed fall on fertile ground. Truth entered your body like a new soul and if cared for, grew inside.

In the three years since I'd met Sensei I'd focused on his every word. I'd concentrated so keenly on him I could read the man, know what he was feeling, anticipate his every command before it was spoken. This wasn't an order, not even a suggestion. But he wanted me to do it. Sensei threw bread on the water and waited to see if I'd bite. With the eagerness and confidence of an eighteen-year-old, I grabbed the hook.

"If the Korean master did it, so will I."

He fixed me with those deep onyx eyes, searching the depths of me.

"A year is a long time, John, not to miss even a single day."

"I'll last."

He smiled wistfully and solemnly nodded his head.

It was easy to make the decision, but it indelibly changed me. The truth is it rearranged the very fabric of my soul. When the winter settled in, I had to walk five miles through snow over my knees. For a week that January it was twenty below zero, so cold I left Ernesto home by the fire. Though I bundled myself tightly in warm clothes, they couldn't brunt the wind. Many, many times the thoughts came: *Isn't it enough that I've walked this far? At least I made it here, I don't have to stay.* Yet this was more than just an agreement with myself. Sensei's eyes and that nod of his head burned in my soul. So I stayed for a full workout—at least an hour—though the blowing snow froze my face numb and ice formed on my whiskers. By the time I made it back there was no feeling in my feet. It took a few minutes in the warm cabin before the dead appendages came back to life.

The bitter cold was nothing compared to the stomach flu in the spring. My strength was gone, I had a high fever, couldn't eat. Three days without food. Each day I wondered if I could venture beyond my bed much less survive the walk, workout, and blood-hungry insects, thick with the first real warmth of the season. I discovered a part deep inside, a place beyond the will that dragged me to my spot and commanded my body to spin, my arms and legs to punch and kick. There was no need to put a pine needle in a jar to mark the passing of a day—I was there *every* day—yet I saved the needles anyway. And when the year was finished, I pushed myself through a second winter. Only after five full seasons had passed did I loosen this daily ritual.

I never spoke about what I was doing. Only Sensei knew. But he wouldn't ask about my progress, though I longed for him to.

And finally he did ask, casually, as if it were something he'd forgotten. No one else would have discerned the expectation in his manner or expressionless face, but I knew every nuance of his voice. Beneath the matter-of-fact tone, it was deep with feeling, pregnant with anticipation.

"By the way, John—did you last the year?"

I ran to my locker and pulled out the jar that held many more than a year's worth of pine needles. I couldn't help standing up straight and throwing my shoulders back. Sensei took the jar and looked at me with that tight little smile. Even his impenetrable eyes let a bit of his pride shine through.

My heart bounded in my chest. My soul pondered the mysteries of being a martial arts master. *Could he have planned this all along?* Surely Sensei must have known what I'd go through, the trials I'd endure. At that moment I knew, beyond doubt, that martial arts was my calling. I'd do anything, even cut off a finger, to win Sensei's trust, to make him proud, to be worthy of his teaching. The highest purpose I could fathom for my life was to follow eventually in his footsteps. My beating heart nearly rose from my throat, I loved him so much.

• • •

Phantom not only knew my rituals, he catered to them. Nuñoz was coming to the East Coast to fight me, and Coach sensed I needed to settle myself. Instead of having me come to the boxing gym in Brooklyn, he drove—two hours each way—to train me at home. It was possible. My four-car garage never harbored a tire or box of junk. Through many a snowstorm my car sat outside. After I started winning fights and had money coming in, I'd had the garage renovated, turned into a high-tech training hall with reinforced ceilings, special floors, and all kinds of equipment. There was good heat, a refrigerator for ice packs, a bathroom with a shower, a little office where we could review sparring sessions, even a cage like the ones mixed martial artists fight in. A large portrait of Sensei hung in the place of honor.

Phantom was savvy as ever in his selection of sparring partners. Where he found martial artists with styles similar to Nuñoz, I'll never know. But one day a different type awaited me, stretching out in the ring: a small, wiry black guy in his mid-fifties.

After quick introductions, Phantom said, "Do a few rounds with Lazio, okay Crandall?" I looked sideways at Coach. I was twenty-five years younger and outweighed Crandall by at least ten pounds. Coach nodded me on.

I started out slow, hesitant to hurt the old guy, but after a few lively jabs that snapped my head back, it was clear Crandall was no pushover. I went at him with quick lefts. He lightly brushed them aside. *Keep on doing that and I'll help you take a little nap.* He was wide open as I shot a straight right. He weaved his head and my right slightly missed. He was still in range so I let go with the left hook, put my body weight behind it, but hit nothing but air and nearly fell over from the miss. Rat tat tat—three blows, not very hard, not even that fast, but precise as a surgeon's cut. I found myself sitting on the canvas looking up. I got up and tried again—same result. The man was practically untouchable. The closest I came to hitting him was his arms.

Phantom was grinning like a cat. "Well, John, what do you think?"

"Amazing! I never came up against a man so skilled in defense he makes me look like a fool. Crandall, I hope you don't catch a cold from all that breeze I fanned your way." Everyone in the gym laughed.

Later, when we had some privacy, Phantom and I talked more about it.

"Johnny, at the height of his career Crandall was ranked sixth in the welterweight division. He never even made it anywhere near champion. You see why I want you to learn this?"

"Sure, but you can't forget that mixed martial arts is a different world than boxing—not taking anything away from Crandall. He's a master! But a few things don't quite fit. Bobbing, weaving, and ducking can be dangerous in mixed martial arts. You could bob right into someone's knee or foot. And the big eight- or ten-ounce boxing gloves change the entire art: it's easier to protect your head. You've seen it, Coach. The gloves we use in mixed martial arts barely cover the knuckles. You try some of the boxing moves with the small gloves and you're just going to get smacked in the face. Besides, I wouldn't be trading punches with a guy like Crandall for five minutes. I'd have used my legs or taken him to the ground."

"Maybe," Phantom said. "If a man's good enough with his hands you might not get the chance to pull off any of your fancy moves before the lights go out. I want you to learn to box real good. It's going to give you confidence."

At Phantom's request, Crandall started training me.

"Whew, buddy! You're *way* too tense," Crandall said deep from his belly in a southern drawl just after his left connected with the side of my head. "You want to fight real good, you got to keep loose and easy. That way you flow with everything. You move in a split second. And if you get hit, you roll with it, you're soft and free like a leaf in the water."

I smiled. Crandall's words could have come from Ting, Sensei, even tantra.

• • •

On a cold December twenty-third, I had my fourth appointment with Cindy. I'm sure she had no idea how unusual it was for me to do something like this so close to a fight. There was almost no traffic on the streets, so I was surprised to find Asia House packed to the gills. A bevy of women I hadn't seen before were standing and sitting against the wall. For the first time Mrs. Li was standing—with a microphone, looking like a stressed-out traffic cop. Cindy was off to the side, waiting for me. The lockers were all occupied, so after bathing we carried my clothes upstairs to her room. I placed them on the floor beside the bed.

"What's with this?" I said. "Why aren't all these men at home with their families?"

"Men get depressed at holiday. December probably busiest month of year."

"Who are all these women?'

"I tell you before, they free agents. Mrs. Li hire them when it very busy."

"With all this business, you're going to lose money doing this."

"Yes, I still have to give Mrs. Li her share."

"What do you pay her?"

"I must pay rent and time both. Rent is the same always for my room, time depend how many customer I have. That how she make her money."

"I didn't realize. It's really sweet of you to do this for me, but I'll give you the money for Mrs. Li. I don't want you to pay for me."

"Thank you for understand. Lay down, I give you massage."

After about ten minutes Cindy stopped. She had a pained look on her face and was rubbing her neck with her hand.

"What's the matter?"

"My neck and shoulders hurt."

"Did you hurt yourself?"

"My neck hurt most of time because of job I do. Massage men, sometimes big men who ask me to press hard. Massage hard work. If you do not do massage you do not know how hard a work it is."

"I do massage, Cindy."

"Ah. Where you study?"

"I learned by myself."

"Oh." Cindy nodded her head but didn't look very impressed.

I turned over and sat up.

"Take off clothes and lie down, please," I said, imitating Kim and Sugi as best I could. Cindy's eyes popped open, surprise stamped all over her lovely face.

"You joking me."

Looking at the expression on her face, I couldn't help laughing. Cindy cracked up too but didn't stop unbuttoning her shirt.

"I hope you not just blow hot air. I could use massage."

"Oh, you could, could you?"

"Yes! I not go to bed unless it three and usually I go up at nine. When I not working—and this very little time not working—we clean and buy food and prepare food. This job probably hardest one there is. I must be polite and bow and I smile smile smile, make my face hurt. We massage and have sex with men and make that we like it. We have to sometimes be with sick or crazy and there always worry about disease."

It must have been a huge act of trust for her to have unprotected sex with me. *Why did she do it?*

"Now you know why I could use massage. Now I wait for you to give to me!"

"So you pretend to like it?"

"Stop it! I tell you already—it different for you."

"Oh, sure! Besides, with me it lasts such a short time you don't have to pretend for very long."

"Stop! You very sweet lover."

"Okay. It will be my Christmas present to you, lie on your stomach."

Cindy flipped face down on the bed. I put myself fully into it. My hands worked on her neck, body, and legs—gently yet firmly, rhythmically, never stopping for a second. I became one with her body.

"You *fantastic!* You must practice for many years, no?"

"I've practiced on and off, but I'm no professional. Sometimes I think when I hang up my gloves I might become a doctor."

"I don't know this about you."

"Healing is the other side of fighting. In the old days martial arts masters learned both. Besides, there's a lot you don't know about me, Cindy."

"That American actor—you know on TV movies sometime in Old West? Very big man, lots of fight, little talk? Joe Wayne?"

"*John* Wayne?"

"Yes John Wayne. You make him look like man who never shuts his mouth." She gently touched my chest. "I am sure there is a *big lot* nobody know about."

I felt the blood heat my neck. Annoyance and the desire to defend myself rose like a flame to engulf me. *How quick I am to jump into a fight!* I took a series of deep breaths. Then I concluded the massage in the classic style of Asia House.

"Massage finished, turn over please." I watched Cindy as she turned over. It made me happy to see all the tension gone from her face. That's what I loved about massaging women. When the stress is taken from a woman's face it brings out her distinct beauty. I had to tell her.

"When you're this relaxed you look like a little girl."

"Thank you." She sighed heavily. "I don't feel like little girl. I don't feel like little girl for *very* long time."

She sat up and looked at me with soft eyes.

"You good man, Johnny. Have good heart. I meet many many men. No man *ever* do what you do for me." She kissed me gently. I returned it. She kissed me longer, with passion in her tongue. She felt me harden and waited, looking at me with innocent eyes, the corners of her lips slightly upturned. We both knew we were not supposed to have sex today. I kissed her again. She pulled me to the bed. We ripped off our clothes; she got on top and started to move quickly. I touched her lips.

"Slow down," I said.

She stopped moving. That gave me time to relax and slow my breathing. I attempted the pelvic contractions, which helped dampen the urge to ejaculate. After a few minutes I should have stopped, but it was so delightful to be inside her. Cindy groaned and started moving fast. I tried to move with her, thought I could control myself, but I came inside her. Cindy's face was a mix of disappointment and apology. She seemed to be waiting for me to tell her it was okay, but I was too shocked to say anything.

On my way out Sugi was in the waiting room with her client. She looked good. She winked and waved. I waved quickly and headed down the stairs.

As I walked onto Canal Street, the traffic was quiet and the hum of the city subdued. Even though I'd failed with tantric yoga, I couldn't help but smile at the look of surprise on Cindy's face. If Sensei had been a fly on the wall tonight, he'd have fallen off at the sight. Massaging a woman! He'd think I was a wimp. But he and I were different people, stamped from very different molds. At the moment my problem with him seemed a little further away, as if I were looking at it from a distance. Inside, I felt warm.

TWELVE

During the prefight so-called staredown, Nuñoz and I barely looked at each other. Once, I shot him a quick glance, but he didn't raise his eyes from the ground. While the ref gave brief instructions, I looked over the audience. For the first time, Sensei was absent. *No surprise there.* The horn sounded for the first round.

"Hit him," Phantom said.

I walked out in a strong defensive mode, my hands in tight protecting my face, my arms and elbows covering my body. Nuñoz and I slowly felt each other out. I flicked out a few tentative left jabs and a weak front kick. Halfhearted as it was, the kick scored in the midsection and Nuñoz retreated. Though our careers were on the line, we were both gun-shy, hesitant to mix it up. The place was packed to the gills with fans expecting a ferocious battle. After a minute there were a few boos and catcalls. Never had an audience booed one of my fights.

Nuñoz preferred to take the fight to the ground, where he was the undisputed master. He dove in quickly for the takedown but I threw my legs and body backward in a sprawl that neutralized his efforts. We were back in the center of the ring, which was more to my advantage. I connected with a double jab and followed with a weak right, then threw a straight kick to his midsection. Nuñoz wasn't hurt, but the crowd, easily roused by any action, cheered loudly anyway.

Again Nuñoz dove in to try and grab my leg for a takedown, and again I easily avoided him with the sprawl. It would have been far more effective had he set me up with his hands and feet or waited to charge until I was coming in for an attack, but he seemed a little off. I hit him with a good flurry of lefts and a single right, then kicked his left leg with my rear right leg. He came in to clinch; I thought he was trying to rest, but it was a ploy. He placed his foot on the outside of mine and spun my body around in a slick takedown.

Quick as lightning he got behind me and applied a rear naked choke. His position was good, he had both leg hooks in and the choke was deep, almost perfect, but not quite. He tried to stretch me out with his legs and cinch the choke in a little tighter. A submission such as this can instantly end the fight, and like a chess master, Nuñoz patiently waited for me to hang myself.

I had to find some way to survive two entire minutes in the chokehold until the round ended. I fought with all my strength to turn my head to give me a tiny bit of space, and at the same time fend off his arms. Nuñoz tried just as hard to manipulate my neck to compress the carotid artery. One fraction of a millimeter deeper and it was lights out. Nuñoz continuously ratcheted and pressed to get his arm in deeper. I was beginning to get lightheaded, getting real close to going to sleep. The round ended just in time for me.

I lay on the canvas, clarity seeping back from a far away, hazy place, my heartbeat pounding in my ears. The ref came over and checked me carefully before letting us continue.

"Goddamnit!" Coach said as I sat on my chair trying to gulp back my strength. "Don't let that happen again! Hit him!"

When the horn sounded for the second round, I pranced in close, my face intensely set, feeling for an opening. *Loose and easy,* Crandall's southern drawl floated into my head. Nuñoz came in aggressively. He threw caution to the wind and tried to land, but training with Crandall made anticipating Nuñoz a walk in the park. He held his head rigid and too high, didn't tuck his chin, and dropped his left hand. My straight right flicked out and connected. His legs slightly buckled.

"Lazio!" Phantom yelled. "He's finished! There's nothing left of him. Take him out!"

I was all over him like ants at a picnic. Lefts, rights, uppercuts rained like a monsoon. He was hurt. I whipped around with a perfectly timed back kick that smashed under his ribs. Nuñoz tried to clinch, but I reached under quickly and pushed his head into a standing guillotine. He tapped out.

• • •

Coach drove me home, yakking all the way.

"Nuñoz can't take a punch anymore, he's washed up, poor guy. So long as you kept yourself off the ground, it's an easy win. It's good, you need it."

I sighed. "Is that supposed to make me feel good?"

The next day, the reviews of the fight made the paper and were also posted on the web: "John Lazio stopped former champ Fernando Nuñoz forty-five seconds into the second round, by submission. Most agree that it's time for Nuñoz to retire."

Phantom called it an easy win, but it hadn't been. My fighting style was the opposite of easy. As much as I hated to admit it, I wasn't as good a fighter as I'd once fancied. I'd won my earlier fights mainly through an aggressive offense. Morales burst that bubble and since then my shortcomings had been clearly revealed, in the ring and out. I was tense and had periods where I lost focus. It had happened tonight. But then Nuñoz wasn't the fighter he once was; his confidence was shot. Knowing that was like looking in a distorted mirror and it bothered me.

• • •

When I returned to Asia House it was already the tail end of January. As I opened the door and walked into the waiting room, Mama-san got up from behind the desk and bowed low from the waist.

"Good evening, doctor," she said in a respectful tone. "Miss Cindy's waiting for you sir."

What's gotten into her?

Cindy came out looking particularly fresh and radiant in her black miniskirt and a white blouse. Her long hair was woven into tight shiny pigtails that hung down her back. She looked so much like a schoolgirl I was beginning to wonder if she was even eighteen. She put her hands together, palms together over the heart and bowed. "Sawatdee ka," she said.

"What's that mean?" I asked on the way to the locker room.

"*Sawatdee* mean hello."

I bowed to her. "Sawatdee ka," I said.

Cindy laughed as if it were the funniest thing she'd ever heard.

"Man never say *ka*—man say sawatdee *khap.*"

"Why does the man say khap and the woman ka?"

"Speech is different for man and woman," Cindy replied. "If you want to say hello as man you must say khap."

"Okay."

As I took off my clothes she patted me on the back. "Kop khun ka!"

"More words! What does *kop khun ka* mean?"

"Thank you."

"Are you trying to teach me Thai? And thanks for what?"

"Yes, I teach you a little Thai, it good to know for when you go to Thailand—and thank you is because you heal me! My neck feel all better after you massage so good."

"It was my pleasure. I'm glad it helped," I said, a little surprised it was so effective.

"You very good! I know. Healing, it in my blood. My auntie gifted to heal. Auntie say, some have gift and others not. You have it."

"I appreciate the kind words, but let's not get too carried away."

"You give to me, I try and give back to you. Why don't you take?"

"What are you talking about?"

"I say you good healer, but you don't open up heart to take it in." She tapped me on the chest. "Why?"

"Okay then, I'm a healer. Thank you—I mean kop khun ka," I smiled.

"Man say khap," Cindy said.

"Okay, *khap.*"

"That better! Mrs. Li think about paying you to look at her bad knee and cure some of the other girls. Did she talk to you?"

"So that's why she called me doctor. But I'm sorry, this really is going too far!"

Cindy punched me in the ribs. "Why say no so quick? You get paid and I see you more."

"Would that make me a regular or a free agent?" I laughed. "I'm coming here enough, it wouldn't hurt to make a little cash to help pay your fee. But there's just one fact everyone's missing. I'm not a doctor. I'm not even in med school. Tell Mrs. Li to forget it. The only person I'll work on is you."

"Okay!" she said. "I keep you to you word."

Immediately, she took off her clothes and lay on her stomach.

"I'm ready," she called gaily.

"I see that you are," I said, staring at her back as she lay face down on the bed. The massage I gave her was real enough, but since our time was so limited, I strategically stroked and kissed her stomach, thighs, and ankles as a type of foreplay. Cindy smiled as I awkwardly got myself inside her. *Take it easy, breathe.* I closed my eyes, focused on a spot between my eyebrows, and made my breath slow and relaxed— another tantric yoga technique. I started to move carefully.

"Don't forget!" She said. "You must tell me how you go to Heidi's house and sleep with her."

"Uh huh."

"Tell me more about that."

I opened my eyes and looked at her. "Cindy! Do you want to make love or talk?" I closed my eyes and returned to the spot between my eyes.

"Who say you have to keep quiet when you make love?"

Good question! But it sure was foreign to me. Heidi and I had always done it in silence. Occasionally we might scream or groan, but never did we speak. I stopped moving. With my eyes still closed I said:

"Why do you want to know this anyway?"

"I not hear of anything like this except in fairy tale."

I looked at her face and started moving again. "You're very lovely," I said.

"Don't change the subject!" She looked away. "And I not so lovely, thank you."

"What? How do you say *beautiful* in Thai?"

"*Suay.*"

"You are definitely suay."

"I average cute, maybe have tiny bit of beauty. That's all."

"You're drop-dead gorgeous!"

"Not beautiful, I black." She pointed to my leg against hers. Look at you." In contrast to her brown skin I was white as Casper the Friendly Ghost. "Look at me," she pinched her arm. "Black."

"You're not black but even if you were, what does it matter? In America we like black. Black is beautiful. In the summer white women bake their bodies in the sun by the thousands. And winter it's the same thing in a tanning booth."

"That crazy! Thai women stay away from the sun. We even have cream that bleaches our skin white. We think it more beautiful for woman to have white skin. We believe that if you born light, you have good karma from last lifetime."

"Now *that's* crazy!"

"And look at this." She touched the bridge of her nose.

"What about it?"

"It so flat." She pouted. "I like your nose. It not flat against the face."

Again, I stopped moving and stared.

"My nose? No, mine's not flat. It's twisted and smashed. You like *my* nose?"

"More than mine."

"Hey, wait! I tell you you're beautiful but you refuse to take it into your heart?"

Cindy's first reaction was surprise, then she broke into a broad grin.

"You give me my words back to me, but you right!"

"Well? You're changing the subject."

Neither the dim light nor her dark skin could conceal her deep blush.

"Okay, then," she said, "I'm a pretty woman."

Her face glowed, uncensored, like a shy little girl beaming at a compliment. My words seemed to reach her heart, and it opened like a rose. Maybe it was because I was inside her body, but something in me also opened. A strong wave of emotion swept over me. I wanted to touch her. Not her body, but *her*.

"Cindy ... you're so beautiful," I said as I moved slowly, pressing my body and soul into hers. I tried to look deeply into her eyes, but she had a way of narrowing them so much I couldn't see into her. She pulled my face toward hers and kissed me. But even though she wouldn't look at me, I could feel it. *She's afraid of connecting to me.*

Sensei demanded we use our inner senses, not just to prepare for danger, but at all times. I'd never dreamed of using them in the bedroom. With Heidi, I—we—were in our own space. She always kept her eyes closed, mine were open. I liked to watch her face. I focused on the sensation of the sex, the visual of our bodies, how close she was to orgasm. Never in the hundreds of times Heidi and I made love did I focus on connecting to *her. Having sex is the physically closest anyone can get, and yet it's possible to be so far away.*

I felt like a scientist who uncovers a natural law right under his nose. Ting had always said the goal of meditation is to disappear. Let go of the ego and self disappears. I'd heard it a thousand times but it went in one ear and out the other. My ears tuned only to what I believed would be useful to a fighter, to what might bring me closer to no mind. But this *was* no mind. You had to bridge into your opponent to know what he'd do; if you could empty yourself and become one with him, you sensed it before he moved. All my performances in the ring, not just Morales, had been the same as the bedroom: a solo head-centered experience. I didn't merge or blend, never read my opponent to the extent that was possible, and I couldn't wait to try.

Even partially focusing on the eyebrows, in conjunction with deep breathing, had been successful. I didn't come, and I was feeling pretty good. Cindy, of course, didn't either, but she seemed happy. I wrapped the towel around my waist and leaned against the wall.

"So what's new?"

"You are going to tell me about Heidi."

"That's not new."

"Tell me anyway."

"Let's talk about something more interesting. I never told you. I won the fight."

"I knew you would." She said it very softly and simply, as if it were a matter of fact. "Tell me!"

I was surprised how eagerly I launched into the story. It was pathetic, really. Heidi was the only relationship I'd ever had. I was like an old man who repeats the same story, holding on to the past because that's all there is.

"Six months into our relationship Heidi told her parents she wanted her own room, some privacy from her younger sister. Her parents agreed, and Heidi moved into the partially finished basement. There weren't decorations on the wall, the floor was just painted concrete, but there was a queen bed and two huge wooden nightstands that sat on either side of the bed. Heidi kept candles burning on the nightstands, kind of like you do here. It gave the room a nice feel. Just before she went to bed she lit a signal candle in the window and unhinged the garage door."

"Signal candle in window? You like secret agent man."

"Yes, well, we had to have some way to communicate that the coast was clear."

"Coast clear? I don't understand."

"It's a military expression that at one time literally meant the coast was safe from enemies. Now the expression means everything's okay, it's safe to move forward."

"See, more secret agent talk. What you do that have so much danger?"

I laughed. "Let me tell you! After her parents fell asleep, I slid under the garage door and crept into her bed. For almost a year we slept as man and wife in her parents' basement."

"That *is* danger! You not afraid her parents find you out?"

"We didn't think it through, we just did it, and caution obviously wasn't one of our strong points."

"They never catch you together?"

"No, but we came close. Once, her dad noticed the garage door slightly open and asked about it. After that we had to be extra careful. But one evening we came within a hair of getting caught. We were a bit too cocky. I arrived early, about nine, while everyone was still awake."

Cindy was so excited she was holding her breath.

"We were already in bed, talking and relaxing as if we owned the place. All of a sudden her mother calls from the top of the stairs, '*Heidi!*

"'What is it?' Heidi says.

"And her mother started down the stairs. Every one of my nerves fired at once. I jumped out of bed just before she saw me and hid in the closet. The mother takes one look at Heidi and smells something fishy.

"'What's going on here?' she says.

"'Nothing,' Heidi says. 'I just want to go to sleep. But you won't let me.'

"'Hold your horses, it's only nine. I want to look for something.'

"'Can't you do it in the morning?'

"But her mother ignored her and to our mutual horror went right to the closet I was hiding in."

"Did she see you?"

It was like I'd hit the replay button of a movie. I could see all the details time had muddled or forgotten.

"Actually, it wasn't a closet at all but a little room where the furnace was. I was crouched by the boiler and so nervous I could feel my heart pounding. I wished I could make myself invisible, and it must have worked—her mother was standing so close she brushed against the hair of my leg. I don't know how she missed me. Really, I wasn't hidden at all, but maybe seeing her daughter's boyfriend in the boiler room was so unlikely it just didn't register. There's no other explanation that makes sense."

Cindy had done it again. Uncharacteristically, words were tumbling out of me as if they had a life of their own.

"There was no way around it, the whole affair was dangerous. Her dad was two hundred pounds, strong as an ox and hot-blooded. If he'd caught us he'd have killed me."

"In Thailand this not happen with poor family," Cindy said. "Our house too small and parents watch daughters." As she said this, sadness took over her eyes. "This seem like very strong love," she said. "How did it end?"

"I guess we were just too young to handle it. After we'd been together for a while we started to fight."

"Why?"

"Who knows? We argued, mostly over meaningless stuff. Both of us were bullheaded. Sometimes she'd get so angry she'd hit me."

"Really? So she has temper like father," Cindy said. "Girls often more like pa than ma. In Thailand we believe if a girl take too much after the mother, she have bad luck in love. What you do when she hit you?"

I hated it.

"I just laughed. 'Is that the best you can do?' I said. But that just threw gas on her fire."

Cindy crinkled her nose. "Gas on fire?"

"Sorry, that's American slang. It made her angrier, and she hit harder." I paused. "The arguing was one thing, but there was also a lot of love. After Heidi got pregnant, things changed—"

"Heidi with child?" Cindy gasped. "So the gods hear you call for baby. *They answer you!*"

A chill went up my spine and into my neck, making me shiver.

"I never thought about it that way."

"I'm sure this what happen. Both of you talk about baby. If you very strong about ask for something, spirits always answer. But you not have baby?"

"Cindy, I was seventeen and Heidi sixteen. We had an abortion before anyone found out. We still dreamed of the day when kids would be possible. But it wasn't meant to be. With the abortion something seemed to die besides the baby."

"In Thai world this make sense. If man and woman call baby and then you kill baby, you kill the love in you heart for the other. Only way to fix this is to honor the soul of baby. You do anything?"

"No, we didn't even think about it."

"That's it then, that what happen," Cindy nodded her head with absolute surety. "Maybe child want very much to come to you. Maybe even now spirit of baby not know what to do. But not too late to talk with baby. In Thailand we have place for this."

"What's that?"

"We call it spirit house. It small house, look almost like dollhouse you have here in you country. We keep it in a high place, out of doors. It is place where spirits and ghost can come. We invite them to come. If we have problem, disharmony in the family, we go to spirit house. We bring dish of food, we light incense to give good smell.

Hom, we say, it mean good smell. Spirit like good smell. That what you do: you build spirit house for your baby and baby can still be part of you life. You call baby and ask it to come, you give it nice things to make it happy. You give it name and make it welcome. It help to bring peace to whole family. In Thai way of thinking this very important."

I nodded my head. Buddhism and Taoism sometimes mentioned spirits and such, but I had no experience that led me to believe in them.

"To be sure killing baby break bond in you heart, but then what happen?"

I probably got pale, or Cindy sensed something. She reached up with her hands and pulled my face toward her, then she kissed me ever so softly a few times on my cheek and ended on my mouth. When we finally drew apart, she asked me to finish the story. I shook my head slowly.

"We were almost like a piece of fruit that rots from the inside. You don't see the problem until it's too late. Our routine stayed pretty much the same. We still made love and slept together. But on the inside something had changed. I guess you really couldn't call it lovemaking anymore, it was sex. And our fighting became bitter—we were hurting each other. The signs were there, I should've known something had died, but I just held on.

"One night I went to her house as usual. The signal candle wasn't lit, the garage door was locked, and Heidi wasn't waiting. I kept repeating to myself, *I'm sure everything's all right,* while pacing back and forth in the shadows of big trees. It seemed like forever, but I'd only been waiting about an hour when a car pulled up. Both doors opened and slammed shut. In the strong moonlight I could see it was Heidi. She was with another guy, a popular boy a couple of years older than me. I watched as they walked hand in hand up the stairs to her front porch. He moved toward Heidi, she pressed her body and lips into his like glue. I couldn't watch anymore and stormed up to the porch.

"It's finished." I said.

"Wait, wait!" she yelled, but I ran off her porch as fast as I could and went home. My heart didn't stop beating fast for days."

"What happen then?"

"Heidi came to see me the very next day, but I was cold, I asked her to leave. We never spoke to each other again. End of story."

"You *never* speak to her?"

"No."

After a very long pause, Cindy asked. "There no one since Heidi?"

"No."

"*No one?*"

"No."

"Why?"

"I don't know."

Cindy's voice held surprise: "You *twenty-seven* and you don't have sex, and no girlfriend since you *seventeen*?"

My face and the back of my neck grew red hot. "Yeah, and actually, I had my twenty-eighth birthday, so it's been over ten years."

Cindy gave a long incredulous whistle.

"What happen? You become monk?"

It was impossible to describe how, in losing Heidi, I mourned her, quietly and inwardly, almost as if she had died. To me she *had* died. Certainly a part of me shriveled with the ending of our relationship. I wandered the streets, stopped at our favorite places. A waiter recognized me and led me to our regular table. Heidi and I didn't eat like most people. We sat side to side, with our bodies pressed tightly together. We sort of held each other even while we ate. But I couldn't make myself call her, I tried to put her and all the memories out of my mind. And now a decade had passed as if it were a mere sliver of time. I'd been alone and for the first time in over ten years had admitted just how lonely I'd been.

"I suppose that's not far from the truth," I said in a strange-sounding voice. "For a little while, I used drugs pretty heavily. I wasn't addicted, I think I was depressed and trying to numb myself. Then I got super involved with training. I started karate at fifteen, was always into it—but after Heidi, my interest became an obsession. I didn't have time for a girlfriend, and now that I'm a professional fighter I still don't."

Another incredulous sigh escaped Cindy's throat.

"You *believe* that?

I looked at the ground and sighed.

"I used to believe it, but to tell you the truth, I don't know anymore. Obviously, I have time to see you."

"I tell you some truth. You get hurt and you don't let you self get hurt again. Love too much danger for you to take chance." I felt the edge of my boundaries being pushed and retreated into silence. Cindy sat up and leaned against the wall. She motioned for me to lean back against her, then she put her arms around my waist. Again I had that foreign sensation of a spring unwinding in my chest, and an uncontrollable feeling of tears building up. *How strange!* Except for watching movies, I couldn't remember the last time I'd cried. Mom said I never cried as a kid, even if I hurt myself. I wouldn't let her comfort me. If she tried to hold me I'd squirm away after a few seconds. Thankfully I managed to control the tears by taking some deep breaths and blinking them back.

Still in her arms I weakly asked, "Do you do this with *everyone?*"

"What?"

"Our time together seems awfully personal. Is this your way with all your customers?"

"No."

"Do you kiss your other customers the way you do with me? No ... do you kiss them at all?"

"No."

"Why then are you so ... kind to me?"

Cindy didn't look at me. "Because I like you very much."

I dared not look into her eyes and said nothing. We were both very much aware of each other.

Late as usual, Cindy hurried off to meet her next customer. I went to the dressing room and opened the locker. Sugi was there with her client. She quickly got the man squared away in the Jacuzzi, then came back, standing only a few inches away from where I sat on the bench. Her perfume wafted over me, compelled me to look up at her. Sugi wasn't good for me but I wanted her anyway. She prodded my groin with her high-heeled foot. As if it had a life of its own, my penis inched slightly forward.

"How's it going?" she asked.

"Okay."

"Why don't you come back to me? You like her better?"

I shrugged. Tension was quickly building in my guts.

"What does she have that I don't?"

The stymied gears were turning so slowly my voice was paralyzed. Sugi tapped her heel on the floor.

"Well?"

My eyes met hers and quickly slid away. "I'll see you one of these days." I smiled grimly to myself. *When I'm ready.*

THIRTEEN

"Ed tells me we can't get a rematch with Morales until September," I told Coach.

"No problem, the longer we wait the better. It'll give me time to get you ready."

"September's over eight months away!"

"Do you really want to climb in the ring with Morales right this minute?"

"Why not? I did okay against Nuñoz."

Phantom sighed. "Don't flatter yourself. You could just as easily have lost. The way I figure it you train hard, take a few fights. Fight Haines last. If you get that far, you'll be ready for Morales."

"Ed says Haines comes next."

"I don't like it, Johnny. It's too soon to fight Haines."

"Coach, you're not the one who has to fight."

"No, but I've got to live with myself. I told you, it can take time to come back from a fight like the one with Morales. This is a delicate thing. It's something on the inside. I want to make sure you're ready."

"Isn't being ready on the inside my responsibility?"

"If a fighter's not prepared to get into the ring with the best, that's *my* responsibility."

"The fight's not till April. Don't you think I'll be ready by then?"

Coach sighed heavily and gave me a penetrating look.

"This means getting serious starting yesterday."

"Serious? What've we been doing up till now?"

"Without the back talk. Are you ready to get serious?"

"I'll do whatever it takes."

"Okay, see you tomorrow."

The following day there was nothing new during the workout. But when it came time to spar there was a fellow warming up I'd never seen before, though his face seemed faintly familiar. He was in his mid-twenties, maybe a few pounds heavier but taller and slenderer than I, with the finely tuned body of a top athlete. Everything about the man was crisp and professional, especially the polished way he moved in the ring. He was obviously in a different league than any of the regulars here.

Phantom made quick introductions. "John Lazio—Jorge Sandoval."

No wonder he looked familiar.

"Jorge Sandoval, the middleweight?"

Sandoval simply nodded, and Phantom looked pleased with himself.

"Yes, Jorge Sandoval. Ranked second in the WBC. One of the best middleweights in the world, and *if* he plays it smart, the next champ."

"It's an honor to meet you, Jorge."

"Likewise. I follow mixed martial arts whenever I can. You're good: I saw the Morales fight."

Seems like everyone saw it.

"That wasn't my best night."

Sandoval laughed. "Nights like those never are."

"Have you ever had one like that?"

"Are you guys here to spar or gab?" Phantom said.

"Okay, Coach," Sandoval said.

"I'm training Johnny to be good with the hands," Phantom said. "He's no boxer but he's got an unpredictable style and might surprise you." He turned to me. "Jorge's also got a fight coming up. I promised you'd give him a workout. So if you want to go hard with someone, here's your chance." Then, to both of us, "We'll do three rounds. Don't hold back. Let's see what we got here."

Nervousness tightened my body. *This'll be only a couple of notches below a real fight.* Every man in the gym, coaches, fighters, and even old Paolo Santomero stopped what they were doing and crowded around the practice ring. I swallowed hard. I recalled the last time with Cindy, tried to center myself and turn on my inner senses.

But Sandoval's left jab was fast and felt like it could have belonged to a heavyweight. His right turned my chin directly into the left hook that followed, and my legs buckled. I backpedaled away.

In mixed martial arts there's at least four ranges. Kicking, punching, knees and elbows, and closer: wrestling, throws, and groundwork. In boxing there's only one range: the fists. That means inside and outside. Sandoval was a classic fighter, really skilled at his game. He kept me outside, just where he wanted me. With my shorter arms I was helpless to hit him. If it were martial arts I would've stayed just outside his punching range and used my legs. I knew I had to get inside, but theory was one thing and reality quite another. Knowing you had to get inside of Sandoval was like knowing you had to grab the arm of a guy who's swinging a baseball bat at your head. Wading into that was awfully risky.

For the first two rounds Sandoval stuck to his plan. He kept me outside and battered me badly. Several of the blows to my head had been powerful enough to produce that little spark in my brain, a sizzle of electric current. Just before the bell rang for the third and final round, I settled into my game.

You never look a man in the eyes when you fight. The eyes will trick you, entrance you. Better to focus loosely at a point on the upper chest: you see everything, and I *did*. After Sandoval threw a flurry of punches, there was an occasional settling back on his feet; for the briefest instant he was flat-footed, had his weight on both legs. Sandoval knew he could keep me outside all day. He wasn't the slightest bit worried I could hurt or even touch him. *That's my only chance.*

Sandoval shot three jabs and the last one knocked me back. He threw his right, I bobbed; his left hook followed, I ducked. *There it is.* There was no way to train for this—it was spontaneous. I didn't plan how I was going to get inside; my body moved by itself. I jumped in the air and hit him with a Superman punch square on the left side of his jaw. I followed immediately with a left hook to the other side of his jaw. It hurt some, surprised a lot, and knocked him into the corner. I clinched roughly, hit him with a right uppercut and some heavy body shots before he pushed me off and got back to the center of the ring.

For the remainder of the round, Sandoval returned to his former strategy: he kept me outside but was a lot more careful.

Had it been a real match, I'd have lost badly. It was a lopsided display of boxing mastery. Except for the few punches at the end, I'd barely touched him. Yet as soon as the bell rang, Phantom was in Sandoval's face, as if *he'd* been defeated.

"You see, Jorge, *that's* what I'm talking about! When you're flat-footed you're a sitting duck. That's the difference between winning or losing right there." Coach drilled his index finger into Jorge's chest and repeated, "That's the fucking difference—right there!" Sandoval nodded.

Phantom was all about working with Sandoval while this was fresh. He glanced at my bruised face. There was a tiny but deep cut on my left eyelid, the eye almost closed from swelling. He grinned from ear to ear.

"See you tomorrow."

Before I climbed out of the ring, Sandoval clasped me warmly.

"Thanks, Johnny, Phantom's been trying to show that to me for months, think I've got it now."

"Thanks for the boxing lesson," I said.

"Don't worry," Coach said. "You'll cross paths again."

"I'll look forward to it." Sandoval sounded like he meant it.

"Same here, Jorge."

• • •

That Phantom's an old fox, never know what he'll come up with next. On one hand I was disappointed with myself. After the countless thousands of hours I'd put into fighting, I should've done better. Once again, I had to go back to the drawing board, had to learn to fight all over again. *It's disheartening! But Sandoval ... he took his medicine without a murmur.* That impressed me.

The session with Sandoval was a contrast between being centered and not—most of the time not. When flustered there seemed to be a movement out of my center, and beyond doubt, the ability to stay grounded was the key to winning fights. When I was grounded, my inner senses turned on. It was as if there were a space around me.

Everything seemed to happen more slowly and I reacted without effort. That's what Crandall was talking about when he said to stay loose. When anxious I was in my head, hesitated, and made mistakes; I didn't seem to be running on all cylinders. But why and how had I settled in at the end? Maybe because it was the last round and I was still standing. More important, what was preventing me from staying centered under pressure?

• • •

"Ai-ya!" Mrs. Li took one look at me and grimaced.

Cindy gasped. "Johnny, what happened to you?"

"Training."

I'd taken a shower at the gym, so we went straight to her room. Cindy touched my eye gently, with pain in her own face.

"Are you going to be okay tonight?"

"It looks worse than it is. Don't worry about it. Lie down."

"You sure? Maybe I give you massage tonight?"

"It's okay, it'll help relax me. Lie down."

Even Cindy's typical five minutes of massage would've been welcome, but I enjoyed massaging her. Her face was transparent as glass and her features reflected how much she loved it. If the way to a man's heart is through his stomach, I was well on the way to confirming my theory that the way to a woman's heart is through massage. Touch relaxed Cindy's body, but more, it seemed to loosen something deep inside. She felt more comfortable, trusted me more. As a surprise, I asked one of the ladies to get some oil from the kitchen. I put it on my hands and stroked it into her skin.

"What's that?"

"I thought you might like to try a massage with oil."

"Farangs love oil."

"*Farangs?* I asked.

"*Farang* is what Thai people call white-skinned foreigners. But now in Thailand, not only farangs but even Thai people want oil. Me, I like traditional massage better. This done with clothes on."

"With the clothes on?"

"Thai people modest. The old way we not show skin."

"How can you give a good treatment without getting to the skin?"

"You have to learn to feel through clothes," she said. "It take much more skill."

As I rubbed a little more oil onto my hands and massaged it into her golden-brown skin, Cindy nodded her head silently, her eyes closed, her eyelids relaxed in rapture, as if she were savoring the tastiest morsel of food.

"Sabai dee! This way of massage different from Thai way, but I like it a lot!"

I winked at her. "I'm glad you enjoy," I said, finishing up.

"You don't know how much."

I'd taken up tantric yoga to be better in bed, but the more I studied, the more intriguing it became. Actually, it had very little to do with sex, which it embraced only because it embraces life. In tantric yoga there is no good or bad. Everything—all of existence—is taken as a perfect whole. Having sex is just as godlike as going to church. Rule number one, if there were any rules, would be accepting life just as it is, without judgment.

I took a few deep breaths and slightly shook out my body the way I relaxed my muscles before a fight. I tried to focus between the eyebrows but the sex didn't last very long. *Hell!* I'd done so well last time, I thought I was over this problem. Worse, I couldn't control the ejaculation. Exhausted from training with Sandoval, I shouldn't have pushed it. Now I'd spent even more energy!

I lay next to Cindy and curled my body around hers.

"You seem sad tonight," she said.

"I'm okay."

"If sex was good with Heidi, what happen now?"

Following each of my pitiful performances, I inwardly burned with shame. Yet I never offered an explanation. I didn't know *what* to say—so I told her everything. About Morales, my life before the fight, the prophecy of the old woman, my struggles to pick up the pieces.

Cindy whistled slowly. "So you get hurt? This make sense."

"I'm not hurt," I said.

Cindy shook her head. "Maybe not outside."

Maybe she wasn't very sensitive tonight—or I was hypersensitive—but she was jarring against my nerves as if my skin were fur she was rubbing the wrong way. She crossed her legs and smiled brightly.

"So, what was it like when you little boy growing up?"

I ground my teeth.

"I don't remember a whole lot, it's kind of hazy, almost like a dream."

Cindy gave me an authoritative nod.

"Thai people say that when you don't remember childhood you *forget* because there are things you don't *want* to remember."

"You know, Cindy," I said with a rise of heat, "you once told me I make John Wayne look like a chatterbox. Well, John Wayne's *horse* is more revealing than you. You know more about me than anyone—you're the only one I ever told about Heidi. I admit it felt good to get some of this stuff off my chest. But you never say anything about yourself. I want to hear about *your* childhood. Tell me about *your* boyfriends, who was *your* first love?"

The smile vanished. She seemed visibly jolted by my words. I reached out and touched her shoulder.

"I'm sorry. I didn't mean to hurt you."

It took a few seconds before she recovered her poise.

"I'm okay, but if you wait for me to tell you about boyfriends you wait long time. I never have boyfriend. I like to hear about romantic things you do because this a new world to me."

"Wait a minute. I've guessed you're twenty, give or take. Unless I'm totally off base and you're a heck of a lot younger, how could you never have a boyfriend?"

"I'm twenty-*five*, only three year younger than you. I am working since my parents send me to work at twelve I too busy to have boyfriend."

"*What?* Your parents *sold* you?"

I'd just seen a special about child prostitution in Thailand and had the image of Cindy as a twelve-year-old, her dark, innocent eyes widening as she was led away from her family home.

"How could your parents *possibly* do that?"

"My parents don't sell me, you hear this on television. But young girls being sold by family not so common in Thailand. It happens more that Lao girls are sold. My parents *want* me to work because we have no money and you make much more money with this kind of work."

"That's not much better." I said.

"You don't understand," she said. "Asian people more real with this."

"More real? You've got to be joking! I can't understand how allowing your daughter to work in the sex trade could be construed as realistic."

"Because it *is* real where I come from, it happen with poor family. You have to live. If there no food you starve. Every day has worry and stress because not enough. You don't understand. I have to help my parents, Thai children must help take care of parents."

"Why?"

"Our parents give us life. They do everything for us. It is a debt that can never be paid. Children *must* help their parents. I *want* to help. I young, I have what men want, and so I do what I can. I proud to help!"

"You were only twelve. Who took care of you?"

"A woman who own house in Thailand. I work there for five year. Then, at seventeen, I go with Chinese woman. She bring me to New York. Her place also in Chinatown, not so far from here. Two years later Mrs. Li give me contract and I come work for her. I here at Asia House since nineteen year old."

A child being treated like property sounded like something out of medieval times.

"What was that like?"

"The years flow into each other, day after day like water in a river." Long thick eyelashes veiled her black eyes as she turned inward. "I don't know what to tell."

"Start at the beginning. What's it like to be a child in Thailand?"

"My family live in a small village in the country. We very poor but poor does not make it bad. We have large family, we spread out all over neighborhood. Everybody call me *Goi*. It mean banana. My aunts and uncles come to the door of our home. Goi, they say, let's go to the market and buy food, or come get some mango juice. With big family, there always someone to care for me when my parents busy with work."

"Banana?" I asked.

"Yes. Many time young girl named after something sweet like fruit. Girl called mango or banana for nickname like American girl have angel or honey. To call a young girl by this name mean she special to you.

"One day, I twelve year old, I know something important happen. Mother all dressed up and she dress me in my best clothes. We go on long trip by bus to see old woman in Bangkok. We go to rich house. Never do I see inside of house so fine like this. Servant bring us to big room where old lady sit in fancy carved couch with thick cushion. She thin with yellow flesh that hang on her body, she dressed in rich black silks and have big chain of yellow gold around her neck that cost five year of my father's wage. On the chain was big figure of Long Bu."

"Long Bu?"

"*Long Bu* mean Buddha. It made of solid gold. The old woman's skin have deep wrinkles. I can't take my eyes from brown spots on her arms and backs of her hand. She smoke American cigarette, Camels, one after the other. She look me over from head to foot. She take my arm with her shaking hand and pinch my flesh between her fingertips, stained more yellow and smell of tobacco. All the time she look at me with cold fish eyes. Like I piece of meat."

"Who was this woman?" I asked.

"She owner of the house. In my mind I call her *yellow lady*.

"Yellow lady look at everything about me. She pull my hair and look at scalp for lice. She open my mouth, look at my teeth and tongue. She put her nose close to my mouth and make me breathe in her face. She take me into small room. She tell me take off clothes and open my legs, she smell there, too. Yellow lady make me sick but I do what she say.

"'She'll do,' she tell my mother.

"I never go back home.

"Ma say 'You grow up very fast, little one.'

"Ma's voice crack with her sadness, but there no shame in her words, *this is how it is for us.* Children must help the family.

"After Ma leave, young girl come and take me to my new place. I sleep in big room with many other girl."

"What was this place like?"

"Like Asia House but not so fancy. This was one of biggest house in Bangkok, hundreds of girl work here. The fee that girl get for customer was very small compare to America but much more than she make in factory. Customer mostly Thai men, but some farang. People come from all over the world for Thai sex house."

"What was it like for you?"

"In beginning I miss my family and my neighborhood very much, I very lonely. When I go to sleep, I cry. But I know it not okay to be sad so I try to be happy. Soon I learn job and fit in."

"How did you learn what to do?"

"Another young girl become my friend, she teach me, she say it easy. You just do what man want. So I learn to please the man, be polite and make like I enjoy."

"You must have gotten to be an expert at pretending."

"Stop it," Cindy said. "Why you make me tell you so many time—it not same with you."

"Sure."

"You learn quick in this job not to get caught into it."

"How do you not get caught in it? It's so ... personal."

"Part of you not there."

"I can't picture a twelve-year-old having to do this. It must have been terrible."

"It is job, like any other."

"How can you say that?"

"The man who fix toilet stick his hand through crap. He not think about it. The man that kill animal learn not to see the blood or hear the cry of the animal when it die. Everyone has to do work and it not always fun. This was the job that was given for me. In Thailand we say: *Mai pen rai,* this mean what does it matter? I just do it. I don't think about it much. With the girls there is family, there is joking and laughter. I make money and send it home. This make me feel good. And job teach me about men."

"What does it teach?"

She licked her full lips and crinkled her brow.

"How to find right word in English? In my country we say every act a man do show him for all that he is. I say, with sex, a man show his soul more than anything else."

"Sex shows the nature of his soul? Makes sense, but what about a woman's soul?" Cindy laughed. I wondered how I stacked up in this pecking order, and at the same time hoped she wouldn't tell me.

"You are gentle, kind man, that why I like you." She touched my cheek softly as the brush of a feather. "But inside something has broken."

I had the distinct sensation of being nailed to the wall.

"Mai pen rai," she said softly. "Everyone have place inside get hurt. When we get big scare part of our spirit go away."

"What do you mean?"

"Spirit leave the body to protect itself from hurt, but sometime it not come back, it get stuck somewhere. When this happen, we not all here and we don't feel right inside."

The Horse Whisperer, the old movie with Robert Redford, flashed through my mind. The friendly plow horse changed its personality completely after it got in a bad accident, became a raging fiend. Redford's character whispered to its soul until it came back and the horse was healed. The concept wasn't *that* foreign. When someone's really spaced out we say they aren't home, but where are they? I'd never thought of it in relation to myself. I laughed nervously.

"Where does this part of us go?"

"Different place. Sometime it stuck where it get hurt, other time it go to safe place, where no one can hurt it again. Sometime it go so far no one ever find it. Old people in Thailand believe that spirit have thirty-two part, and live in different parts of the body. I had friend, she older than me. One day she get in accident with her motor bike, she fall on the street break her leg. She not herself after that. If very close to someone you see when they lose something. I ask her, are all parts there?

She say I don't know. But I see she different. If this happen you must get help to bring part back."

"How?"

"We have a special healer that call back part that go away. Healer light incense, bring gifts and foods that person like. Family and sometimes whole village gather for this. The healer call out for spirit to come back to person."

"I never heard of this. Is it special for Thailand?"

"No, most of Asia have same belief but it is lost by modern people, even the modern Thai don't think much about this anymore. But old people believe if don't bring lost part back we can't be whole. We think to have good life, whole spirit most important."

"I think maybe I lost a part of my spirit in the fight."

"Maybe you lose part of spirit with fight, maybe not," Cindy said with eyes half closed, "but, *for sure*, you lose part with Heidi, and I think before."

I remained silent. Cindy continued.

"Thai people believe life is mystery, and everyone we meet is for reason. I think this is why we meet." She paused and I realized I was holding my breath. "We help each other," she said. "I help you bring back part of you, and I think *you* help *me* to bring back part gone for long time."

"Really? How am I doing that?"

She lifted her eyebrows. Her dark eyes sparkled with glee.

"I think it the massage. So you want my spirit to come back, I need a lot of massage. I mean *really* a lot."

She tried to hold a straight face but cracked up laughing.

I laughed with her but went down the stairs feeling strangely shaken. Finally, it clubbed me over the head. No amount of physical preparation could possibly make anyone free and easy. It happened at the core and spread to the periphery. No matter what the game, to perform at high levels you had to be relaxed on the inside. It was crucial for winning in the ring, or in bed. Cindy's life had been incredibly hard, her profession scorned by society, and yet she was at relative peace with herself. I'd always considered my esoteric lifestyle laudable, as if I were some martial arts hero sitting atop Wushan

Mountain. But Morales and my time at Asia House sabotaged that fantasy from different angles. Even after many years of training I was still uncomfortable in my skin.

I never pondered why I was so attracted to the martial arts. I wasn't the macho, bad boy type. Some mixed martial arts fighters seemed to like violence and hurting others. I didn't want to hurt anyone, and sensitive nerves screamed under a thin skin. Perhaps somewhere in my misty unconscious I knew fighting would give me a chance to face my fears and grow. But now that I was at the crossroads of actually facing myself, I wondered if I was up to the task.

And the time was flying. It was late February, only six weeks to the fight.

FOURTEEN

Haines was the new golden boy of the lightweight division, undefeated in seven professional bouts, winning by knockout or submission in every fight. His professional name was Rolland "The Robot" Haines, so named because he was consistently efficient and powerful in his attacks. He had a relentless, overwhelming style somewhat reminiscent of Tommy "Hit Man" Hearns, except Haines also possessed ferocious kicks to match his punches. To top it all off, his grappling and submissions were formidable.

A native Texan, Haines was super clean-cut, with a shaved head and close-cropped goatee. He was the real serious type, not a second spared for nonsense. Only twenty-two, he already had a wife and three-year-old girl. Like me, Haines was known for training severely. He'd climbed Mount Everest, and pictures had been circulated of him throwing a kick at extreme altitude. Another showed him meditating in the snow with a glacier behind, wearing only a pair of sweats, no shirt.

In the prefight interviews Haines got in my face foaming at the mouth, said he'd destroy me as he'd done with his first seven "victims."

"You'll have to be carried out, Lazio, just like with Morales." Usually that kind of infantile crap never bothered me. This time it touched a raw nerve.

"I know Haines is a tough guy," I said when it was my turn. "I'm expecting a hard fight."

My manager called. "It's a fucking circus, John. You know the game! You want to sell tickets, you could talk a little tougher than that."

I was growing weary of the circus.

Phantom procured every tape with Haines fighting anyone, even a couple of scratchy home videos of him practicing.

"You got to be real careful with this kid," he said. "To my way of thinking, Haines's the most dangerous fighter in the division, much tougher than Morales. There's a reason why the champ's avoided facing him like the plague. His offense is near perfect. He's young, super-confident, and always in terrific shape. It's almost impossible to wear him out."

I was only six years his senior but felt so much older.

Phantom spoke low as if telling me a confidence.

"Haines's only weakness is his strength."

"Are you turning philosophic on me? What's that mean?"

"He's just a trifle *too* cocky, he don't think he can lose."

I remembered how that felt. It seemed like a distant memory.

"You see, his offense is so strong, he's never really had to use his defense. Never been tested by a fighter of your caliber."

Yeah, right.

"You've got to get him off balance, interrupt his timing."

"How?"

"Offense is faster than defense. Hit him. Use his strategy against him. If you lay back and try to defend, this guy's gonna hurt you, he'll roll over you like a freight train. Hit him first and hit him hard. Hurt him, put the fear of God in him."

Interesting choice of words. More and more often I experienced a strange uneasiness. It wasn't only in my conscious, everyday life. It was deep beneath the surface. My once sound sleep was disturbed with dreams that left me with a feeling of panic—disjointed dreams of being out of control, lost, not being able to find my way back, my body not responding to my wishes. One night I dreamed I was lying on a stretcher on my back, two men hurrying me along a corridor. It must have been in the hallway of the hospital going toward the Intensive Care Unit. I thought I'd been unconscious the entire time but now it seemed that the bright light from the ceiling was bothering me. I tried to turn away but couldn't move my head. I woke with every muscle tensed, sweat oozing from my pores. I couldn't go back to sleep but lay in bed—my adrenal glands pumping overtime, my heart racing, my guts winding into knots. I jumped out of bed and into my sweats and went for a long run.

Maybe Phantom was right about it being too soon to take on Haines. Just a passing thought of the upcoming fight sent wild spasms of energy up and down my chest, throat, and stomach. Fear seemed to be intensifying inside me, as if a mad scientist were flipping a lever that hyped the voltage. It had to be explored.

A bell went off in my head, a Hemingway story that had made a strong impression on me in high school. I'd forgotten the name but easily found it in the library. I stood, nearly breathless, reading "The Short Happy Life of Francis Macomber." It's all about fear, and in describing Macomber, Hemingway could have been writing about me. Macomber goes on safari for a lion, but when face to face with the flesh-and-blood king of the jungle, he taps into elemental fear and bolts like a rabbit. The white hunter, the safari leader, tells him to forget it, it's all over. But Macomber knows it isn't.

Hemingway writes:

It was neither all over nor was it beginning. It was there exactly as it happened with some parts of it indelibly emphasized and he was miserably ashamed at it. But more than shame he felt cold, hollow fear in him. The fear was still there like a cold slimy hollow in all the emptiness where once his confidence had been and it made him feel sick. It was still there with him now.

Macomber has another lion to face, a second chance to overcome his fear.

Macomber heard the blood-choked coughing grunt, and saw the swishing rush in the grass. The next thing he knew he was running; running wildly, in panic in the open, running toward the stream.

This story hit too close to home. Macomber had his lion and it was the same as mine: *raw fear. But fear of what?*

Macomber found his courage hunting the huge African buffalo. They were driving in the car and suddenly came upon three bulls. There was no time to think. Macomber jumped into action. When it was over, he was a different man: no longer afraid at all. Even in the face of danger, only excitement and elation remained.

Hemingway called overcoming fear a coming of age that has nothing to do with years. It sometimes happens, he said, during war.

Fear gone like an operation. Something else grew in its place. Main thing a man had. Made him into a man. Woman knew it too. No bloody fear.

Yeah, but then his wife shot him in the back of the head.

• • •

Phantom outdid himself, more even than usual, to prepare me. He found sparring partners—the same style and build as Haines—formidable opponents, contenders in their own right. One after the other they showed up. Not just mixed martial artists but the cream of New York's boxers. I never knew what to expect. One day it was Sandoval; another, the middleweight champion's top sparring partner. Still another day it was a bruiser heavyweight, a lightning-fast welterweight, and Crandall. Every day different. Guys aggressive as tanks, only one gear on them: forward, full steam ahead. They pushed me to my limit.

I dreaded even waking up. As soon as my eyes opened, the peace of unconsciousness shattered, my heart fluttered, and fear tightened my stomach. It was a struggle to show up for training. More than anyone I pushed myself, but it was a push from the inside. I forced myself to run and work out with the team. When it was time to spar, my hands shook slightly as I wrapped them with tape. I turned away so no one would see. My thighs were stiff and the muscles fluttered as I walked into the ring, and yet I grimly steeled myself and fought every match Phantom lined up. I did the best I could. Most days Sandoval could still outbox me, Crandall still made me look like a fool, but other days I did well against them. After a few seconds in the ring, I always felt more relaxed. And when the day was over there was the relief of getting through, of surviving another day. I went to bed relaxed, but sleep was poor, and every morning it was the same: as soon as my eyes opened, the fear was back—I had to pass through it again and again. But as the weeks flew by I learned I could survive no matter how much anxiety I experienced.

• • •

Four weeks before the fight, I'd finished the workout. I didn't leave right away but sat and watched the other fighters. Coach looked at me thoughtfully, then pulled up a chair.

"How's it going, Lazio?"

"I'm okay."

"Are you?"

"Maybe I should've listened to you. Maybe I shouldn't have been so anxious to fight Haines."

"I feel okay about you in the ring—with anyone. It's your attitude I'm worried about."

"Yeah."

"If you don't feel up to it we can cancel the fight. I'd rather say you got hurt in training than put you in a place you aren't ready to be."

"I can't back down now."

"Don't do something you're not ready for. If you try to force open this door it'll blow up in your face, then you'll never come back."

"You always talk like this. Back from where?"

Phantom tilted up his chin and pulled at his jowl.

"I've watched lots of fighters, you know. It's become a real interest of mine."

"Yeah?"

"A man's fought before, been hit hard plenty of times, maybe even knocked out—but this time it's different. He gets pushed to some inner edge. After that he's a different man, something's missing. He acts different, talks different, different reflexes. The man's jumpy, hesitant, gun-shy."

It was like hearing Cindy all over again.

"Does a part of him really go away?" I said.

"Regardless if anything goes or not, he's got to get over the fear of it happening again. That's the big nut."

Fine sweat sprouted on the small of my back.

"Why?"

"Fear grows roots in the muscles, brain, and nervous system. That's why I say getting over this is so delicate. It's like pulling out a cancer whose roots go deep into the flesh, can't be rushed. It's what separates the men from the boys. The real champ isn't the undefeated kid on his way up. Once this kind of test comes—and sooner or later it always does—most of these hotshots never come back. There're a hundred hopefuls. All of them have the physical skills to be champ. Only a few have what it takes inside. It gets down to this: Do you want the championship bad enough to go back into that place and come out the other side?"

I questioned Phantom with my eyes.

"Don't play dumb with me, Lazio. You know exactly what I'm talking about. That's why I'm pushing you so hard."

I was surprised. It's bad form to talk about fear in a training camp. It's a taboo that's rarely violated. Until now I'd suffered with mine internally, shared it with no one. And yet maybe there was one man with whom I could speak.

Fifteen

I went into the little room Master Ting let me use and tried to still my mind. My stomach was tight and little twinges panged in my chest and shot up to my throat. Fighting was my life. I'd fought so many times. *Phantom has my number, damn it.* Fingernails brushed against the door.

"Come in."

Ting swished softly into the room, a faint scent of incense clinging to his flowing orange robes.

"Master Ting! We've been together many years now. In all that time you never spoke to me, but lately you talk with me every time. I like it, really appreciate it, but why have you changed?"

Ting laughed. "In the past you wanted to be by yourself. Now? I give you back your own question: What's changed in *you*?"

"I hardly know where to begin."

Ting sat cross-legged on the floor and fixed me with his fine listening eyes.

"I've always considered myself a fairly relaxed guy, but after losing that fight last September, I've been afraid. It's more even than fear. It's a feeling of not being safe. I have a tough fight coming up and I feel as if something terrible is going to happen. I've never been like this before."

"I tried to tell you this might happen. As one develops the strength to face himself, more of his sickness comes out."

"Sickness?"

"My illness is called Ting and yours, John Lazio. Few know the bliss and joy—what we really are—inside. Most are firmly convinced they are their mind: the sum total of their patterns, neurosis, unresolved trauma, and all such rubbish. Of course, no one wants to admit that the mind itself is sick, but just go inside and watch it. We cover our sickness with busyness and pretend it isn't there. But deep down everyone knows it *is*, lurking just below the surface. We don't want to feel it—will do anything to avoid it, distract ourselves any way possible. Meditation suggests the opposite."

I nodded.

"But that doesn't mean the process is easy."

Ting attempted a smile, but his lips seemed cemented in a tight line.

"With your master Omura, you know what it means to train under a traditional teacher. I *lived* with my master. He could do whatever he wanted with me. At seventeen, he put me in a room for a month. There was a small bed, a cushion so I could sit on the floor. Once a day, a small bowl of rice and vegetables was left outside my door. There were no books, music, or talking. For one month I didn't see a living thing, not even a plant. I tried to meditate but my mind was driving me crazy, and there was no way to escape it. It got so I couldn't stand it anymore. The days were unending. At night I was absolutely certain I'd go insane. To maintain even a bit of composure, I saved one grain of rice a day and wrapped it in a handkerchief. It was cheating, but many times a day I occupied myself by taking out the rice, counting how many days had passed and how many were left."

"Wow!"

"For two years my master alternated. One week I worked in the hospital helping the sick and dying, the following week I was back in complete solitude, trapped in my own suffering. I'd been meditating for over ten years, but fear, insecurity, and negativity came out. I relived my entire childhood, all the things I'd repressed: anger, hate, sex, greed—it all began to surface. I was horrified. It wasn't proper for a monk to feel such things. After a few months I doubted my path. I didn't think I had it in me to continue, I didn't know who I was anymore."

"*Yes*," I said, "I understand perfectly."

"If you go deeply enough into meditation, sooner or later you tap into fear—deep fear. It can't be avoided. It's there, waiting. You say you've never felt it before? You weren't ready. The ego's a watchdog, it protects. On a profound level we have to give ourselves permission to feel what's buried—to relive what is buried—or else it won't come up."

"I haven't given any permission. I'd rather go back to not feeling."

"If you didn't want it, the inner door wouldn't be open, the sickness would stay repressed. Stay with it, John."

"I've tried but it's not helping. Constantly watching myself makes me feel like I'm going insane …" I laughed. Ting had used the exact same words.

Ting smiled sadly. "Let yourself go deeper. When the pot's boiling you *will* go insane, but you must if you are to reach sanity."

"Why?"

"The ego is terribly threatened. It doesn't want to lose control. It doesn't want you to see it's no more than an insecure, petty dictator. If you get close to severing your identification with the mind, it will panic, try to pull you off center, distract you with every trick it knows. You'll want to flee, you'll do anything to escape from yourself. You'll feel you can't go on, that you're going crazy, that you must lose your mind."

"You're exaggerating? Truly lose your mind?"

"Madness is the first passage. It's a leap over the cliff without looking where you'll land. It's difficult beyond belief, but you *must* jump to find peace. Most spend their lives at the edge afraid to jump because the hell of their own mind is so horrifically frightening. Even death does not guarantee a person will jump—we hang on even in death. But this is torture, far worse! Get it over with. Jump right now! Then you can live. This is the peeling of the onion."

"What happens when the onion is peeled?"

"Nothing."

"Nothing?"

"You become clear, and even if it's for but an instant, you know what you really are."

"Is this no mind?"

"If you have the experience, you'll never have to ask what it is."

Ting left me alone to sit. He was dead right. I'd sat at the edge of my fear but never allowed myself to fully jump in. The tip of it was like pulling the tail of a serpent. I didn't really want to get its attention. It might turn around and bite me. I was afraid of the fear itself.

My mind raced. I did exactly what I wasn't supposed to do: lost all awareness, got stuck in my thoughts. *Fighters die in the ring. It's a fact.* There's a primitive fascination with fighting that goes far deeper than suspense as to which contender is most powerful and skillful. Fans watch fighting with the same eyes as they did in the days of the gladiators—with a thirst for blood, for weakness, even for death.

Death. I kept coming back to it. Death is what makes fighting so profound. But fighters, like most people, rarely think about it. I couldn't stop thinking about it. *How many men have died in the ring?* In America, most recorded deaths occur in boxing, which obviously has a far greater history than mixed martial arts. But who knew how many matches in Asia, after thousands of years of contests, ended in death? The cause? Usually cerebral hemorrhage, the very thing the doctors feared after I'd been knocked out by Morales.

One bleeding artery and it's all over.

Me afraid of death? I never thought so. I'd always fancied myself a brave man. I had the courage to get in the ring with powerful men. But at the core, I was afraid. A coward. No more than a strutting peacock covered in bright feathers, big muscles with a slimy yellow core. I was a coward and a faker and I hated myself. Meditation was impossible.

I got up to leave. Ting was nowhere to be seen. *All the better.* I bowed to the empty room as I closed the door quietly behind me.

• • •

Mid-March, the city received a fresh dusting of snow on top of the old. My feet walked softly on fresh powder, occasionally crunching on a hard crust of ice. It was midnight, and due to chilly temperatures, the throbbing of the city was at a lower pitch than usual; it was a night to stay home and eat hot soup. There'd been almost no traffic and I arrived at Asia House about a half hour before my appointment with Cindy. Mrs. Li called her, and she wasn't with anyone. When she came into the waiting room to greet me her hair was brushed back, falling behind her shoulders in a sheet of radiant black.

Almost a whole month had passed since I'd last seen her.

"Where you been? You forget about me?"

"I think about you all the time."

"Then why don't you come?"

"When I have a fight I must concentrate all my energy on it."

"I tell you already, that not *all* we can do together! Maybe you call me and we go to lunch?"

"If you wanted to get together, why didn't you call me, Cindy?"

"It not my place to call you. If man want to be with a woman, he tell her."

"Not always in this country,"

"Always in *my* country," she said. "Anyway you early. I not ready yet, I about to eat. You want to wait for me in my room or come with me?"

"Maybe I'll come with you."

"In Thailand a woman say maybe. A man say yes or no."

"Yes, then, with you."

We walked through a long dimly lit hall that opened to a large kitchen. It probably once had been one of those spacious office kitchens that never got much use, but now, even with worn yellow Formica countertops and warped linoleum floors, it was the heart and soul of the place. Two electric ranges, a couple of hotplates, three refrigerators, and four long tables cluttered the room with a homey feeling. An arrangement of fresh flowers sat on each table. Ten or so women were scattered about, sitting and eating or standing at the stove preparing food. It always seemed warm at Asia House but the kitchen was a notch or two warmer. It was a good place to be on a cold night.

Cindy placed me at a table with six women. She went to the cupboard, grabbed a plate, took a generous helping of white rice from the rice cooker on the counter, and heaped meat and vegetables on top.

"It's too much, I'll be so full I'll just want to go to sleep."

"You can't have that!" a woman called out. Cindy laughed and put some of the food onto her plate. The woman poured a steaming cup of tea from a kettle on the stove and placed it next to me. "Let's wake him up a little." Everyone laughed.

The chatter and giggling of women that pervaded the room reminded me of the rich music of birds in the jungle, or of children playing. How pleasing it was to just sit and be part of it. Then an attractive Japanese girl, barely twenty, said her older sister had died recently while giving birth to a baby girl. Half the ladies spontaneously rose to comfort her, and soon most of them were crying. But within a few minutes, tears were dried and everyone was smiling or laughing again. As I basked in this unique experience, some deep part of me took notice. These Asian women fed each other, fulfilled a deep elemental need.

Cindy looked into my eyes and saw how much I was enjoying myself.

"Do you want to stay here or come with me?"

"You can leave him here with us," one of the women said.

"I bring him back sometime, Taka," Cindy said.

"What shall I do with my plate?" I asked.

"I'll take care of it for you," Taka said.

I said my goodbyes and followed Cindy through the unfamiliar part of the building until we reached the main hall that led to the stairs and up to her room.

Since last time Cindy had apparently changed her tune about oil. She kept a small bottle with her makeup and toiletries. As we walked, she held the little plastic bottle, absentmindedly moving it from one hand to the other. When we were seated on her bed she silently handed it to me—with a flourish, almost as if it were a ceremony between us. The oil was warm from the heat of her hands. I squeezed out a few drops on my palms and sniffed it: it faintly smelled of her perfume.

I kissed her; her mouth tasted of the spicy pork we'd just eaten.

"Lie down," I said, then put the oil on her back and stroked it in.

"What do you want to talk about today?" Cindy said.

"Nothing. Relax, let's be quiet for a little while."

I felt strangely vulnerable, wide open, as if all defenses had fallen away. Taka's sister's baby would never know her mother. Death again! *Hell, women are bolder than men.* A woman faces death every time she has a child. I took in Cindy's little room, the candlelight flickering on her naked brown body.

I'd reached a certain point in all of this—fighting, my study of karate, meditation, and spirituality—a critical point. Too many concepts were floating in my head: loose, flexible, easy, no mind, losing a part of me, accepting parts of myself I despised, duck, bob, weave, slip, be free, natural. Theories and techniques were conflicting, colliding, smashing against each other. There were no answers, nothing to make of it. Everyone says something different, but ultimately it's all the same. It was like going to sea alone, without a map or compass, and the voyage was beyond theory, books, or teachers. I'd read that the road to spirituality is littered with billions of corpses. I finally understood the metaphor.

Cindy sighed heavily and turned slowly onto her back. In her exhaustion she'd fallen asleep. I watched her childlike face, so beautiful in its peace. Without thinking I reached out and softly touched her face. She opened her eyes and looked at me.

"What?"

"Nothing," I whispered.

She wanted me to come to her. Her invitation was wonderfully subtle: ever so slightly, she moved her legs apart.

Looking down at her naked body, I understood why tantric yoga suggests approaching a woman's body with reverence. I bowed to her.

She laughed and raised her eyebrows.

"What are you doing?"

I shook my head, put my finger to my lips, and got on top. Her belly was warm, almost hot. Involuntarily I shivered; she held me closer. It had been a little chilly standing naked in her room. I did no contractions, no deep breathing, nothing. I felt frustrated, empty of technique, too weary to try. I melted into her body. *Her smell ... a woman is such a gift.*

We made love in silence, my eyes closed. It was lovely! I easily avoided ejaculation. Cindy didn't come either, but that was natural. Who'd expect a working girl to have an orgasm? It was flattering enough that she seemed to enjoy it.

The less I tried, the better I was. I recalled the most important thing I'd learned during my year in the forest: the mind is the enemy. The mind is never in the present but always taking the past and projecting it into the future, always going down a "what if" road.

Anticipating the "what ifs" is where fear comes in. Letting go, I was in my heart.

Time to leave. I whispered: "I won't be here for a couple of weeks."

"Do I make you upset with me?"

"Not at all, I have a big fight coming up. When it's over I'll come back."

She looked at me half seriously but with a smile in her eyes.

"You promise?"

"I'll come back."

"Chok dee, Johnny. It mean good luck."

"Thanks."

Cindy grabbed me and held me tight for what seemed a long time.

When I got home and into bed it struck me: with Haines, not going down the "what if" road would be an awfully good idea. I slept well for the first time in many weeks.

SIXTEEN

April ninth. After a particularly intense training session, Phantom tapped my shoulder as I was leaving.

"This'll be the last official workout before Haines. I'll meet you at the airport on the fourteenth. Until then take it easy. And don't overtrain with your martial arts buddies! Most important ..." He tapped me on the head. "Don't think too much. We trained hard—you're ready. He's not Superman, just another contender. You can beat this guy, Johnny. For the next few days just relax, *please.*"

That was fine by me. I was tired of working out. A diversion from coaches, fighters, gyms, and holy men was sorely needed. I'd be fighting Haines in Texas, his hometown. My preference was to arrive early and settle in. In the few days before leaving, I'd meditate in the forest as much as possible.

The next morning I did an easy five-mile jog to my spot. I tried to still my mind but was distracted by the sounds of the birds and even more by morose thoughts. Was I man enough to beat Haines? *Don't go there.* After a couple of hours I got up, stretched my legs, and walked around, throwing a couple of lazy kicks. The air had been chilly but by noon it was already high in the sixties.

On the first hot day of spring, it was my ritual to jump into the ice-cold stream that snaked through the deepest part of the gorge. It was a secret spot, hidden from the road. The first time I'd heard the sound of water I went looking for it. Water fell four feet, crashing into a deep pool framed by ferns, rocks, and fallen trees. Only a few weeks earlier the land had been buried under two feet of snow. I took off my clothes and eyed the stream. There was no going in slowly. If you stuck a foot in, the icy cold pained the ankles and spoiled the will. I dove in and swam to the end of the pool, getting out quickly, gasping for breath.

Yet it was worth getting beyond my comfort zone. The contrast of my overheated body and the intense cold produced a euphoric high. Every molecule of my body was supercharged.

I returned to sitting. After an hour of deep concentration, I opened my eyes. I had an overpowering urge to see Cindy. None of my friends would think it was a good idea, but then all my friends *were* fighters, coaches, or holy men.

• • •

Mrs. Li put me on hold as she looked over the book.

"Yes sir, Miss Cindy has one opening. Seven o'clock."

"I'll take it."

That afternoon it got into the seventies and stayed warm. My watch said a quarter to seven as I walked down Canal Street. The city was humming with motion; the heat brought people out like ants. Nature's sexual quickening of erupting seeds, buds, bees, and flowers was mirrored in the way women and men watched each other.

Cindy was waiting up front, oil bottle in hand. As I entered the room she placed her palms together over her heart and bowed. We walked together to her room.

"I surprise when Mrs. Li tell me you have appointment. I thought you say you not coming? Why you change your mind? You miss me?"

"I just wanted to see you."

She smiled and handed me the bottle of oil.

"That's good for me."

This time as I worked on her body she gave me a little tutorial.

"Better to press longer with palm of hand. Count to three before you let off pressure, don't use end of thumb—too sharp. Make thumbs flat—ah, that's it—and in Thailand, not good to just come and massage neck or head. We begin at feet, the head come last."

"And why is that?"

"The head is holy, close to God, feet are lower. It insult to point at people with feet. If you point with feet, people get very mad. When you pass people who talk, it good to move head so it lower than theirs. You don't touch anybody's head, and a man *never* touch woman's head, or *any* part of body, without ask okay first. Thai people very modest.

When I was little girl, men and women don't even hold hands in public."

"How is it that the Thai are so modest they don't even touch a woman in public, yet you allow your children to work in the sex trade?"

"Many thing in life not what they seem," she said. "Like us. Something good happen with us, don't you think? Maybe we get together outside this place, maybe I take day off and we go out on the town, spend night in hotel room? What you say?"

"Sounds like a plan to me. That is unless you expect me to massage you all night long."

"No, not whole night, just most of night."

"Okay, then. Maybe you could show me around Thailand sometime? It sounds like a paradise."

"We start with one day." Cindy laughed. "Maybe later we talk about Thailand." She sighed, had a faraway look in her eyes. She seemed to speak as much to herself as to me.

"Thailand *very* special place. In the south it always warm. North get cool in winter, but cool for Thailand still hot for America. Many Thai people poor, but food is cheap, fresh, and there is enough for most. We have many food you never see in America. Some vegetable and fruit go bad so quick they not last a day after they picked. Even with jet plane, they never make it to market here. There is a huge nut with spikes on the shell. When cracked open it smell little bit like gas, and if eat too much you get fat. But it very good, it healthy as meat from animal. It called *turian*."

I massaged into the muscles of her shoulders and neck. She had a lot of tension for a young woman.

"Ouch!"

"Sorry," I said. "I'll use less pressure."

"No, don't—I like pressure firm."

Uh-huh. I grimaced as I worked.

"In Thailand we have best of many things, Johnny. Thai food taste so good and is so healthy. Our Thai boxer best in world, and our massage! Let me tell you. When Thai people think something good we say *dee.* When bad we say *mai dee.* If very good we say *dee mak.*

Massage in Thailand *dee ti suit,* the best, number one. You should go to my country and study."

"I thought you liked my massage." I was teasing her, but she took me seriously.

She quickly said, "You good, but study massage in Thailand make you better."

"Perhaps someday I will."

"You love Thailand. Many men think Thai lady most beautiful in the world."

"I can vouch for that. Suay mak, mak!" I said—very beautiful.

Cindy eyes got soft and I could tell she was pleased. Since she was in such an open mood I pointed to the two golden-framed pictures that hung on the walls. I'd been meaning to ask her about them. One was a man sitting on an ornate throne who had the bland benign countenance and blue-blooded look of aristocracy. In the other picture the woman, presumably his wife, was smiling broadly.

"Who are they?

"They king and queen of Thailand."

"Why do you have a picture of the king and queen hanging on the wall of your bedroom?"

"All Thai people have king and queen in their home and business. Thai people have good king! It is good luck to have picture."

"Few in America would say that about our government."

Cindy nodded. "We don't like the government so much but we love our king." She went back to reminiscing.

"All of Thailand is market. Merchant line up for blocks, pack like sardines, sell gift, fruit, vegetable, fish, clothing, shoe. We have stand where you get fresh juice from mango and papaya—you never taste anything so good. Get food right on street. For a dollar you have meal better than fancy New York restaurant.

"Some merchant carry shop on their back, come before sunrise and set up. When day over they pack up and go home. Many shop open late and Thai people love to go out with friends and have fun."

"Do you miss it?"

"Very much," Cindy said. "Thailand is special place. In ancient times there are bandits and fighting, but we have peace now for many year. My country have thousand-year-old temples and statues of gods all over. Some statues of Buddha are higher than this building. When you in Thailand you can feel it—you stand on special ground."

"Sounds like the people are spiritual," I said.

"We see things different than farang. Farang want to figure out everything with the head. Thai people believe there is more than what happen on the surface. We believe in spirits and ghost. But our beliefs don't make us heavy, Thai people love fun and adventure. Thailand used to be called Siam, and the spirit of Siam that grab the heart of the people for thousands of year still alive today! I miss this the most."

Cindy spoke quickly. It tickled me to watch her speak with such excitement.

"Of all southeast Asia countries, Thailand is special. It is boomtown. You get what you want from modern world yet with all the change Thailand keep the old ways. Thailand's place where old and new not at war. Orange-robed Buddhist monk smoke cigarettes while wait for bus, they walk street with begging bowl and pass by girl on street trying to make wage."

"Sounds like a paradox."

"What is paradox?" Cindy asked.

"Paradox is when something is in conflict with what we might expect, like a monk smoking cigarettes or begging for food on the same street where a prostitute is working."

Cindy nodded. "We accept life the way it is. So yes, Thailand is country of paradox. Our climate is warm and so is our blood. We have generous heart—Thai people bend over backward to help you. A man spend half his day to help if you are lost. We cook food for you, we help in every way. But at same time, the whole country is for sale. If you have enough money you can buy whatever you want. Even our sacred art has been sold."

"Is that right?"

"Most people honest but some have no guilt over taking you out of all you money. They play like game."

"How's stealing money a game?"

Cindy had a guilty look on her face. "Most Thai people good heart."

I nodded.

"But some Thai people not so good. They make fancy scam to take you money. It funny, unless you are person that get his money stole. We are Buddhist country and most people raised with the Buddha teaching, but some will even use Buddha to make scam."

"How could Buddha help anyone pull off a scam?"

"All right, not possible to use Buddha, but in a very sneak way the holy temple."

"How?"

"You go sight-see to temple and find Thai person worshipping on hands and knees. You don't know they hang out in temple just waiting for farang. They get up and talk to you. They very polite, very nice, tell you about their lives and family, you like them. Then they talk about some big happening at the export center. Then you meet another Thai person, she tell you same thing. Taxi driver also talk about it. You don't know everybody in on scam, so you curious to see what's going on. Next thing you know, you bought a few thousand dollars of gemstone not worth much. In Thailand," Cindy said, "*many* way to take your money."

"Like what?"

"There is sick buffalo story. Person make new friend with you. After you like them, get to trust them, they tell you they have trouble. They need money for mom sick, or house or car have problem. You *lend* them money but never get money back."

"That happens everywhere," I said.

"Some things only in Thailand. One lady I know marry man from Japan. He live in Japan and come to Thailand to visit his wife every few months. He buy nice home and send money to wife every month."

"Yeah?"

"After Japanese man leave, lady get second husband, a Thai man. He and his parents come and they all live together in the house. Nobody work. Everyone live on the money Japanese husband sends."

"What happens when the Japanese guy comes to visit?"

"Thai husband and parents move out. When Japan man leave they come back."

"That's pretty sneaky. And the whole family goes for that?"

"People do what they need to survive."

"Not very fair to the Japanese man."

"No, but little lie okay in Thailand if it help you parents."

"That lie's not little!"

I looked sideways at Cindy. She had a smile on her face, her eyes gleaming. It was fun to be around her. I smiled back.

"You seem to know an awful lot about this type of trade. Are you sure it wasn't a side business of yours?"

"Oh yes! After see customer all night, I teenage scam artist. Very nice of you to think this of me."

"I didn't mean to hurt your feelings, but you sure have a quick temper. I thought Asian women were supposed to be sweet and polite."

Cindy made an exaggerated bow.

"So sorry sir." She didn't raise her eyes. "This what you like? I hope you different, maybe you want woman to be herself and not little fake doll who put on act, but I wrong about you."

"I'm sorry, Cindy. I want you to be exactly who you are. I came to see you tonight because I thought it might take my mind off the fight."

She looked up and smiled. Her anger was like the flame of a candle: easily ignited, blazed intensely, but went out with just a puff of air.

"Mai pen rai," she said. "We learn more about each other all the time, that good. Now you lay down, I take care of you. Lay on stomach, I give you quick massage." Her touch was gentle, soothing. In a minute I'd dozed off. Her voice woke me. "Massage finish, please turn over."

I turned on my back and watched Cindy putting away the oil bottle. How was it possible? She didn't work out and yet her body was perfectly toned. Soft curves of stomach tapered to wonderfully shaped hips, abdomen, thighs, pelvis. Extreme beauty in a woman had always intimidated me, yet with each visit to Cindy I was getting more comfortable.

"Suay mak mak," I said. Cindy put her index finger to her lips.

"We be quiet tonight, Johnny, the way you like."

"I don't always want to be quiet, just that one time."

"Shhh," she said, and got on top of me, her skin like warm, fragrant silk.

With the fight so soon I was apprehensive. But Cindy said she was going to take care of me, and for once I let her. She was exquisitely gentle; she kissed me and moved ever so slowly. Concentrating between the eyes and breathing slowly was rapidly becoming my favorite technique. It took my attention off the genitals and made the encounter something like meditation. I didn't come and lasted much longer than usual. Cindy still didn't come close to orgasm, but again, who could expect her to? I felt relaxed and energized as we walked downstairs.

As we stepped into the locker room a booming voice pierced the air. A very large man, stripped to the waist, held Sugi tightly by the wrist.

"You fucking whore," he yelled at her. "It took me a long time to save enough to come here. Is that all I get for my money?"

I suspected he may have had as fleeting a sexual experience with the seductive Sugi as I had. Still holding her by the wrist, he kicked the locker, caving in the metal. In a burst of frenzy he slammed another locker door shut. It hit with a loud slam and bounced back. The metal hinges groaned under the strain, and the door hung oddly.

"This place is a fucking rip."

This outburst of violence was shocking in Asia House, a quiet oasis of carefree pleasure in a stressful world. Two scantily clad women and their customers stood frozen to a spot. Sugi's face was stark white, her body trembling.

I scanned the details of the small space, the locations of the benches, the exits, all the people. The room became a single entity. Not even the movement of a finger escaped my peripheral vision. We were in my world now.

He was six foot four and weighed over three hundred pounds. His arms and chest were massive and well muscled, but a big belly hung over his beltline. His thighs were easily twice the size of mine. His washed-out blue eyes were flat and surprisingly small in such a huge face. Another man slouched on the bench propping his head up with his hands watched with a little smile. I assumed he was a friend of the big man, whose behavior apparently was not uncommon.

I walked into the center of the room, tapped one of the frozen women on the shoulder.

"Call the police," I whispered in her ear as I moved slowly and carefully toward the man, who was glaring at me.

"What the fuck do you want?"

"Let the girl go."

"What business is it of yours?"

The way he slurred the last few words told me he'd had a lot to drink.

"Sugi happens to be a friend of mine. You're scaring her."

The man looked at me carefully. I was already feeling more at ease. Real fighters don't talk much and this guy's asking a bunch of questions—he's no fighter. But still, I wasn't going to take chances. I lowered my voice to barely a whisper, fixed my eyes into his, and spoke not to his face but to a point behind his head, since I knew this gets a person's attention. There was no trace of threat in my words, but they held the absolute conviction of authority.

"Let go of her arm."

Surprise registered on his face. It is said that a mouse can frighten even the mighty elephant. As a small man, I knew from experience it's true. A person's energy field is what makes him seem large, small, or intimidating, and I made mine intimidating. A shred of doubt wormed into his confidence.

"Now!" I said, louder. I flashed my eyes at Sugi and motioned with my hand for her to come toward me. She grabbed my hand, and I gently pulled her away from him. He didn't try to restrain her.

"Get out of here, quick," I told her and the other women.

Guys do rash, stupid things when women are watching.

The man sitting down on the bench shook his head and chuckled.

"Holy shit, Mike! You let that little pipsqueak tell you what to do?"

The big man lunged at me, trying to grab me with a bear-like left arm. I stepped back and easily avoided his clumsy attempt.

"I don't want trouble with you," I said. "But you're about to get more than you can handle. The police will be here in a minute. You can leave now, maybe stop off and have a few drinks. In the end you can laugh about this. You might still have a good night. But keep going, and a night in jail will be the *least* of your worries."

The two of us locked eyes and read each other.

"You're nuts!" his friend informed me. "This guy just took the bar down the street apart. Three people were carried out on a stretcher. He's gonna kill you."

Mike watched me to see how that information registered.

I kept silent.

"Who *are* you?" his friend said. "Are you some kind of kung fu expert? If not you must be the stupidest guy on the planet, 'cause you're sure gonna get your ass kicked tonight."

I stood just out of Mike's range, my arms by my side. He was twice as strong as me. I remembered Peter Urban—a grandfather of American karate—saying that the average two-hundred-and-forty-pound stevedore can kick the shit out of the average hundred-and-forty-pound black belt. If this guy got hold of me it could be dangerous. But he was drunk and out of shape, and I wasn't planning on letting him touch me. I didn't want to fight but was already measuring the distance to his throat and the vital areas of his body. I'd hit him five times before he could raise his arm.

My eyes bored into his.

Mike looked at me. In my eyes was the unmistakable willingness to go to war. There was no bluffing. Win or lose I'd go all the way. In Mike's eyes was uncertainty, even fear.

"Go home, man," I said. "We don't need to fight."

Mike grabbed his clothes and headed quickly down the stairs. His friend trailed behind—with Mike gone he had no one to protect him.

The police arrived shortly after they left. I heard Mrs. Li talking.

"Thank you, officers," she said. "Yes there was a disturbance, a customer was being rough with one of the girls here, but the man has already gone, we have no need for you." She answered the officer's questions and had them out in five or six minutes. Uniformed police in the waiting room was the last thing she wanted.

• • •

The incident created a snafu in the well-oiled hourly schedules of Asia House. Usually there was a short period of time in between customers. A woman might need to clean herself, fix her makeup, or grab a bite to eat. With the scuffle we ran right into Cindy's next appointment. The customer, about forty-five with graying hair and a wedding ring, was seated in the waiting room when we finally walked out of the locker room.

Cindy's dark eyes regarded me with amused respect as she twined her arm into the arm of her customer. It felt weird to see them walking together through the red curtains. Though I understood her profession and thought I'd accepted it, I felt a twinge of possessiveness, which felt even weirder.

Other eyes had been on me. The self-proclaimed martial-arts expert, the man I'd seen before, had been sitting and watching. All of Asia House must have heard, but he hadn't made a move to help.

The instant Cindy disappeared, a freshly made-up Sugi, still slightly pale, walked into the room, also with her next customer. She motioned with her finger for me to wait. She hurried her customer into the locker room, put him in the shower, and then ran back to where I was standing. She kissed me on the mouth, grabbed me around the waist, and cooed in my ear.

"Thank you so much for saving me, honey."

"I couldn't let you get hurt ..."

She held me in her arms. Her breath was warm on my ear and her perfume flooded my senses.

"Why do you stay with Cindy all the time?" she whispered. "You should come back to me." She took my earlobe in between her teeth and gently bit down. She pinched my nipple and kissed me again on the side of my mouth.

"Next time you come see me, no charge. You like that?" As if by a will of its own, my head nodded. She winked and walked back to her customer.

Shit! My hands were sweaty, my mind was reeling, and my heart beat fast in my chest. Tonight had been a roller coaster—way too much sensory input. I had to get out of here.

I turned to leave and walked smack into Mrs. Li. Her hawk eyes had been watching Sugi and me. She beamed from ear to ear and bowed low.

"Thank you so much for helping us tonight."

I barely managed to croak out, "You're welcome."

Mrs. Li cleared her throat. "Cindy has told me you'll soon be a doctor. I was wondering if you might consider looking at my knee? It gives me a lot of pain."

Her question caught me completely by surprise.

"Perhaps one of these days," I said. "But now I have to go."

"My low back is also a problem," she said with a pained look on her face. "It bothers me most all the time."

I nodded my head weakly as I edged my way to the door.

"Good night, Mrs. Li."

"With my knee and back I can't tell you how difficult it is for me to go up and down these stairs."

"Goodbye, Mrs. Li."

Mrs. Li closed her eyes and bowed in defeat.

"Thank you doctor, maybe another time?"

As soon as I hit Canal Street I began shivering, couldn't stop. I took some deep breaths as I walked back to my car.

On the drive home I went over the evening in my mind. I'd played my cards well. The big man was a bully, and as a mugger will only prey on the weak, a bully only picks on those he knows he can beat. If you can strike doubt or fear into his heart he'll usually back down.

Omura trained us to win without fighting, to perceive the energy of a situation and diffuse it with the least ruffling of feathers. The highest accomplishment would be to turn the situation around so skillfully you'd not only avoid the fight but also part with your would-be attacker as friends. I'd won without fighting. Perhaps I should've been proud, but I wasn't. My training had merely given me the tools to psychologically intimidate a drunken lummox.

I gripped the wheel a little tighter and let out a long sigh.

Sugi! There was still a slight sore spot where she'd pinched my nipple. I adjusted the rearview mirror so I could look at my reflection.

There were two sets of dark red lip prints on my face. One was above the upper lip. The other was just off my mouth on the cheek. I reached up and gently felt the stickiness with my fingertips. I rubbed the lipstick with my fingers, brought it to my nose. I put my fingers to my mouth and tasted it. God, what a woman! "You come back to me," she'd said.

Should I? A part of me wanted to fuck her like she'd never been fucked in her life. This same part thought it every time I saw her. Another part felt a strange, strong loyalty to Cindy.

I'm losing my mind. It's not like I'm in a relationship. We're not going steady, we made no vows. She's a prostitute, for god's sake. She's getting fucked right now by that guy with the gray hair. And after that there will be another man, every hour on the hour. Life's putting a sweet dessert right on my plate. Why shouldn't I eat it? Why shouldn't I have fun?

But that type of fun would have to wait.

SEVENTEEN

From my locker room I heard the crowd going wild as Haines entered the cage. As was my ritual, I recited Kipling, lulling myself into an almost dreamlike state. The words had always inspired me, helped me center in rough times.

> *If you can keep your head about you when all about you are losing theirs ... if you can trust yourself when all men doubt you ... if you can force your heart and nerve and sinew to serve your turn long after they are gone ... you'll be a Man, my son.*

Step by step, I walked slowly toward the ring. Never in my life had I felt more like turning around and going back to the dressing room. *Macomber "lion-hearted" Lazio.* The prefight knot in my stomach was tighter than ever, like a snake coiled in my guts. I walked through the gate and into the cage. Chok-dee, Cindy had said. Good luck—I could sure use it.

The crowd booed as I stood numbly in my corner while Haines danced wildly around. Phantom was by my side, tight and reserved. He didn't feel good about this fight, and who could blame him? I'd been off from the start and everyone knew it. Bad attitude in a fighter is like a virus that affects the entire camp. You can smell it as soon as you walk into a gym, like the wrong spice in a dish of food. My moroseness and anxiety, despite Phantom's best efforts, had pervaded the training and still hung in the air.

"Hit him first," Phantom said as he made the sign of the cross. He had his own rituals.

Finally the referee called us together for the prefight instructions. I stared at the floor. I didn't have to look at Haines, I could feel his energy: powerful, brash, and confident. Nothing about him was slow.

Even though he stood without moving a muscle, he wasn't quiet inside. If Haines were a panther in a cage, his tail would be whipping back and forth in annoyance. That's why his style was so kamikaze: it was in his makeup to be fast. I felt his gaze and glanced up to see steady hazel eyes piercing into mine. Hard and unrevealing—there was no seeing behind them. I made an attempt at a smile but was sure it looked more like a grimace. Haines was perspiring lightly, his shaved head gleaming in the bright lights. Muscled like a Greek statue, he reminded me of a young, exceptionally healthy animal. We touched gloves. No words.

I got off a few half-hearted kicks before Haines tagged me with a stiff flurry of punches that snapped my head back. The old familiar spark went off in my head and slight fuzziness spread through my brain. Nothing new. It had happened many times in fights and even during sparring matches. I almost liked it; it woke me up, made me focus. *Get down to business!* My butterflies disappeared and my jaw set with determination.

We both charged in like rams intending to smash our heads together, Haines a machine, unstoppable. He threw a blinding flurry of punches and kicks. Automatically I backpedaled, bobbing and weaving to neutralize his attack. I slipped under a few, some bounced off my arms, but a right-hand lead caught me on the side of the face and a vicious left hook sent me sprawling to the canvas. *He hits hard.*

The crowd cheered. Haines jumped on top, and I wrapped my legs around him. He was in my closed guard, but he controlled my body with his weight and position. Elbow jabs rained hard on my head, but I tucked my chin and tried to protect my face. The point of Haines's right elbow hit the top of my skull, making a surprisingly loud crack inside my head, the force reverberating all the way down to my toes. There was blood on Haines's face and I wondered if somehow I'd cut him. But then I felt it, warm and sticky down my neck, pulsing with each heartbeat. In an instant, I was bathed in my own blood. It soaked my hair, pooled under my back and head, making it slippery, easy for Haines to jerk me around the floor of the cage.

The ref stopped the fight, called the doctor. He examined my head and shrugged his shoulders. Phantom looked at the cut and my eyes carefully. His face mirrored his concern. "Lazio," the ref said.

"You want to fight?" I nodded. Phantom said: "Are you sure Johnny?" I nodded emphatically. "I'm sure."

The ref set us up in the same position as before the fight was stopped, Haines on top, me on my back with my legs around his body. Bent on finishing me, Haines dropped short, hard punches and elbows to my face and head. He was trying to smash the cut, open it more.

In his haste to end it Haines made a small mistake. He was pushing forward, trying to pass my guard, and he ducked his head. I grabbed his right wrist with my left hand, whipped my right leg around his neck and got him into a triangle, a very dangerous hold that could easily choke him senseless. Just one more inch and I'd have the leverage to end this fight. I grabbed his head and pulled it down, while squeezing with my knees. Haines tried to posture up. We struggled, the strength of man against man, strong men of equal weight pushing not just against muscle and nerve but also against the heart of the other. He forced his head out. I grabbed it again and tried to reposition my leg for a tighter triangle, but I just didn't have the hold deeply enough, and we were both slippery with blood. Haines dropped a final elbow on my head as he muscled out. We stood up.

Both of us were now standing in the center of the ring. Haines moved forward with his buzz-saw attack. He hit me with a strong left and straight right. As I stumbled back he drove a hard kick to my chest, just over the heart. Haines measured me with the left and let go with a powerful right. It happened in slow motion: the roar of the crowd, Phantom yelling—*Hit back!*—I felt myself flying through the air, hitting the canvas, sliding back. Something clicked like a gear slipping into place: *I'm not going to be knocked out!* I got up.

When Haines moved in to finish me, I stood and yelled at the top of my lungs. Samurais developed this scream, a sharp expulsion of air known as a *kiah*. A warrior could stun his opponent with the force of his voice, freezing the blood and paralyzing the nervous system. For the slightest instant Haines was startled, and in that instant I got in a hard left and right. He landed a couple of wicked punches but they didn't faze me. I lashed out with my legs and fists until Haines fell to the canvas. I didn't stop until the ref pulled me off. Haines was senseless.

I stumbled back toward my corner. The referee raised my hand. Haines had regained consciousness but was still too weak to stand. He rested with the doctor.

"Three minutes sixteen seconds of the first round ... Johnny Lazio ... the winner ... by knockout!" The crowd that had been rooting for Haines now clapped and yelled wildly for me. Texans like a good brawl no matter who wins. The media man came into the ring.

"Great win, Lazio. I guess this will silence the critics who didn't think much of your last fight with Nuñoz. Incredible! This is the biggest upset we've seen in a long time—looked like Haines had you finished. The elbow to the head, all that blood! Tell us, Lazio, were you hurt? What were you thinking to stand there and trade punches with a guy like Haines? Why did you yell? Can you tell us what happened out there?"

I was slowly coming out of a state similar to the deepest meditation. It took a second to make my mouth work. I'd been hit so hard it felt as if my jaw had been wired shut.

"Haines is truly an awesome fighter, one of the best in the business. I was definitely hurt, yeah there was lots of blood, but it didn't obstruct my vision. I don't know how I stopped him. It was instinct and a lot of luck. As to the yell, I don't know. It just happened."

"You're a gracious winner, Lazio. Everyone watching, know this— when Johnny Lazio is pushed, he'll push back! Johnny, who would you like to fight before the rematch with Morales? And how about the champion?"

They expected an enthusiastic ham-it-up response, but I wasn't up to it.

"I'll take it as it comes."

"Well then, we'll be looking forward to seeing more of Johnny Lazio here in the winner's circle."

When I said I didn't know what happened, it was true. Yet I knew something I couldn't explain to anyone. Haines had pushed me to a place I'd been before, took me up to the brink of where I was with Morales: my body beaten, my senses failing me, the electric shock flaring in my brain. Just as I was about to black out, I willed myself, forced myself back to my body, fought—went berserk—with every ounce of my strength to keep myself from going back there again.

• • •

Phantom drove us back to the hotel.

"I didn't follow the plan," I said.

"You sure didn't, Johnny. You made a lot of mistakes, almost got your ass handed to you. Did you forget everything we did with Crandall and Sandoval? But let's not go there just now. You pulled it out, son—big time! That fight proved what you've got inside, and the shaking up you got? Let's just say there's no money can buy that kind of education. You just might have what it takes, boy."

"Takes for what?"

"To be champion of your division. Still want it?"

"Sure."

"You don't sound so sure."

"We've been working on this for a long time. I'm not going to quit now."

"You're not a quitter, Johnny."

"Do you think I'm back?"

"You made a good showing tonight," Phantom massaged his jowls with his thumb and forefinger. "But you'd know better than me."

We sat in the car, neither of us speaking until I reached for the door. A spasm of pain in my chest made me groan. Phantom nodded.

"You'll stiffen up pretty good tonight."

Gingerly, I touched my bruised face. A wave of gratitude passed over me. "Coach, I can't thank you enough for all you've done. Without you I'd never have won. You're a genius."

"Don't mention it, kid."

• • •

Back in my hotel room I lay in a hot bath, soaking my bruised body, sweat beading on my forehead. Pinkish fluid still oozed from the raw gash on my scalp.

Lao Tzu once said: "Those who speak don't know." Omura added to Lao Tzu and said: "Those who speak a lot know the least." Asking Phantom if he thought I was back only confirmed I wasn't.

Doberman pincers and German shepherds are both trained to be guard dogs, but they have vastly different personalities. Dobermans are territorial and nervous. If a burglar breaks into your home, a Doberman feels threatened—its world is disturbed. It will jump at the slightest noise and bark before it attacks. If a burglar breaks into the home of a German shepherd, the dog lies in the shadows and waits. Calculating. At the perfect moment he bites the burglar without a sound. A shepherd's much more grounded and centered. The Doberman goes wild; its aggression is fear-based. A Doberman is more tightly wound, more out of its body. I'd been a Doberman. I aspired to be a shepherd.

But can a dog, or a man, be trained to change his character?

• • •

By the time we got back to New York, the rematch with Morales was in the bag. But the fight still wouldn't take place until late September. They said I should keep active with a contender or two out west.

Phantom adamantly agreed: "Keep fighting! Now's not the time to slack. You've got to stay sharp."

The outcome was that I'd take a fight in LA.

"We need to get out of town," Phantom said. "Let's set up camp in California for a few months."

"I prefer my home routine. I've got my team, the gym, and … everything else. Why can't we train here and just fly to the fight a few days before like we always do?"

"Sometimes it's better to break routines, clears your head. Lots of good guys to work with out west."

Next time I saw Coach he was bursting at the seams.

"Wait till you see where we're going to train," he said. "We're going to set up a little gym at Mammoth Lakes—a homestyle gym, similar to yours. You're gonna like this place, Johnny. It's real quiet and our camp will have it all to ourselves. Five or six hours from LA, way up in the High Sierras. You never saw mountains like this—snow till July. The altitude's seven thousand feet. You feel like you're at the top of the world, and training that high is the best thing for your wind."

• • •

I'd made an appointment with Cindy for one a.m. on Saturday, the night before we left for California. It was a sweltering early summer night in New York. During the day the temperature had been in the nineties, and it was still terribly humid. Even at this hour, I couldn't find a parking spot. Running late, I put the car in the garage and jogged down the sidewalk of Canal Street. Women were in shorts and skimpy tops; men went shirtless. Pungent odors of sweat, food, and garbage hung in the still air. There was the languid tension that comes with the first real heat of summer. The denizens of Manhattan hadn't adjusted to the quick change. I thought of Mammoth, California. It was hard to imagine snow anywhere in the United States.

The waiting room was air-conditioned but it must have been over ninety in Cindy's room. A small fan on her dresser cast out a semicircle of humid air. A thin layer of sweat sprouted evenly from my pores. I started to massage her but she pushed me off.

"Don't tell me you're going to give me a massage for a change?"

"Oh," she mimicked me, "you don't remember. I give you one before you last fight!"

I felt a rise of anger. *I ran here for this?* I turned on my stomach.

She performed a couple of half-hearted strokes. In a few seconds I felt the sharp pinch of her fingernails on my flesh.

I cried out, "Ouch! What was that?"

"You got zit on you back."

"What're you doing, squeezing it for me?"

"It all part of my full service," she said.

"Are you going to give me a massage or not?"

She didn't even bother to answer. I was annoyed and turned over to look at her. She kissed me. Immediately, I stiffened. Cindy glanced at my impressive erection and carefully got on top. I must have never been this erect; her vaginal canal was so short I went all the way to her cervix. It wasn't a smooth sensation, but Cindy didn't seem to care. She moved hard and fast, making little groans. I settled in and relaxed completely.

We made love in cycles of movement and stillness. The resting cycles were perfect. I was able to contract my pelvic floor muscles, which helped me to be less sensitive. Even though there had been no foreplay, Cindy's desire was mounting: I could feel her wetness and the passion in her tongue. Her eyes were closed. She arched her pelvis and her fingernails clawed at my back. While she moved I rested my hands on her hips. When we kissed I held her close. I'd always longed to make love to her, to *really* make love, the way it used to be with Heidi. Even though it was unclear what Cindy and I meant to each other, or why we were brought together in this bizarre relationship, there was something between us. I wanted to show her with my body how I felt.

A half hour passed, then more. The cycles of stillness were getting shorter. Our lips and tongues were together. Cindy rocked back and forth, grinding against me harder and harder. She wasn't giving me time to rest. Her breath came quickly and I could see her heart pulsing in the soft part of her throat. Her forehead was shiny and a few beads of perspiration dripped down the small of her back. I touched the wetness with my fingertips. Her eyes were closed in rapture. My eyes were open, watching her face. She was beautiful, exquisite.

The instant before I came seemed to hang in time. I was deep inside her, the soul of her womanhood. I didn't try to hold it back, nor can words describe the orgasm. The closest experience was when I was a boy of nine or ten, swimming in my friend's pool. There was a record player set up on a rickety wooden table just outside the pool. The record had finished, my friend asked me to change it. I got out, dripping wet, and bumped the table. I reached out to steady it and touched the metal spindle. The current engulfed my entire body. I couldn't let go for what seemed forever. White energy traveled through my spine. My body shook and lurched out of control until the electricity released me from its grip.

I felt a snap and crackle just that strong as the current gripped our bodies. It engulfed me like an enormous wave, crashing and sucking me under the crest, leaving me pulverized, completely helpless in the grip of its power. Tears rolled from my eyes. My face contorted into a wild grin, and though I tried to hold it back a loud sound—half laugh, half scream—erupted from my body.

I hadn't known such pleasure was possible. Cindy was yelling just as loudly as she climaxed at the same time. We lay in each other's arms, gasping, until our breathing returned to normal. While making love there'd been no room, no bed. Two people had not been. Together, as one, we'd gone somewhere else.

• • •

Cindy lingered on top with her eyes closed for a few minutes even after I'd gone completely soft. When she opened them they were wide with wonder. She lay down next to me without a word and placed her head on my chest. There seemed to be an oasis of peace in the dimly lit room where the king and queen of Thailand watched solemnly from the wall. The only sounds were the monotonous droning of the fan and the occasional siren or truck from the street. From her breathing I could tell she was getting sleepy. We must have been close to the end of our time. If she fell asleep she'd be late for her next customer. But I didn't wake her as she drifted off. I wanted this experience.

Sleeping in each other's arms in the afterglow of sex is an act of intimacy natural for a couple but not at all for a prostitute and her customer. If this tiny act were stacked and tabulated in the universe of intimacy between men and women, it would be enormous. Cindy falling asleep in my arms was a bigger event than my sneaking into Heidi's bed and sleeping under the roof of her parent's house.

I didn't sleep. I lay awake, eyes open, watching Cindy while she slept. I jealously hoarded these brief parcels of time, like a taxi meter ticking or sands running through an hourglass. I lay listening to her soft breathing, waiting for the inevitable loud rap on the door. It came all too soon.

"Cindy, where are you? You fifteen minutes late! Your customer is waiting."

She shot up quickly, not sure what time it was or what she was supposed to be doing. She looked at me, surprised for a few seconds, then groaned and jumped to her feet.

"Fuck, I don't believe I do this!" She hastily put on fresh lipstick and ran out the door without even a kiss goodbye.

I walked myself down the stairs, dressed, and chatted with some of the girls. On my way out I passed the front desk. Mrs. Li stood up and slightly bowed. Of course she knew I was the cause of Cindy's lateness. She was angry, but only for a second.

"Good evening, doctor."

"Good evening, Mrs. Li, and yes! It's a good night, a very good night."

Mrs. Li raised her eyebrows. "Does this hot weather agree with you?"

"Not particularly, it's just good to be alive." I said.

Mrs. Li looked at me the way people look at Hare Krishnas handing out Gitas at the airport.

"Well, since you feel so good, perhaps now would be a good time to look at my knee?"

I thought of Sun Tzu, the most esteemed of all ancient Chinese generals. Mrs. Li certainly was a crafty fox. She'd waited patiently for the perfect moment. I was about to tell her the truth, that I was tired of this nonsense, calling me doctor. Instead, I tried to out-general her.

I smiled and said, "Perhaps, but there's no place where I could give you a proper examination or treatment, and it's so hot."

"Let's go to my office," she said. "There's a table, and my room has the best air conditioner in the house." Without giving me time to answer, she picked up the microphone. Within seconds, a woman came to cover the front desk and was given instructions that we were not to be disturbed for any reason. Mrs. Li was the superior general. There was nothing else to do but follow her as she limped stiffly down the hall.

She opened the door to her office with a brass key on a large keychain. Scrolls of Chinese calligraphy hung on the walls and colorful porcelain vases sat on richly carved teak tables. An Oriental rug of rose and gold with deep violet highlights made a striking contrast against the hand-hewn bamboo floor. This wasn't the look of taste and luxury Asia House attempted to portray in the waiting room. These were the real goods.

Mrs. Li sat on the table and rolled up her pants.

"Take a look at this, would you, doctor?"

I put my hand on her knee. It was hot and swollen. I'd never massaged anything but young flesh; this was a world different. I ran my fingers gently over the sides of her knee. The bone seemed jagged and misshapen. *How does the body get like this? Is it possible even to make a change?*

"Okay, Mrs. Li, lie face up on the table."

I put a little oil on her kneecap and rubbed it in. The knee is mostly tissue and bone, hardly any muscles at all. I didn't have a clear idea what to do, but I'd heard that in Japan the best healers are blind. I closed my eyes and focused, tried to feel through the fat and inflammation. I found tiny tight swirls of knotted tissue, presumably ligaments, and pressed with my thumb. The way her body stiffened told me it was painful.

"I don't mean to hurt you, Mrs. Li."

"Sometimes you have to go through pain before it gets better."

"That's what we say in martial arts."

She nodded. "After the way you handled that man bothering Sugi, you've become a celebrity here, and also a mystery man. Everyone wonders why you come here."

"The same reason any of your customers come."

Mrs. Li turned her head and gave me a strange look.

"Could I get you to lie on your stomach so I can check the back of your knee?"

The muscles directly behind her kneecap were stiff. I pressed on the sore points and stretched her leg out gently.

"Stand up and let me know how the knee feels now."

She put weight on it and walked carefully around the room.

"Much better. Cindy's right about you, you're a miracle man. I can hardly believe it, thank you, doctor."

"Okay then, I'd better get going."

"May I please impose on you to check my back as well?"

I stayed another forty-five minutes. When Mrs. Li got up there was something different about her face. Gone was the habitual narrowing of her eyes, the look of chronic pain her polite smile could only partially hide. *She's in pain all the time.* For the first time I really understood that this was how some people live. I'd done my share of inflicting pain, but this was the first time I'd ever helped take it away.

• • •

My watch said five a.m. as I pulled into my driveway. A doe that had been sleeping under a tree startled and vanished into the deep shadows of maple and oak like a wisp of smoke. The air was cooler and more fragrant. Judging from wet spots and puddles, a brief but intense thunderstorm had passed through the Hudson valley without touching the city. The rain-washed air exuded rich scents and had lost some of its stickiness. Leaves and small branches littered the ground. Parched plants rejoiced with crystal beads of water still resting on their leaves. In the east, a band of apricot light had begun to show and birds were flitting about, enjoying the rain-replenished birdbath.

I helped Ernesto down the stairs. His arthritis was getting worse. I made a mental note tell the neighbor kid, a teenage boy who looked after him while I was away, exactly how to handle him. After he did his business, Ernesto lay on the cool grass. I sat with him. He'd been my loyal companion for almost twelve years. With Mrs. Li's treatment I'd been gone for almost six hours. He was an old dog and he needed me more than ever. But I was compelled to creep into the city during the wee hours, staying up most of the night. Even now, with Ernesto's head in my hands, thoughts of Cindy flooded my consciousness.

What was she doing? Probably taking a shower, eating, or just getting into bed. I wished she could experience the quiet peace of the morning. She had mentioned getting together outside of Asia House. *Why not here?* I smiled as I imagined her walking up the steps of my little cabin at the base of a hill, walking in the front door. What would she wear? Her black miniskirt would certainly raise the brows of my church-going neighbors. What would she look like in blue jeans, out of the dim light of Asia House? Most of all I wondered what it would be like to sleep with her in my bed.

In the still of the morning I did my karate and yoga practice. By the time I finished the sun had risen in a great ball of orange fire, burning a hole through the hazy sky. Even with the rain it would be another hot day. I sat down to meditate but my thoughts turned back to last night. I felt strangely connected to Cindy, as if by some inexplicable magic of lovemaking our souls had flown together. When at last I reached a relative state of focus, my head dropped to my chest. I lay down on the ground and fell into a deep sleep.

At eleven I drove back to the city. Phantom met me at Kennedy airport.

"You look like a cat with feathers on its mouth," he said. "What the fuck are you so happy about?"

"Just enjoying life."

"What's her name?'

"She's just a friend, Coach."

"Stop with that bullshit. I was born at night, but it wasn't last night."

"That's for sure."

"Goddammit, Lazio, what's her name?"

"Cindy."

EIGHTEEN

Any man in the lightweight division had winning potential, and "Ax" Martinez, my opponent for the LA fight, would not be taken easily. Martinez was a Brazilian-born Ju-Jitsu player, a submissions expert who also loved to stand up and strike. He was a little tank: same weight as me, shorter by two inches, and much more solidly built. His legs were thick as a heavyweight and he used them to chop an opponent's legs out from under him.

Ax was especially known for his fortitude. He never gave up, refused to submit, even if he took a pounding. Any fighter hoping to make a dent in the lightweight division had to first get through him.

"Martinez and you are the same," Coach said. "You're both marks to get through. It was just a matter of time before they got around to seeing which of you is the higher." In mixed martial arts the marks were always changing.

During the day we trained intensely. A couple of Brazilian Ju-Jitsu black belts from my team traveled with us to strengthen my groundwork. Sandoval also came along to make sure my hands stayed sharp. Phantom pushed us all to our limits. After training I had long afternoons and nights to myself. The air was cool that high in the mountains, the sun scorching hot. I hiked for miles up steep hills and burned my fair skin to a crisp meditating on mountaintops. I missed the lush greenness of my eastern forest, but the beauty of Mammoth Mountain was beyond any imagining. Peaks of snow-covered rock jutted twelve thousand feet into cloudless cobalt skies. From the top of the mountains I gazed out upon an alpine wilderness so vast it seemed endless. I'd traveled all over the Colorado Rockies, but these High Sierra peaks were the most magnificent I'd seen.

Phantom had been right: it was good to get out of town. I had everything I wanted ... almost. In the rarified light of the Sierras I was almost able to see my ties to Cindy as cords of energy holding us together. *But she's a full-time prostitute.* She made her living by having sex with men. Not occasionally: she had sex like clockwork, one man after another, day after day, month after month, year after year. Not once did I imagine she'd become my little woman, yet I couldn't help but think of her with the thrill a man feels toward a woman he cares about.

Maybe it was the intensity of our last visit, but images of her kept floating in and out of my mind. She was a prisoner of her profession. Her life consisted of walking from her room to the waiting room, to the locker room, to the shower, and back to her room. With customer after customer, her footprints wore a rut into the dull beige carpets of Asia House. The sun rarely touched her body. Even on days off she seldom left Manhattan. Since I'd known her, she'd never been on vacation.

It was a fantasy, but I wanted to share the inner treasures of my life. Little things, like walking quietly through the woods, watching sunsets, swimming in a stream-fed lake on a humid afternoon. We'd float on our backs in the cold water looking into the fathomless blue sky alive with swirling clouds. I'd wrap her in a soft towel and we'd sit, our feet in the water and the wind on our skin. Right now I longed for her to know what it was like to be here, on the top of the world in June. I yearned to show her the places I loved. But it was unlikely she'd ever leave her world and come to mine.

It was quite a stretch for me to write. Not keeping in touch, with anyone, was a marked deficiency of my character. Yet my desire to give her even a taste of my adventures was so strong that I picked up the pen—finding myself painfully aware of my stumbling inadequacies in the English language in the process. I couldn't find the words to describe my feelings. It was the first time I'd even tried to express them. Past letters had been simple affairs that could have been written by an eight-year-old. I innately knew poetry was the only form capable of expressing the feelings that smoldered deep within and even tried to awaken this faculty. But after an hour I realized it should remain undeveloped.

"Our souls travel through time and space and continent,

To meet in a dark little room filled with light."

Shit! I crumpled up the miserable attempt, threw it in the waste-basket, and went back to a simple letter.

In the weeks to come I wrote several letters and addressed them to Asia House, attention Cindy. It felt good to write, to connect with her. At the time I didn't think it odd to be writing letters to my hooker, nor did I see the irony in writing a woman whose last name I didn't know. Really I didn't know any part of her real name—Cindy was a made-up stage name, like Madonna.

• • •

Martinez was a brutal warrior. I had the utmost respect for him. I've never met anyone, especially a submissions specialist, who loved to stand up and brawl as much as he did. He pushed the fight from the start and never stopped. My legs were so sore and fatigued from his kicks I could barely stand. I narrowly won the first two rounds because my hands were a little faster, my moves a touch crisper, and my defense a little better, thanks again to Phantom's entourage of great boxers. Crandall had drilled the slip, bob, and weave so arduously it had become second nature.

Martinez had trouble landing clean punches, and I took advantage of it. We both gave our all. Halfway through the third round, Martinez got tired of getting hit. He faked, rushed in, picked me completely up off the ground, and slammed me to the canvas. In the scramble, he maneuvered my leg into a kneebar. He had it tight. The pain was excruciating. I could feel the ligaments of my knee straining; I knew the knee was being damaged, but I couldn't tap out. I couldn't let myself lose. Still thirty seconds before the round ended. It was torture, the longest half minute of my life, but I managed to last and won the decision.

The media man standing next to me said, "Rip my leg off if you will, but I'm not tapping out. Right, Lazio?"

"I guess that about sums it up," I said.

I limped out of the ring, and that night the leg stiffened up to the point that walking was really difficult.

• • •

When we returned home Phantom took me to Vito's to celebrate. After a couple of glasses of wine and some antipasto I was feeling good.

"You're a freaking pit bull," Coach said. "What the hell's gotten into you?"

"For the hundredth time, Coach, thank you!" I shrugged my shoulders. "Without you I'd never have gotten this far."

"You're getting better each fight. Makes me happy to be part of it. Very smart, the way you handled Martinez. You made a good showing."

I nodded. Things had certainly gotten better in the ring. I could will myself to take care of business without hesitation. I'd passed though the eye of fear and made it to the other side. *And isn't that bravery?* But being brave wasn't as sweet as I'd imagined. I'd been thinking a lot since the Haines fight. A brave man is just as fearful as a coward. But for an instant, a brave man steps out of his fear. That's the only difference. *The fear is still there.*

"Making your hands top-notch made all the difference. Didn't I tell you?"

"You were right."

"You never took a fighting name. I think we're gonna have to call you Johnny *badass* Lazio. How does that sound?"

I smiled and tipped my head in a bow.

"Jumping Jack Jesus! What the fuck is that?" Phantom shook his head. "I got nothing against karate. Tell the truth, I like all the kicking and grappling. You martial arts guys are allowed to do more than boxers. But maybe you can clear something up for me? What's with the bowing? Every time you see your teacher it's like you got a hinge on your back. You look like a Japanese puppet."

I laughed so hard the wine went out my nose.

"We have to bow," I said when I calmed down.

"Why?"

"Omura's from the old school. The very first lesson, before he even taught me how to make a fist, was to make sure I understood that the student acts with respect, loyalty, and gratitude toward his teacher. It's a matter of etiquette, which Omura says is the most important aspect of karate. We have to bow to Sensei as soon as we see him, even if we meet him on the street."

Now it was Phantom's turn to laugh like a maniac.

"I'll never get why you karate guys take to all that bowing and scraping," he said when he collected himself. "Hell, you do more than take to it. Shit, you lick the bottom out of the dish."

"Respecting your master is an important part of the program."

"*Master?* Now that sounds like a real healthy relationship."

"It's a title of respect."

"I'm your coach but we're sitting here as equals. You call me by name and I call you by yours. And if I catch you prostrating yourself in front of me?"

He didn't have to finish the sentence.

NINETEEN

After being in the high altitude for almost two months, my heart seemed to be pumping in slow motion. Energy streamed through my body as I walked up the stairs of Asia House. It was just a few days before the beginning of August. Some of the freshness of the mountains still oozed from my pores, and I had the deepest tan of my life.

I greeted Mrs. Li. She got up from her desk, put her hands together, and bowed, a trifle deeper than usual.

"Hello, doctor." She beamed. "My leg is so much better after your treatment. I'd tried physical therapy, painkillers, and steroids, but they did nothing for me. My physician wanted to operate. But under your care, I believe surgery won't be necessary."

"I'm glad you're feeling better, Mrs. Li."

"Of course, I'll need more treatments. Perhaps you and I can make some sort of deal? I'll make it worth your while."

"I'm pleased the treatment helped, but you've got to drop this doctor routine. You must know that being a doctor is barely a thought. I'm not even in medical school yet."

"Yes, I know that," she admitted for the first time. "But you helped me so much! You're better than my doctors. They took X-rays, they did tests, but they barely touched my leg. You're like the doctors we have in China, who really know how to fix the body."

"I'll think about it, Mrs. Li." But just then I saw Cindy walking through the red curtains with Sugi. They were talking and laughing. When they saw me, they both came up and kissed me at once. At that very instant Len Takuchi appeared, took in the tableau, and blinked in surprise. Caught off guard, as if I were doing something I shouldn't, I nodded my head in a bow. Len raised an eyebrow and smiled.

"When I first brought you here I never dreamed you would become such a sensation with the ladies. Did you just enjoy both of these lovely women?"

I laughed uneasily. "No, one is enough for me."

He punched me lightly on the shoulder. "Not for a young stud like you! Never say never—right, Johnny?"

"Sure, Len. Well, I'd better get going, take it easy." Then, to Cindy, "I didn't know you and Sugi were friends."

"We all family here."

We passed three women in the hall. Two I'd met, but one must have been new. She pointed at me. "Is that him?" she asked. Her companions nodded their heads and all three women giggled.

Cindy gave me the bottle of oil when we reached her room, took off her clothes, and lay face down. I rubbed some oil into her back.

She sighed happily. "I miss you, Johnny."

"Did you?"

"You bet, and my body miss you massage a lot. My neck really sore."

That wasn't what I expected.

"Everyone heard how you help Mrs. Li, it wonderful."

"How is it to work for her?"

"She has very hard life but she treat everyone fair. Of three owners I work for, she the most kind."

"You told me about the place in Thailand where you worked as a girl, but you never said anything about another place."

"I *do* tell you. Maybe you forget? After I work for the yellow lady in Thailand, a Chinese woman take me to New York. It was my second house. From her I go to Mrs. Li."

"I don't remember."

"Yes, it just off Mott Street in Chinatown, not far from here. That by far worst time of my life. After I leave Thailand I very homesick. It winter in New York, and that make it worse. The new house was very bad place. Customer almost all Chinese men that use me with no respect. I don't know how to say. Of the men that visit girls like me, some show kindness toward women, some treat woman with a little respect. These men act like we something to spit on. They beaten men that never smile."

I reached over and kissed her back.

"It okay," she said. "They were poor men, poor in money and spirit. In their sex was frustration and anger. You stay with men like this, they come into your body, they put their energy into you and you start to feel like them. In that place I lose myself. I try to be happy but even the other girls not laugh or joke much. I wake up late in the morning, sun already high in sky. But sun never touch that place.

"From the windows we see only walls and shadow of tall building. Sometimes I climb to the roof to feel the sun. I look over the rooftops. I raise my hands up and say: good morning Chinatown, like they say on television show Good Morning America. But I can't be happy no matter what I do. The owner was a cheap hard woman who treat girls very bad. I'm so happy when she let me work for Mrs. Li."

"If you're happy, I'm happy."

"It different here. Customer almost all American men. They treat us pretty good, and you best of all."

I thought back to the giggling in the hall.

"Why do the women point and stare at me when we pass them?"

"They jealous of me."

"Why?"

"Because no girl have man like you."

"Like me—what are you talking about?"

"You young and handsome. But more way you treat me. No girl have someone kind, write letters, massage them. You very romantic man. You create little fairy tale with women. You do it with Heidi, now you do it with me. It not common with man. I lucky girl."

Hot red blood coursed into my face. I stopped massaging her.

"How do they *know* these things, Cindy?"

Cindy sat up and arched her eyebrows.

"*Everyone* here know you," she said.

"They do?"

"Oh yes."

"Who, pray tell, is *everyone?*"

"All the girls."

"Great."

"We tight family. We have fights, get jealous, but mostly we take care of each other. After we got you letters—"

"*We?*"

"I read letters to everyone," she said, as if it were the most natural thing in the world.

The image of the women sitting around the breakfast table laughing at my letters was mortifying.

"Well, that certainly explains why the hell they look at me the way they do," I said.

"It not bad thing," she said. "They like you. And after reading the letters we all think same thing."

"Oh really," I said. "What do you *all* think?"

"That you look for girlfriend."

I almost choked. "*What?*"

"Isn't that what you do here, look for girlfriend?"

The whole thing hit me like the first well-timed blow of a boxing match, that little jolt of electricity that wakes you up and makes you pay attention to what's going on. I liked Cindy and enjoyed her company. Sure, a man can "fall in love" with a beautiful woman, especially if he's having sex with her, but to the extent that I thought about it, Cindy was part of my training: she helped fix something that was broken in me and I paid her for it. She was a hooker. I was safe.

But what had been really going on was a very different story. I'd been pouring out my heart as if she were my steady girl. Which might be fine for an eighteen-year-old football player with his cheerleader sweetheart, but for a man a decade older who supposedly had his act together it was pathetic. A cluster of emotions hit me at once. Waves of panic welled up. I was pinned to the wall, wanted to escape. I stood there like a mute, as if her question hadn't been asked. Yet the words still reverberated. They rang with conviction, with undeniable truth. All of my defenses slammed into place.

Drowning so deeply in my own soup, I almost failed to notice there was no judgment in her voice. Her statement was a feeler, she'd thrown a line out on the water. In her soft eyes was a trace of hope and even of longing.

I tried to pull myself together. I knew that for Cindy, sharing my letters with her friends was natural. Like she said: this was her family. Oh, what the hell! It wasn't likely anyone would be telling anybody about my escapades. If, by some long shot, Takuchi were to blab, I might become a laughingstock. But who hasn't done a few things they didn't want publicized? So I wrote a few letters.

Sitting on her bed next to a half-naked Cindy had a remarkable effect on my emotions. Her perfect breasts with their slightly upturned dark nipples were only inches away. I wanted to be close to her. She sat and appraised my face, her forehead slightly crinkled. She also wanted to be close. She leaned over and kissed me gently. I felt the stickiness of her lipstick on my tongue. I loved the feel and taste of her mouth, the fragrance of her body. With her kiss, the last vestige of my anger turned to passion.

Her face broke into a happy smile.

"You come back to me."

I smiled back. Cindy raised her eyebrows.

"Johnny, I have surprise for you."

"What is it?"

"I knew you come tonight, and I tell Mrs. Li I not feel good until you come. All day I take no customer. I have long bath, wash very good."

"So?"

"I try to … I know you like …" Her face was three shades darker. "Today I am clean for you—okay? You understand now?"

"Oh—you mean … Ohhh!"

"Yes." She patted her crotch with the palm of her hand.

Now all thought evaporated. Nothing existed except the offering in front of me. I was terribly excited but made an effort to go slowly. I took her in my arms and kissed her tenderly, slowly working down her body. With my fingers I eased the elastic of her underwear and gently peeled it off. It clung a little to the place where she was already moist. I slowly moved the dark lips apart, pink and wet inside. *Beautiful! Slow, go slow. Loose and easy, Johnny. Breathe!* I kissed around the edges. The scent of her drove me crazy. Her wetness was *Amrit*, the sacred nectar of the yogis.

Maybe the Chinese had it right: men are yang and women are yin. Without the cooling yin fluid of a woman, a man's fire can burn out of control. He can go crazy. I think I'd gone a little crazy so many years without women. I had to have her slippery fluid inside my body; it was essential, it was food. I didn't stop until she moaned in orgasm.

"Cindy *chob*, Johnny," she called out. "Cindy *chob*."

Aroused beyond belief, I got on top. She moved fast and hard under me. Her eyes were closed and she groaned with pleasure—

Through the paper-thin walls we heard loud footfalls, someone running down the hall. The feet stopped at our room and a fist banged hard on the door. My heart jumped in my chest and I went limp.

"What!" Cindy yelled. Inwardly, I jumped again.

"Mrs. Li said to get you. You late again. Your customer is waiting."

Cindy touched my chin and drew my face up so I could see her eyes. They were soft and apologetic.

"I'm sorry but thank you. You great. Cindy chob."

"*Chob?*"

"Like."

"You like?"

"*Chob mak.* I like very much."

She took me in her arms and kissed me gently. She whispered, "We *must* get together—away from this place. I take day off and we go to hotel. Spend whole day and night together, nobody interrupt. I promise. What do you say?"

This hour had been another roller coaster of emotions. An entire day and night together? *That would certainly be a test.*

"I'll make the time," I said. "Call me, let me know when you can get away."

TWENTY

W e'd left it that Cindy would call. With her scent and *chob mak* etched in my memory, I'd thought of little else. But ten days passed and I figured it wasn't going to happen. Then the phone rang.

"Yeah," I said.

"Johnny? *Sabai dee, mai ka?* Means, how are you? You sound unhappy. You upset about something?" Her voice sounded different on the telephone. I felt the wings of my heart unfold and the stuff that makes blood boil surge through my spine.

"Hi, Cindy. I'm good, sabai dee. What's up? So you want to get together after all?"

"Yes but also I want to ask you big favor. Okay you can't do it, but I don't know anyone else to help me."

"Of course I'll do whatever I can. What do you need?"

"I need someone to write check and I give you cash back."

"I'm not sure what you mean."

"I have lots of cash but since I don't have legal job I can't put cash in bank."

"If you can't put cash in the bank then what good is a check?"

"If we call it a gift it okay, a gift legal. Then I can start bank account. Nobody know you get money back. Maybe you be able to do this for me?"

"How much money are we talking about?" I asked.

"Maybe thirty to sixty thousand American dollar."

"That *is* a lot of money." Despair was rising in my gut. "I'd like to help if I can. I'll do something for you, I just don't know how much. I'll tell you what. The next time we meet I'll bring a check and we'll figure out the details then."

Cindy sighed. "That really big help to me. Let's say we meet at hotel. We could go to really fancy place. Oh, I never do anything like this!" She sounded excited. "What do you like?"

I took a long breath. In our time together she got to relax, didn't have to bow and scrape, and like a ridiculous puppy, I massaged her—and she got paid for it all. Now she wanted to use me some more.

"Let's just meet at Asia House like we always do," I said.

"Why? I thought we were going to get together, away from there."

"Yeah, well, maybe some other time. This money thing is more important right now, isn't it?"

"If I make you unhappy let's go to hotel. Forget about money."

"No, let's meet on Wednesday. I'll call Mrs. Li for an appointment."

"If that what you want, I see you Wednesday."

I hung the phone up and went straight to bed. It was close to midnight. The air was humid and motionless. A family of owls that lived in the forest surrounding my home called to each other from the pines. Normally I loved to hear them, but tonight they made only the faintest impression. I lay there feeling awful, unable to sleep.

• • •

My accountant told me the federal government and IRS would be alerted if I deposited ten thousand dollars or more into my account. I'd have to declare how that money came to me, and money made by prostitution was illegal.

"If you're fool enough to do it," he said, "exchange a very small amount." And so I went, blank check in hand, to meet Cindy.

It was almost midnight when I arrived at Asia House. We dispensed with all amenities. There was no bathing; we went straight to her room. When she put her arms around me and kissed me I barely returned her embrace.

"I brought the check," I said.

She seemed bewildered at my coolness but pointed to a large bag.

"And I have cash," she said.

"How much do you need?"

"Thirty to sixty thousand. But if you can do it, I have lot more—over two hundred thousand American dollar."

Knowing that she worked on the hour, I had a vague idea how many men she fucked for a living, but I never did the math. To see a huge bag of cash made it real and tangible.

"Look, I don't have anywhere near that kind of money. I'm not sure you know how difficult it is to do this. It's not like I can just deposit the cash in the bank any more than you can—for the same reason, in a way. I'll have to keep it liquid and pay what bills I can with it. It may take me years to disperse it."

"It big risk for me," Cindy said. "I take you word that check you give me is good. If not good—I lose everything. You don't know how hard I work for this!"

"I think I do know."

We sat on the bed together, just as we'd done nine times before. The tension seemed to be hanging over the room like a dense fog. I'd not seen this side to Cindy. The money seemed to be an anchor of great weight—and why not? It was the tangible product of years of hard work. Money was a ticket out of slavery, money represented a life where she could have a modicum of normalcy. Money also represented a new level in our relationship, one of mutual trust. We sat inches away from each other, our eyes unfocused, staring into space. We were both lost in thought, miles away from each other.

Cindy broke the silence. "Buddha say that helping others is important, but you only help if you feel good about it. So if not feel good, don't do it."

I was in trouble. Now she was bringing Buddha into it.

"I do feel good about helping you, Cindy. I'd love for you to have money in the bank and not sitting in a burlap sack. But I'm wondering what's the best way? Could we somehow buy a diamond on the street and sell it ... get a check that way? Maybe we could get you a sleazy tax lawyer to help bend a few rules. There's no shortage in this town."

Her forehead creased.

"Tell you what," I said, bargaining like a jeweler. "At least give me time to look into this. If nothing pans out I'll write a check for twenty thousand. But that's all the money I can do."

"That is big help."

"Okay, done. I'll start asking around tomorrow."

Cindy was so deep in thought she didn't move a muscle.

"No, Johnny," she said finally. "Forget it. This too much to ask for you."

"I said I would and I'll honor my word."

"No, I feel it is problem. I don't have right to ask this from you, I find other way to take care of it."

I was secretly relieved. Cindy leaned close and started kissing me. Some part of her wanted to remove the wedge that had sprung between us. I quickly took off my clothes. Both of us climaxed in minutes, but the tension remained. It seemed neither of us knew what to do or say. I got up to leave. It was the first time we hadn't pushed our hour to the absolute limit. I took out my wallet.

"*Mai pen rai ka!* You no pay today, not visit," Cindy murmured softly.

"Another date night?"

She tried to smile.

I peeled off her usual fee and dropped it on the end table. She stared at the bills and shrugged her shoulders. She didn't protest further. Money was money, something never to be refused. Just as for me, sex couldn't be passed up.

"Good night Cindy." I closed the door, leaving her sitting on her bed with sad eyes. I flew through the waiting room with barely a nod to anyone. Mrs. Li called out—"Doctor!"—but I was out the door before she could utter another word. It was the only time I couldn't wait to get away from Cindy. I walked with a firm, hard step toward my car. It was near one a.m. and still brutally humid. The breezeless heat had made the streets an unpleasant place that smelled of stale air and garbage. I crinkled my nose.

"*Mai dee,*" I said out loud, then caught myself.

Outside I was calm and quiet. Inside I was shriveling up like a days-old balloon. I'd been here with Heidi, I knew how to handle it. Run as fast as you can. Shut down as tight as you can. It was finished. I *would not* call her. *Would not* call Asia House for an appointment. Women were not to be trusted. It was really for the best—time I learned once and for all. Sometimes you had to go to the bitter end before you knew for sure.

The Henry Hudson Parkway was under construction. A crew of over fifty workers was operating massive equipment, tearing up the roads. Huge portable overhead lights made it bright as midday. Fixing the roads at night makes sense in a city as large as New York. Closing down even one lane during the day was like a clot in a crucial artery. The traffic backed up for hours. But here it was, one-thirty in the morning, and I was sitting dead in traffic.

My patience was paper-thin, and after half an hour of crawling I turned off the West Side Parkway and sped all the way across town to the FDR Drive. It was clear going for a short time, but then smack— right into another traffic jam. *Only in New York!* A car had hit the dividing rail. It was past three when I got beyond the wreck. By the time I made it to the Taconic Parkway I was driving fast. The Taconic originally was a winding two-lane country highway made for leisurely country drives in a Model T, not for the speed or volume of vehicles that now travel on it. Over the years it's been widened, but once you pass Yorktown Heights the Taconic becomes what it originally was: a narrow, windy, potentially dangerous road. I'd seen some messy accidents and more than one fatality.

My speedometer read eighty miles per hour. I kept my foot on the gas and passed car after car. Suddenly a yellow cab pulled up right on my tail. I increased my speed to ninety, but the taxi tailgated only a few yards behind me. I pulled over to the right lane and let the taxi by, then increased my speed and got right behind him, just the way he had. He pulled over and I passed him. He flicked me the finger. He looked crazy. No problem, I felt crazy too. I gave him the finger right back.

I passed him, and once again he got several yards behind me. I almost felt like tapping my brakes, but we were going way too fast.

The taxi lurched into the right lane and tried to pass me from the right. We were neck and neck on the narrow, windy road, the speedometer just over a hundred. This part of the Taconic was probably meant for speeds not more than forty-five or fifty. A hundred and five—we were still neck and neck, just a few feet separating our cars. It took every ounce of concentration to keep the car where it needed to be. I turned a little too quickly and the back skidded slightly, coming mere inches from the steel dividing rail. The taxi pulled slightly ahead. I floored my Fiat and caught him.

Whether it was fear or common sense, I decided beating a taxi driver in a road race wasn't worth killing myself or him. I took my foot off the gas and let him pass. The taxi gunned his engine, gave me a last finger, and left me far behind. I had the performance car, he was driving a Chevy. *He's a better driver than I am.*

As I pulled into my driveway I felt disappointed. Not because I'd backed down from the race but because I'd lost my cool so many times this evening.

Every fiber of my being was exhausted. Sleep was what I needed. Wanted. I'd left the air conditioner on, so the house was pleasantly cool. *At least I did one thing right.* But only my body was comfortable. I kept replaying the evening with Cindy.

And finally I got it: it was the sick buffalo scam! And I had stuck my neck right in the fucking noose. What a schoolboy sucker! But at least now I knew. Cindy didn't care about me. Everything she'd said was calculated. *Hats off, she's a genius. So believable!* Had me eating out of her hand. I needed to wake up from my fairy tale and get down to business.

It was already dawn. The riot of calling birds made me realize, once again, the degree to which I was going against the grain of my normal life. Finally, my mind let go. The last feeling before I drifted off to sleep was regret. Tonight was the first time in all our meetings that I felt we'd done anything sordid.

TWENTY-ONE

N ow I understood why Phantom and the other trainers insisted on staying away from women. It just doesn't work. A man needs to focus and prepare, not dissipate his energy fretting over women. The fight with Morales was just weeks away. Last night with Cindy had left me tense and agitated, the opposite of how I needed to be. I managed to make it through the day's training, but everyone noticed my foul mood.

If only there were some semblance of normalcy in our relationship. I wanted to talk with Cindy, but I didn't want to go through Mrs. Li. I wanted her to call me, however unlikely the prospect.

The sun was setting on a warm summer evening and making dancing shadows on the walls of my cabin. The phone rang.

"Sawatdee ka."

My spirits lifted. Maybe I'd been wrong.

"Sawatdee khap. Kun sabai dee mai?"

"Sabai dee ka," she said.

At least one of us is fine.

I asked, "What's up?"

"Darling."

Darling?

"I hate the way we leave last night. Please let's go to hotel like we plan. We take bath and eat together, whole day and night."

"When?"

"How 'bout tomorrow night?"

"What about your work? Don't you have customers?"

"I cancel. This more important to me."

"Where?"

"You decide," she said.

I was no authority on Manhattan hotels, but I'd been to the Algonquin before, and it wasn't hard for Cindy to get to.

"Fine, meet me at the Algonquin at three. It's on West Forty-Fourth between Fifth and Sixth."

"Okay, darling. I see you at three."

Darling again.

"In the lobby, okay?"

• • •

I arrived fifteen minutes early. Cindy was already waiting on the edge of an overstuffed chair, immaculately dressed in black pants and a long-sleeved white silk blouse, her back straight, almost as if she were meditating. She wore a gold necklace with a diamond pendant, and on each wrist were intricately woven gold bracelets. Her gold looked somehow more golden, more deeply yellow than the gold manufactured in America. The jewelry seemed to add another layer to her beauty—not that she needed any help. She was twenty-five, fresh, and radiant. Mystery exuded from her body like delicious, compelling perfume. Her face lit up when she saw me.

"Sawatdee ka."

"Sawatdee khap," I said as I took her hand and helped her up.

Heads turned as we walked to the front desk. I felt strangely proud.

"You're lovely."

"Kop khun ka."

I selected one of the nicer suites and took out my credit card. Cindy touched my arm.

"I pay."

"It's okay," I said.

"Let me pay for us."

She must be trying to show me money meant nothing.

"If you really want to, go ahead."

"I want to do this for us."

"Thank you."

Cindy paid in cash, nearly five hundred dollars. We took the elevator up to a spacious old-fashioned room on the seventh floor.

She put the contents of her bag neatly away and surveyed the room, looking with fascination at the little soaps and shampoos provided.

"This is first time I stay at hotel."

"That's hard to believe."

"When I home there never any reason, and I work ever since."

I walked over to the window and stood watching silently. Though born and bred in the city, I found looking at the people and traffic below fascinating. Cindy came up from behind and put her arms around me. She held me for a second, then led me to the bed. We lay together without speaking. She reached up with her nose and rubbed mine like an Eskimo kiss. When I gave her a real one, she put her finger to my lips to gently stop me.

"We take bath?"

The deliciousness of it! No rush, no knocking on doors, no customers. She screamed as I licked her, but I didn't stop until she begged me to make love to her. I got on top. It was so different from being at Asia House. Maybe she held herself in some sort of check there. But here? She completely lost control. Her body was bathed with sweat as she writhed; her face looked pained as she moaned and screamed. "Faster!" she cried. But I couldn't thrust as quickly as she wanted. She got on top and started moving rapidly, grinding against me until she came with a loud cry. She had several orgasms before I finally came. Afterward she curled up in my arms and I dozed off. When I opened my eyes, she was looking at me.

"Good morning," she said.

"Morning? Don't tell me I slept the whole night?" I said. "I don't want to waste any of this time with you."

"No, *Tirak*, you not miss anything. We have the rest of the night and all of tomorrow morning."

"*Tirak?*"

"*Tirak* is darling."

"Tirak," I said, "I have a surprise for you."

She smiled like a kid who's just been told she's being taken to the ice-cream parlor.

"What is it?"

I'd gone back and forth about doing this, but in the end I couldn't resist.

"We're going out to dinner, and for dessert we've got tickets to *South Pacific.*"

"What's *South Pacific?*"

"You've never heard of *South Pacific?* It's an old musical, one of the most famous ever."

Cindy looked at me apologetically. "Going to play not part of my usual life." I smiled, then she took my hands in hers and laughed.

Before we left the hotel, Cindy made sure my shirt was properly tucked in. At dinner she put food on my plate. When we got up to leave she wiped a bit of sauce off my lips I had failed to catch and tucked my shirt again. Her attentions weren't servile but profoundly caring. Never had a woman treated me this way, and it touched something deep inside me.

I'd thought Cindy might enjoy the hit musical, but I had no idea how much. She sat holding my hand, hardly moving for the entire performance. I was more interested in watching her. *How genuine and unaffected she is.* Her breath inhaled sharply in tense moments and she laughed and cried easily. Cindy was mature and intelligent yet wonderfully unsophisticated. As soon as the show was over, she called her mother and sisters. She spoke fast and loud in Thai.

"I tell them I at Broadway play," she said, her eyes shining.

We got back to the hotel late.

We showered together and got into bed. Cindy called Thailand once again to talk to her sisters. She was chatting and laughing.

"My sister say hello to you, Johnny."

"Tell her hi from me." I started to fall asleep.

"Are you tired?"

My eyes were already closed. "I'm really relaxed, maybe a little, how about you?"

"*Nit noi*—a little."

She lay down next to me, kissed my nose, softly, in the place it had been broken, then put my whole nose in her mouth.

It was nearly dawn before we switched off the lamp. We rested in each other's arms. Cindy kissed me sweetly.

"Thank you, Tirak. Today was best day of my life."

"You know, I can't think of a better one in my life," I said. "I had a lot of fun with you."

A second later, my eyes were closed, almost asleep.

Very soft, she said, "Tirak?" A slight pause. "I love you." Her lips were like the brush of an eyelash. I heard but didn't stir. She fit her body snugly against mine and we slept, exhausted, for six hours.

• • •

We must not have moved, for Cindy's body was still pressed against me in the same position the next morning. As soon as I stirred she woke and held me tighter.

"We have just enough time for a quick shower and breakfast," I said. "Are you hungry?"

She checked her breath by blowing in her hands and smelling it, then shrugged and kissed me anyway. It was fine with me. I preferred her scent to toothpaste. She kept on kissing me until I pulled back and looked directly into her dark eyes.

"Johnny? What is it?"

I wanted to say *I love you*, but the words wouldn't come out. They lodged somewhere in my throat. I chickened out.

It was almost twelve when we got dressed and packed up our stuff. Just a few more minutes before we had to leave. What had she said once? *If a man wants a woman he should tell her.* I needed to say something. I motioned for her to sit on the bed, sat down next to her, and took both of her hands in mine.

"Cindy, I care about you a lot. If there's anything you need, just let me know."

"There *is* something. I speak to Mom on telephone last night. They have bad storm at home. The wind is very strong and have thunderstorm, roof get broken and water come in the house. I need to send money very quickly."

I felt my stomach clench, but I looked into her eyes.

"A couple of days ago you say you would give me a check. I say no, not right for you. But now, after this time together, I feel it okay.

I need to help my family. Do you remember you say you would help me, Tirak?"

"Yes," I said. "Remember I was going to check out some way to help you? I've already asked some people. The bank says you can send a small amount with Western Union even if you don't have an account."

"That won't work. My parents need a lot of money now. They can't wait."

Of course not. But what if I was wrong? I wanted to trust her. "Okay, Cindy. Give me until tomorrow afternoon. If I can't find a way to help you by then, I'll give you the money myself. Can you wait one more day?"

Cindy looked anxious. "I guess I can wait one day." She kissed me tenderly. "*Kop khun ka.*"

"*Mai pen rai krap.*"

TWENTY-TWO

During the day, I made some calls. Nothing could be done as quickly as Cindy would have liked. I went to bed early, resigned to giving her the money. I was tired but woke at one-thirty with an inexplicable urge to talk to her. It was ridiculous. I'd seen her less than twenty-four hours ago. We'd arranged to talk sometime tomorrow. What was I going to do? Check up on her like a jealous boyfriend?

I tried to relax by listening to the owls. One was right by my window. Another answered further away, and in the distance, barely discernible, came the faint reply. Finally I drifted into an uneasy zone, halfway between sleep and wakefulness. At five my eyes shot open and I got out of bed. Cindy was still strong on my mind. Technically Asia House was open twenty-four hours, but most everyone was asleep by three or four on the weeknights. Cindy didn't get up until late morning. I wasn't sure why, but at ten I couldn't wait any longer.

"Hello Asia House, may I help you?"

"Hi, Mrs. Li. Could I please make an appointment with Cindy, as soon as possible?"

"Johnny." Mrs. Li's voice sounded different. And she never used my name.

"Yes?"

"I was just about to call you. Cindy's not here. She went to the moneylender last night and never came back."

"What are you talking—"

"Cindy needed to wire money to her parents. She doesn't have a bank account. She wanted to give cash for a bank check she could wire immediately."

She didn't even wait long enough for me to help her!

"Who is this moneylender?"

"A Chinese man named Lu. A robber, really. He charges fifty percent interest, and if you don't pay there's trouble. Everyone in Chinatown knows him ... two-bit gangster. Some say he has connections with the Chinese mafia." Mrs. Li's voice cracked. "I don't know what happened, I'm afraid for her."

"How could you let Cindy go to a place like that?"

"I tried, Johnny, but I couldn't stop her! She said she understood moneylenders, she could handle herself. She was willing to pay the fifty percent. You know her, you know she has a mind of her own."

That she does.

"I know you care about Cindy, Mrs. Li. Why didn't you give her the money?"

"I don't do that with the girls. I can't, Johnny. No exceptions."

She seemed so miserable I couldn't be angry with her. Anyway, there wasn't time.

"Where is this guy?"

"Lu's office might be hard to find if you don't know where you're going. There's no sign, not even a visible address. It's on the second floor directly above an herbal shop, between Mulberry and Mott Streets. There's no separate entrance. You have to go through the herb shop."

"Okay, thanks."

"What are you going to do?"

"I'm going to make sure Cindy's okay."

As I walked down Mott Street I realized the idiocy of what I was doing. The intelligent thing to do was to call the police and report a missing person. But an overwhelming desire to protect her had exploded in my chest. I'd never had a wife, sister, or child, but the thought of Cindy being hurt filled me with pain. If I'd only given her the money when she asked. Ting had spoken about jumping off a cliff. Maybe this was it. Cindy, her sweet child's eyes, her happy spirit ... *fuck it all, I loved her.* If I could spare her from harm, I'd do anything.

I hurried to find the herb shop.

The three-story building was just as old as Asia House but poorly maintained. The herb shop was near the center of the block. Garbage cans and bags sat on the concrete. The smell of rotting Chinese food wafted up from the sidewalks even though they had recently been hosed down. As I opened the door, a bell clanged loudly. The doctor, an old Chinese man with kind, sad eyes surely witness to a lifetime of suffering, glanced up. Several people sitting on wooden folding chairs waiting for the doctor also eyed me suspiciously.

"I'm looking for Lu."

"Up the stairs," he said.

The narrow staircase was littered with clutter, every bit of it caked with dust. I walked slowly up two landings to a closed door. I took a deep breath and knocked.

An eye peeked at me through the glass peephole, the door cracked open, and a large Asian man removed the chain and opened the door. He wore dress slacks and a sport jacket and no expression whatsoever. I felt a tightening in my guts. While he looked me up and down, I scanned the room. It was large, dirty, and colorless with old-fashioned slat window shades.

"What do you want?" he said.

"I'm looking for Mr. Lu."

"What do you want with him?"

I hadn't thought about what I'd say. I tried to stall.

"I'll tell *Mr. Lu* my business."

"You tell *me* or get the fuck out."

"I'm here about money."

"Nobody's here, come back tomorrow."

I turned to leave but it was as if my feet were rooted to the spot.

"Don't you hear good? I said come back tomorrow."

Just as he started to shut the door I heard something dropping or thudding, a man's growl, and a woman's voice cry out. I turned back.

"I thought you said no one's here?"

"Get the fuck out."

He reached up to his jacket pocket. Before his hand made it, I'd whipped my index and middle fingers onto the side of his neck, interrupting the pressure in the carotid artery, and quickly hit the side of his neck with the knife edge of my hand. He crumpled to the floor. I moved quickly down the hall and stood outside the door. All I could hear was muffled noises. I opened the door a crack and looked in.

One man was having sex with Cindy; the other two stood naked waiting their turn. Cindy lay on her back on the bed, totally passive. She had bruises on her cheek and a cut on the bridge of her nose. Her face was set in a mask, her body a shell. Inside she wasn't there, her spirit not in her body.

I was berserk with anger but kept my center. I had to. This wasn't a contest. This made the fight game, brutal as it is, seem like softball. You could get hurt in the cage, but the ref would nearly always stop the fight before things went too far. Here there was no sport. Violence took on an entirely different quality. These guys were the experts, the pros. They'd kill you without qualm or hesitation.

They were so occupied they didn't notice me. I pushed open the door, grabbed the man with Cindy by the hair and yanked him backward off the bed. I spun him around and hit him so hard with my right he flew all the way to the other end of the room, smashed into the wall, and fell down. I kicked the second man in the ribs. He raised his arms to defend, but I hit him with a jab and straight right to the nose. Out of the corner of my eye I saw the other man coming toward me. I grabbed him by the head and spun him into the first man. Now both were on the floor. I kicked, smashing the ribcage of one, then pivoted and dropped my heel on the bridge of the other man's nose. It's not like the movies. One well-placed kick to a vital spot, and it's lights out.

I saw the first man up again, but not soon enough to block the unpredictable angle of his knife slash. It cut into my right side, slicing deeply into the flesh. I stepped back. No matter how good anyone may be in empty-hand fighting, you have only a fifty percent chance at best to beat a man with a knife. And this guy was obviously skilled. Again he slashed with an unorthodox angle, looping upward, trying to cut my stomach and throat. I blocked, but the blade cut into my forearm.

I shoved him against the wall, trapped his arm, and smashed it hard against the wall. The knife clattered to the floor. I held his right wrist in my left hand and with my right arm forcibly straightened his elbow, snapping the bone. Still holding his broken arm, I jerked him off his feet and lifted him into the air. With my right leg, I swept out his unsupported legs. He flew sideways and hit his head on the floor with great force. He lay face down, moaning. I jumped on top, snaked my arm tight around his neck in a rear naked choke, my favorite submission hold. I felt him go limp.

I glanced at Cindy as she lay on the bed. All it would take was the tiniest bit of pressure for a few more seconds and this asshole would never bother another woman again. I felt his breathing slow. Before it stopped I let his body slide out of my arms and onto the floor. The whole encounter had taken less than thirty seconds.

Cindy still hadn't moved much. I helped her up and to get dressed.

"You okay?" She nodded. "We've got to get out of here fast." I put my arm around her waist and supported her as we walked into the main office. The man was still out on the floor.

"My money," Cindy said.

"What?"

"My money. I came here with ten thousand dollars. I can't lose it."

"Cindy, we've got to leave it. These guys are going to wake up soon, there's not a second to lose."

I practically dragged her out through the herb shop and we took a taxi to Asia House.

"Ai ya!" When she saw Cindy's face, Mrs. Li told a girl to call a doctor and said she'd take Cindy to her room. "Do you want me to come with you?" I said.

"I just want Mrs. Li," she said. "Please, you can go."

I turned to leave but Mrs. Li stopped me with a wave of her hand.

"Wait in my office. When the doctor is finished with Cindy, He'll look after you."

I propped myself tentatively back on Mrs. Li's couch. Until now, I hadn't felt the pain in my side or noticed my blood-soaked shirt. After twenty minutes, a soft knock, then a casually dressed Chinese man in his sixties entered carrying an old leather doctor's bag. "Did you see Cindy?" I asked. He nodded. "Is she all right?"

"She'll be okay," he said with a trace of sadness.

I wasn't sure he had a license to practice medicine in America, but he seemed to know what he was doing. He removed my shirt with a gentle hand and examined the wound. "It's lucky, my friend, there's damage only to the flesh—no major artery or organ has been hurt."

He put twenty-five stitches in my right side and twelve in the left forearm.

He gave me pain medication, and when I got home I fell into a deep sleep. The next day I woke with a groan. The stitches had tightened. It was difficult to hoist myself out of bed. I picked up the phone.

"Hello Asia House," the familiar voice of Mrs. Li answered.

"Mrs. Li? How's Cindy? I know she's been badly shaken, but I'd like to see her today if possible—just to talk—and Mrs. Li, I know this is irregular, but is she available now? I'd consider it a big favor if you let me speak to her." There was a long pause. "Mrs. Li?"

"Yes, Johnny, I am here, but Cindy isn't."

"What! Where is she now?"

"She's gone back home."

"Home?" I said. "To *Thailand?*"

"She left just a few hours ago. There's a letter here for you. I have it at the front desk. You can pick it up anytime you want."

"How about right now?" I paused and thought for a minute. "On second thought, if she's already gone, I'm hurt too and maybe it's better if I rest up a little."

"Come whenever you want. I'll be here."

TWENTY-THREE

I hadn't shaved for nearly a week, and the beginnings of a thick black beard sprouted on my face. I climbed the stairs at Asia House as quickly as possible with my stitches.

Mrs. Li smiled, opened the top drawer of her desk, and drew out the letter.

A bunch of girls walked into the waiting room.

"Hey Johnny," Taka called out. "You grow beard! Huh, you mountain man—I think I like this! You come to see me, right?"

"No, you skinny cat!" said Clara, a plump woman with large breasts. "Why would he want you? He's here for me."

"My date tonight is with Mrs. Li."

Mrs. Li tottered up from the desk and raised her eyebrows. "That's right, you girls can all sit down! I may be old, but I still know my way around the block better than you young chickens. I can show him a few tricks you haven't learned." Eyes widened and jaws went slack. Mrs. Li couldn't hold back her mirth any longer, her face broke into a smile and she cackled like an old hen. The entire room screamed with laughter. The blood rushed all the way to the top of my head. Only one did not laugh. Sugi stared at me with her large beautiful eyes.

"Let's go to my office, it will be quieter," Mrs. Li said. As we walked down the hall she said, "You look like hell, Johnny. How are you feeling?"

"I've been better, but let's talk after I read the letter."

Surprisingly, there were a lot of men at this hour. The locker room was full. Other girls I knew smiled and greeted me. But it was a different world now. With Cindy gone—

"You can sit there." Mrs. Li opened the door to her office and nodded toward her desk.

She pulled up a chair and sat across from me, watching my face as I tore open the letter, written in a meticulously neat hand:

Sawatdee ka, Tirak,

I never have boyfriend, and I know you not real boyfriend, yet I feel with you I find little taste of what this feel like. I want you to know that everything I tell you was real. I love you, Johnny. I look forward to our time together. Our times bright spots in a long line of gray. I will never forget you letters and especially you massage. You good with you hands and you make a great healer. Don't forget to study in Thailand. The massage in Thailand is dee ti suit, the best in world.

I feel I have been healed. Not by massage, that is joke I have with you. I heal from everything that happen with you and me. You romantic ways, you make me feel comfortable about me, and like me again. I feel lost part of me come back. Months ago I know it time for me to go, but I stay because I enjoy our time together and I dare to hope for something more. But now there is nothing here for me. It time to go. I go home now to my family. Maybe I start my business.

I sorry I must leave before I say goodbye and thank you for helping me.

Always you friend and always love you.

Lots of hugs and kisses, Cindy

Time and space disappeared while I read the letter. The lump of sadness that formed in my throat was so uncomfortable I couldn't speak. I looked up to see Mrs. Li staring intently at my face. Her eyes were not at all hard but soft and kind.

"Did you read this?" I asked.

"She read it to all of us before she left."

It only took me a couple of beats.

"Of course she did," I said. It even seemed kind of comforting, this sharing of intimate information.

"Cindy was torn about leaving," Mrs. Li said. "She wanted very much to see you, but I made her go. Lu knew her line of work and it was only a matter of time before he'd come looking for her. Cindy was a loose end, and these people don't keep loose ends hanging. You'd better be careful yourself, Johnny. Lu and his associates play hard."

"I'm not sure they had much chance to get a good look at me. Or time."

"All the same, after what you did, they'll be searching for you. They'll go to every house in Chinatown looking for you and Cindy. Sooner or later they'll show up here. But they'll get nothing from us. We Asian ladies know how to keep our mouths shut. Still, you'd be smart to stay away from Chinatown."

Mostly to myself, I said, "Why didn't she call me? I would have come to say goodbye."

"It is a delicate matter, hard for a man to understand. That you saw her raped was too much for her. She felt degraded, lost face. There can be embarrassments too great, even for a prostitute."

Mrs. Li let me use her personal bathroom to take a shower. I was clean and shaved and it was time to leave.

"Thanks for keeping that letter for me, Mrs. Li. Do you have Cindy's phone number? I'd like to call."

"I have her address. I'll write and ask her to contact you if you'd like."

"Yes. Goodbye, Mrs. Li."

She cleared her throat. "Now that we're here, I wonder if you're feeling up to giving me a treatment?"

I wasn't ready to sever my connection to Cindy, and in Mrs. Li's presence I was somehow still linked to her. Mrs. Li lay on her stomach and I worked on her back.

"I once knew a man like you when I was a working girl. He never massaged me, but he treated me very well, and I believe he loved me. At least that's what he told me." After a pause she added, "I loved him."

"Who was he?"

"A young American soldier named Charles. He was leaving for Vietnam, and his friends made a going-away party for him. They bought him a 'date' with a prostitute. I was working at a place near here in Chinatown. He picked me out from all the other girls."

I pushed hard on Mrs. Li's lower back, using my palm the way Cindy had taught me. I counted to myself: *one, two three,* the deepest pressure, then let off slowly *two, one.* While I pushed she didn't speak; when I eased up she resumed.

"The week before he left he came every night. When he shipped out I pleaded with him: 'Be careful! I want you to come back to me in one piece.' 'Don't worry,' he said, 'nothing can stop me from coming back.'"

"Did he?"

"He came back, but not to me."

Mrs. Li hoisted her tired, overweight body and turned face up. There were trails in her makeup, and the face cradle was wet. She sat up for a second and wiped away the tears with a tissue.

"I'm sorry, I shouldn't have pried," I said.

"No, it's an old story, a *very* old story now. They say touch may loosen feelings that linger in the body. It has been a long time since anyone touched me in a kind way," she added, so softly I barely heard it. For a few moments she was silent, then she picked up the story.

"Charles thought me very beautiful when I was young. You see that picture on my desk? Pick it up."

A vivacious young beauty in classical red Chinese silk stared back with haughty eyes. She looked so fresh and alive. I glanced at Mrs. Li's heavily lined face and fatigued eyes. It was hard to believe it was the same woman.

"That was me when I was twenty-five."

"You were quite the looker." I began to conclude the treatment by working her neck and head.

"Time slips away like babies growing up," she said softly. "There's nothing can be held."

Her face was expressionless, her eyes deep and far away. I gently massaged the rigidly tight muscles of her face.

"You feel that?" Mrs. Li said. "That comes from years of smiling too much."

I nodded. "Cindy has the same thing, but yours is worse."

Mrs. Li lay with her eyes closed and began to speak.

"It's a strange profession we're in. People think of us as whores. But you treat us as women."

"They don't sell their bodies for money, but a lot of the people I know seem more like whores than the women here, Mrs. Li."

I finished her massage and Mrs. Li sat up. She motioned me over to a couple of massive carved wooden chairs with plush red cushions. She patted the seat for me to come and sit next to her while she fixed her hair in the mirror.

"Ah, thank you my friend!" she said. "I feel so much better, and I look ten years younger, no?"

"Fifteen at least."

She sat facing me, appraising me through long eyelashes. Her dark eyes shone like agate.

"Most of my girls would be happy to take Cindy's place with you. Maybe you can take one away from all this?"

Even though I was beginning to get used to the unusual honesty and openness these Asian ladies displayed, I still felt embarrassed.

"I'd like to talk to Sugi."

"I'll call her for you."

Sugi gave me her patented seductive look as she walked up.

"Can we talk?" I said.

"Let's go to my room."

As we walked up the stairs, the eyes of other women followed. I sat on Sugi's bed. She wore her hair up, and a few strands fell over her forehead. She was beautiful as ever. She sat close and smiled.

"I'm so glad you come back, honey! Remember you don't have to pay me this time."

"Let's talk."

"Talk? We could have lots more fun."

"I'm not coming here any more and I wanted to say goodbye, Sugi."

"Then let's have goodbye you never forget."

She was so tempting. *Why not?* Sexually, I was ready. This was the moment I'd been waiting for. She started to unbutton her shirt, exaggerating, flourishing the undoing of each button. I curiously watched her breasts jiggle out of her bra, but there seemed to be a space around me. A part of me was watching my mind, almost like a hawk watches a mouse from above.

"I can't do this," I said.

"Okay you give me massage then. Cindy say you give good massage."

"No thanks."

"Something's changed in you," she said heatedly. "And I liked you better before. You used to be a lot more charming."

Sugi was beautiful but she was playing a role. She wasn't even fully here. Cindy was real.

"I just wanted to say goodbye." I gave her a short hug and went down the stairs.

Mrs. Li coughed and straightened up from behind her desk. "I wish you the best of luck, Johnny. I know you'll find what you came here to look for."

She bowed deeply, and in the ancient form I was so well schooled in, I bowed back, even more deeply.

"Goodbye, Mrs. Li."

I turned the doorknob and pushed open the door. I was almost out in the hall when Mrs. Li called out to me.

"Do you want my advice?"

I turned back to look at her.

"Pick one woman and settle down, Johnny. Stay with her. Discover she is a flesh-and-blood woman and not a fantasy."

I nodded, smiled, and bowed again, then chuckled as I walked down the stairs. *She's right.*

Quick as a submission hold, it was over. There was a deep hole, but in a bittersweet way, I was happy Cindy had left. Her long term of indenture to men and mama-sans had ended.

Twenty-Four

P hantom knew I'd been hurt, but he groaned when he saw the stitches.

"What the hell are you into, Lazio? On second thought, don't tell me. All I want to know is are you going to be up to fighting in ten weeks?"

"I've been rubbing the scars with coconut oil and stretching every day. It's not going to hold me back."

To prove it I trained hard, probably too hard. Like a machine I ran five miles a day, did fifteen hard rounds on the heavy bag, and mechanically disposed of my sparring partners. The sweat dripped from my body, and the weight dropped off. Coach watched with a slight frown.

"I don't think that gash in your side is going to hurt you, but inside something's not right. Listen, we still got almost nine weeks before the fight. I'm going to do something I've never done with any fighter. It's unconventional, it don't make sense, but I want you to take a couple of weeks off."

"What about training?"

"Keep running, but other than that do whatever you want. You're in great shape, and you don't need the training as much as getting your heart right. Do whatever it takes. See that friend of yours. What's her name, Cindy?"

"That's not going to happen."

"Then go into the woods, why don't you? You love that."

I shrugged my shoulders. "Thanks, Coach. Maybe I will."

• • •

I hadn't seen Ting since the Haines fight, and I wasn't sure why I'd come now. Ting, however, seemed to be expecting me. He clasped my bicep in greeting.

"John, your muscle is strong as ever, but inside you're a different man. Your face has completely changed."

"How do you judge that?"

"Your eyes are humble. The starch has been taken out of you, you're not so sure of yourself."

"And that's good?"

"Nothing is sure. How's the meditation going?"

"Not so well. I'm feeling off."

"Good."

"Sometimes it feels like you're playing a game with me. Why is all this good?"

He smiled as though I'd said something profound or clever.

"You may not know it, John, but you have asked for it. Deep in your consciousness you struggled for truth, and so you have attracted the circumstances to find it. But truth doesn't come easy. You have to earn it.

"As I've tried to tell you, everything you don't need will be taken from you, a profound surgery. You must face the depths of yourself. It takes great effort, much suffering, death. Yet only through death comes new life.

"So when you tell me that you are off, I say good. You tell me the carpet has been pulled from under your feet and life is crumbling in little pieces and crashing over your head? I say excellent!"

I laughed. Ting shrugged his shoulders and smiled.

"You want to sit?"

"I've promised myself someday I'd give myself a few weeks of sitting. Where there's nothing to get in the way. Like you did when you were a boy."

"What a marvelous idea!"

"I've got the space, and my trainer gave me time off. But I'd prefer to practice in the forest if that's possible."

"It's possible, of course … more challenging. When meditating in nature there's more to distract, but there can be advantages."

"I've been meditating outside for years, Master Ting."

"Then do as you like." Ting paused for a second while stroking his chin. "This will seem contradictory, since I'm always harping about staying in the now, but to find the place you're reaching for, go back to the fork in the road."

"Meaning?"

"If a tree falls into a stream, the stream is permanently altered. The water flows differently, must go around the tree. The sand and mud build in different places and will affect how the insects, fish, turtles, and birds live. A single tree changes the ecosystem of the entire stream. So your wounds leave an imprint in your psyche and your life is never the same. To retrieve your pure nature, go back to the fork in the road."

"How?"

"If you re-experience the tree falling into the water with complete awareness, you'll see your original face, know what you were before."

"What should I do?"

"When sitting in meditation or lying down to sleep, allow yourself to travel backward. Start with a day, then two days, then a week. Set yourself free to wander back. At first it will seem contrived—as imagination, memory—but soon it will become real. Stay in your center and watch it all like a movie."

I thought of Cindy. "I think the process has already started."

Ting laughed.

"How far should I go back?" I asked.

"Sit and see what happens. When you are at the crucial point, surrender."

"Surrender? To what?"

"Have you ever been in someone's car when they're driving fast and recklessly? You watch the road, you become afraid, and your heart races. You are concerned, and justly so, for the very safety of your life. But the driver is unmindful of your discomfort. He continues to drive even faster and more dangerously. You become obsessed by watching the road, the body tenses more and more. Soon you're in an acute state of panic. But what can you do? You're not steering. Things are out of your control. At the crucial point stop watching the road. Go inside, give up, let go."

"And when is that?"

"When the time comes, you'll know."

• • •

And like a bird instinctively returning to its home, I went to the forest, back to my spot by the waterfall. I hadn't come to practice martial arts. I sought stillness of mind, and I vowed to sit until I had answers. August was warm and the days long. Most mornings I arrived before first light and stayed into the night. If hungry, I ate brown rice wrapped in seaweed. For Ernesto I brought canned sardines, one of his favorite treats. If tired, I slept on the soft forest floor, and when hot, I walked to where the dancing water had carved a deep pool through solid rock, jumped in, and returned refreshed to sitting.

Some mornings were clear, and dew blanketed the ground in cool wetness. Later the sun beat down, scorching my flesh. On rainy days I came anyway—and these days were some of my favorites. The warm rain drummed a beat on the canvas hood of my poncho, and the scent of musk exhaled from the clay. On foggy mornings the sky was white and mists hung close to the earth. As the sun rose, the fog moved and swirled on a faint, almost imperceptible breath, leaving transparent drops of moisture on the ferns.

Besides old Ernesto, who mostly slept by my side, my only companions were the creatures of the forest. A family of squirrels lived in the large oak near where I sat. From morning till dusk they gathered their winter stores. They danced through the branches and chattered noisily to each other, and occasionally to me. At about the same time every day, a fat rabbit wandered out to eat grass a few yards away. Soon all the animals went on with their business as if I weren't there. Even a family of deer who at first froze then ran at my scent got used to my presence and considered me part of the landscape.

Three weeks passed to the sounds of water falling over rock, wind swishing through leaves, and intermittent birdcalls. The forest was peaceful as ever, but try as I might I couldn't concentrate. My mind swirled and churned with forgotten thoughts and memories that surfaced like bubbles rising from the muddy bottom of a lake. Snippets of conversation popped in and out of my head, violating the stillness.

Master Ting's voice: "If you can't still your mind and sit for an hour without moving, you haven't learned to focus. The Buddha sat for days without food or sleep."

Sensei: "Many are called to the path but few go far. You must let nothing come between you and your training."

Heidi: "You're the man for me—I'll love you forever."

Cindy: "There something good between us, we should get together outside this place."

When restless, I wandered through the forest, discovering hidden places I never knew existed. Most surprising was a dilapidated house that must have been built in the seventeen hundreds, hidden in an overgrown jungle of plants and nearly invisible. It drew me back again and again. I crawled inside and climbed up the rotting wooden staircase. Old furniture decayed in the living room, and a pine headboard and frame sat on warped oak floors in the bedroom. Sometimes when it rained, I meditated in the attic listening to the rain hitting the roof. The place smelled like the forest. I wondered who'd lived here, and what had happened. Why had the owners left without their furniture?

Outside were remnants of an ancient garden. A massive, tangled climbing rose was in riotous bloom. During a rainstorm, I tipped an open flower to my nostrils. To my delight, fragrant rainwater poured over my face like wine from a cup. From that day, whenever it rained, I made a special trip to the old garden and filled my belly with rose-scented rainwater from the heavily-laden blossoms. With my thirst sated, I splashed the water on my head and enjoyed its dripping over my body.

When tired of wandering, I returned to sit.

• • •

A conversation with a therapist at sixteen. Mom made the appointment because my grades were poor.

"What's your family like?"

"My family, why?"

"It may help me understand you better."

"My family's okay, I guess."

"Tell me about your father."

"What does my father have to do with good grades?"

"Just tell me about your dad."

"He's dead. He died when I was nine."

"I'm sorry. What did he do for a living?"

"He drove trucks. He had eight trucks and a dozen men working for him."

"What was he like?"

"Thomas Lazio? Second-generation Italian, simple guy, hard-working, hard-drinking. Warm, kind."

"Really?"

"Dad liked to laugh, and he made everyone feel comfortable. Dinner was his religion. He'd invite neighbors and friends, and there was lots of food, lots of wine. We had a huge table that could seat a dozen. Everyone had a great time, my friends loved to hang at my house."

"He sounds like a happy man."

"Most of the time."

"What did you do together?"

"Lots of stuff."

We'd wrestle and play all kinds of sports. He had the strong body of a working man, wasn't tall but had big muscles. I was proud to see my dad next to my friends' fathers who had bodies like the Pillsbury Doughboy.

Dad let me and my friends drink wine, even as little kids. We loved it. Mother hated it. After her alcoholic dad, she'd sworn she'd never marry a drinker and purposely avoided the Irish as potential mates. When they were first married Dad didn't drink much, but as time went by he increased the frequency and quantity. He went on long binges. Something seemed to snap—it was as if he were another person.

Two years before he died, Dad got sick. He lost all his muscle and finally died of cirrhosis of the liver. Yet for all his drunkenness, he was a man of great feeling. He was sensitive, he noticed little things. If I was down he saw it right away and tried to cheer me up.

"He died young. You must have missed him?"

"Sure. But at least I knew him before he got sick—my younger brother doesn't have many memories."

"How old is your brother?"

"Four years younger, but those years make a big difference."

"How did your mother manage?"

"After selling Dad's business there was a big chunk of money."

"I see. So ... how did that go?"

"Okay, I guess."

• • •

Though Mom revealed nothing to others, Dad's death affected her profoundly. Things got real shaky. About four months after the funeral, Mom who detested alcohol and berated Dad vehemently for using it, went out with a friend and had a few drinks. It seemed to help her mood and she began drinking more and more frequently. Soon it was every night, and she couldn't see that it wasn't helping anything.

Memories began to loosen and stir, memories I'd long pushed to the basement. For two years, nearly every night, Mom would get drunk. She'd go to bed early and leave me to take care of Nicky. After Nick was asleep I'd hear her crying. I'd creep softly into her room, not wanting to disturb her, but also feeling that I needed to do something to help. My stomach was tense as a drum. I prayed she wouldn't hear me—that's when I stopped believing in a God that hears prayers because she always sensed when I was in the room. I wondered if maybe it was all an act to get attention. I still don't know for sure. I stood frozen by her bed not knowing what to do. "Hold me Johnny," she said. Every molecule of my soul recoiled, but I climbed into bed and put my arms around her. She was completely tanked, and with me cradling her like an infant, her eyes rolled back in her head and she went deep into her pain. "Why did you leave me Thomas?" she wailed hysterically. "Two children and all this to take care of alone." Her breath stunk terribly. The room was dark but there was enough light I could see the whisky bottle on her dresser and the clear little glass. The house was still, and sometimes I listened to the wind pushing the bushes against the house. Inside me was emptiness, and as the pain poured from her soul, my heart contracted. I held her while she cried herself to sleep. Deep inside, I vowed to protect her. Dad left us; I would fill the void.

But I was only ten years old.

Mom held conferences to discuss family business. She consulted with me, wanted my opinion as if I were an equal. "You're the man of the house," she'd say. For two years I *was* the man of the house. But when I turned twelve she got a boyfriend: a drunken, ineffectual slob she had wrapped around her finger. Suddenly, all her crying and drinking vanished as if it had never happened. I was expected to be a kid again, but I never fit into the mold of her expectations.

Mom dreamed of a scholar who would raise a family and grow into a pillar of the community. She revered academics and considered scholarship a set of keys that could open any door, a permanent ticket that could take you over the rainbow. I was never good with school and she never failed to tell me about other kids who were "successful" students. At thirteen I fell in with some of the neighbor kids. We used to smoke pot in their attic.

One evening I came home reeking of dope, my eyes pinned like a zombie. I tried to slip quietly to my room, but Mom saw me and went ballistic. To discipline me, Mom would first yell, then slap. As a last resort she'd use a belt. At thirteen I was already too strong for her and she tried to enlist her boyfriend. The poor clod tried to step into my father's role, grabbed me roughly by the shoulder and spun me around. "Who the fuck do you think you are, mister, to come here in this condition?" I grabbed his leg and dumped him hard on the floor. He never touched me again. *Not long afterward I met Sensei, and it filled a deep hole.*

I was my brother's hero growing up, but the older-brother worship didn't last. Nicky wasn't an athlete, much less a fighter. He excelled in school. Now he was a successful lawyer with a wife and two kids. He was living the American dream, but I could tell by the deep creases on his forehead and the worried look in his eyes he wasn't happy.

Other than Thanksgiving and Christmas at Mom's, Nick and I rarely spoke. This time in the forest was about isolation and silence but I impulsively whipped out my cell phone and called him at his office.

"I'm preparing for a trial," he said. "Can we talk later, Johnny?"

"Okay, but the years pass and we don't know each other any more. I hardly see you or your wife, and I'd like to spend some time with your kids."

"I've always wanted to get together, but you never seemed interested, or maybe you're too busy with all the karate stuff. What's changed?"

"I've been doing a lot of thinking. You're the only brother I'll ever have."

"Come over this Sunday for dinner?"

"I've got a big fight coming up at the end of the month, but right after that, I promise."

"Sure, Johnny. Sure."

• • •

Most nights I brought my sleeping bag and a blanket for Ernesto. I'll never forget those glorious nights. Soft curved hills bathed in moonlight, dark silent sky, mysterious call of the night birds, and thick oxygen-rich air pulsing with fireflies. As if a switch were thrown, each plant and tree popped alive, the earth began to breathe. Cindy had said spirits were all around us. I began to believe it was true. They seemed to brush my hair, whisper in my ear, and pull me up to play with them. Wandering through the living air, I felt like a hummingbird flitting from bush to flower.

Minute, long-forgotten details of life with my dad floated through me like a waking dream: Dad pushing me in the carriage, holding me, looking into my baby eyes. Things I'd never known. And, of course, his death.

It was at the hospital, just me and him. My mother and brother were at the store. He'd been off painkillers for weeks. He knew he was going to die and decided to stop taking them. Dad wanted to be clear at the end, and he got his wish. But he paid a price. He grew depressed, remorseful. He apologized for not being a better father.

"Giovanni ..." He looked at me. He was very weak, but his eyes were brimming with love. I took his hands in mine. "You know son, I named you. Your mother wanted you to be called Patrick, but the second I saw you the name jumped out at me."

I nodded. I'd never liked Giovanni, was embarrassed by such an ethnic name. I preferred to be called John or Johnny. Dad paused for a long moment, then continued.

"It's so strange. No bags to pack, I'm leaving with nothing. Nothing but what's inside. Most of what I did with my life was worthless, amounted to zero. If I could do it again, I'd spend more time with you and Nicky."

I started to interrupt. He put his finger to his lips.

"You're nine years old, Giovanni. I wish I didn't have to leave you." He looked down, then raised his eyes to mine. "Promise me, Giovanni, you'll never be like me, you won't lose yourself. Promise you won't forget what's important."

No words came. I just stared, in a state of shock. The light in his eyes faded. I stayed holding his hand for half an hour, until the nurse came in.

She checked Dad's vital signs, then looked at me. She put her hand on my shoulder.

"Are you okay?"

I wiggled away from her. "I'm good."

• • •

But I wasn't good. Even at nine years old, I covered my feelings, hid the profound loss and fear I felt at his death. I now saw that it had enabled me to deceive myself as well as the people around me.

I got to my feet and leaned against a tree. I'd forgotten how I loved him, and how much Dad loved me. My throat closed and long-repressed tears coursed down my face. Eventually I fell into a broken sleep. When I woke I felt as if I had a father again.

This was the strangest meditation I'd ever experienced, more torture than anything. It seemed as if the lid of my psyche had been pried off, and subconscious ghosts were spewing forth like an upchucking beast. I might have considered checking myself into the nuthouse had Ting not warned me.

The end of August. I'd been in the forest every day for a month. I called Phantom.

"Coach, I think I'm going to need a little more time."

"The fight is in five weeks. Take another week or two if it'll help. Then you got to come back to the gym. If you're in good spirits, two weeks is all I'll need. Well, what the fuck you doing out there, Lazio? Having fun?"

I went back to sitting.

On a humid afternoon in early September I'd sat for two hours, entering into a deep state of concentration. I took a break, jumped in the frigid stream, and swiped the water off my skin. By the time I climbed back up the hill to my sitting spot I was already sweating, but inside I felt refreshed. I crossed my legs and sat for another hour or so until a cool shadow crossed my face. I opened my eyes. The sun had gone; it would soon be dark. There was my friend, the well-fed rabbit, munching on the last grass of the season. A strong wind picked up a few yellow leaves, which made an almost imperceptible swish as they fell softly on the rocks. The swaying of the trees captured my attention. They creaked and groaned, and the leaves turned upside down and flapped. The entire forest seemed to be rocking. My body swayed slightly, back and forth in rhythm with the forest. A mosquito landed on my arm. I didn't notice it until its sting pierced my flesh. I squashed it. My senses were so acute I could smell the iron in the good-sized blob of blood that splattered on my arm.

Suddenly a huge brown hawk flashed through the twilight, pounced on the rabbit, and instantly broke its neck. The rabbit died with a single human-like wail of pain. The hawk strained for an instant, then flapped its wings and resumed flight with the lifeless body dangling from its talons.

I felt unsafe. Waves of panic poured over me. I tried to repress it but the feeling intensified. It felt like I was going to die.

A faint bubble floated from unknown depths and shifted into focus. Impossible! How could this be remembered? I never knew it happened! I sat in meditation and watched as if it were a movie, but the feelings soon became real.

Six years old. I was in the hospital under anesthesia. My appendix was being removed. The doctors were so focused on the operation they didn't notice I had vomited. Or that vomit had filled my throat and nose and was cutting off my air supply. I was unconscious, choking on my own vomit. I was dying but no one knew it!

I knelt on the forest floor. Darkness had descended like a claustrophobic blanket. There was no moon. I hadn't been afraid of the dark since I was a little boy, but I felt an elemental fear now. I wanted to escape, run away, flee, but there was no place to go. I wondered if I'd lose my mind, and that filled me with more panic.

Let yourself go, a voice said.

I put my head down on the ground. Though I hadn't eaten since breakfast, a huge amount of vomit came up. My throat, diaphragm, and abdominal muscles strained but only bile came out. Still the urge persisted. I held my head in my hands and dry-heaved, terror gripping my guts. Stomach acid shot out, with the faint odor of anesthesia.

Fear. Completely out of control. Every muscle and nerve was firing. Elemental panic. I was plunging into an abyss of fear, a beginning swimmer suddenly in deep water, weightless, over his head, nothing beneath the feet. I wanted to touch ground, scrambled to reach, but it was fathomless. There was nothing I could do to help myself.

I was fighting to keep control, but control of what? *If you can keep your head when all about you are losing theirs...* I thought desperately, *force your heart and sinews—*

No, Kipling was wrong! *Stop fighting.*

Now is the crucial moment.

I leaned back against the tree and allowed the fear to engulf me. Death was near me. No—it was within, part of me, but, this time, I didn't fight. I let it take me, relaxed into it, surrendered.

The transformation was instantaneous. I was a leaf on the water, taken by a powerful current. Relaxed, effortlessly centered, I was here, really in my body for the first time in my life.

A striking realization: I had never known who Giovanni Lazio was. Perhaps there never was a Giovanni Lazio, only a confused man trying to be a clone of someone else. I'd tried to be a confident leader like Sensei, to possess the childlike serenity of Master Ting, but my knowledge was borrowed from Lao Tzu, Sun Tzu, Buddha, Krishna, Jesus, and Confucius. I followed instructions. When the shepherds blew their horn I did what was expected. But I could never be like my teachers. *I no longer wanted to be like them.* It felt as if I were wearing a hundred layers of other people's clothes. More than anything I needed to take them off, to be naked. I needed to be me.

After thirteen years of intense effort, all I'd achieved was deep frustration. I had to laugh out loud. There was no possibility of finding peace or easiness. You can't find no mind by trying; you have to stop trying.

A tremor began somewhere in my body. I tried to find its origin and traced it to the inside of my leg. I watched it as it spread out stronger and stronger, until my whole body was shaking like a chicken trying to hatch out of an egg. If I was going crazy, so be it. I no longer cared but laughed like a madman. I had to get up and move, start dancing to an unfamiliar rhythm. How long this went on I'm not sure. It could have been an hour or minutes. My mind went blank, and with the cessation of thought a deep bliss replaced the numbness that had engulfed me for years. I was alive, incredibly alive. My eyes were closed but I didn't need to see. I felt each tree, leaf, and blade of grass pulsing with energy. It wasn't just energy but consciousness, awareness, and love. And this also was me: I vibrated with pure awareness, pure love. Only the faintest remnant of Giovanni Lazio remained like a faraway dream. Mostly I was part of the forest, part of all life.

After some time the vision faded, and I knew I'd never be the same. I'd seen what I'd come here to find. The old had to unravel, fall completely apart. This was Shu's little death. I understood now. But there was something more—what Cindy and Phantom had hinted at—and they were right! It had happened to Macomber, and to me.

When tapping into primal fear, it's natural to want to run away, to escape, to flee in panic as quickly as possible. But with some situations, such as being pounded senseless, or choking to death on your own vomit during anesthesia— you can't escape. The body can't go anywhere. Something on the inside, a part of you, goes instead. You could call it back, train yourself to will it back into the body. That had become my specialty; that's what Kipling did. He willed it back. But it's not enough. A shocked soul is like a rabbit ready to bolt. When the fear comes, you're gone like a whiff of smoke. Until a man makes peace with death, real death, or even more profoundly, death of his identity, fear will always haunt him. He won't be at home. His soul won't be rooted in his body.

All my life I'd sought to be a man but never knew what that was. Being a kick-ass fighter doesn't make you a man, nor does being a great lover. It's *this*. When a man's in his body he can be counted on, and he can count on himself to see the small details.

I gathered my few possessions and made my way through the moonless night, no longer fearful or brave but strangely neutral, in between fear and courage, unconcerned as to what would happen next.

TWENTY-FIVE

Ten minutes before the fight, the usual knock came at the door of my dressing room. I was expecting Phantom to stick his head in as he always did, but again, a steady *rap, rap, rap.*

I called out, "You know the door's open!"

"It's Omura. May I come in please?"

I stood up and opened the door wide.

"Of course!" I bowed. "Come in, Sensei."

Omura took a deep breath and sighed. His eyes were quiet.

"I've studied karate a long time, but the older I get the more I realize how little I know."

I just looked at him and waited.

"Evangeline brought me the DVD of the Haines fight."

"Lena did that? Why?"

"To get me to look at things differently. She feels very strongly about your being in our lives. The DVD sat on my table for a week, but finally I watched it. I've thought about it for a long time."

I looked at Sensei's face, saw that he was struggling for the right words.

"In Japan failure brings shame. That's how I was raised. Here the way is different, people are different. What I said to you, it's not so black and white." Omura paused for a long while. "There are some students in the dojo I'd like you to work with."

"I'll stop by next week," I said.

He bowed.

I bowed back, and almost as if my body had a will of its own, I gave him a brief hug. It was surprising and a bit awkward. In all our years together we'd never even shaken hands, always bowed.

What physical contact we had was in sparring, throwing, or his correcting my posture. His impenetrable eyes gleamed.

There was another knock on the door. Phantom came in and took in the whole scene. He looked at Sensei, put one hand on his stomach and the other on his back, and bowed low like a butler. Then slapped me in the back of the head.

"You ready, kid?"

I nodded.

Morales had stated with great assurance that he'd beaten me before and he'd have no trouble finding my number again. There was a slight prefight knot in my gut, but inside I was loose. I listened to the ref's instructions. We touched gloves. This time there was no "Good luck, Johnny" or flashing smile. *How unbelievably strange!* Here was the man who hit me so hard I almost heard angels sing. But there was no ill feeling. On the contrary, I felt deep respect, the camaraderie of brothers. I'd bowed a million times, but this was the first time I understood exactly why men bow in karate.

Morales moved out throwing crisp jabs. He pressed me tightly. He and his trainer must have gone over the tapes of my fights just as carefully as Phantom and I had looked at his. His strategy was obvious. Last fight he'd been hurt by my legs, so he tried to keep me at a fixed range: too close for me to kick and just far enough away so he could use his reach and boxing skills to advantage.

He threw leather fast. He connected with a left that hurt, but not so much as a jab of Sandoval's. A short straight right hit my arms, and he twisted his body into a hard left hook. I moved my head slightly and Morales hit nothing but air, stumbling slightly off balance. I jumped into a thrust kick that pounded his open flank. At this point, all preconceived strategies dropped away. Focusing intensely, we circled, throwing hard punches and kicks, looking for an opening and watching for the slightest sign of weakness.

I increased the pace with stiff leg kicks that knocked him off balance. But Morales blocked my straight kick and caught me with a looping overhand right. The old fizzle of electricity burst in my brain. Morales was all over me with strong punches. He backed me into a corner and surprised me with an uncharacteristic roundhouse kick to the ribs. The audience cheered loudly. It was a brawl right from the start. *At this pace someone's getting knocked out.* I wormed out of the corner and back to the center of the cage. Morales followed.

He was far more polished than the last time we'd fought, and even with all Phantom's help, his lightning hands were still quicker than mine. I slipped his left, ducked under a right, and got tagged by a right uppercut left hook combination that put me on the canvas. I got up quickly. Sensei and Lena were sitting only a few feet away in the first row. It was pretty much the exact scene as our last fight, only a year later. Sensei had that same perturbed expression. Lena's face was pinched white with concern.

But although the outside may have been similar, the inside wasn't. I was strangely passionless, devoid of emotion, almost like a mirror. Every move Morales made, my body reflected. He threw a long left; I took a half-step back and came in with a right hook that opened a small cut above the eye. Blood began flowing into his eye and he was forced to wipe it with his left hand. I tried to hit the cut with my left to make the bleeding worse but the horn sounded, ending the round. During the break they staunched the bleeding in Morales's corner.

The next round, he charged in throwing punches I mostly deflected by hitting his bicep. I rolled with the few blows that connected. I'd always had trouble with Morales's overhand right, and I didn't see the one that hit my cheek, sending me back against the cage.

Morales charged forward. *He thinks I'm hurt more than I am.* Though a common strategy in combat, never in my fight career had I even dreamed of bluffing. I was always too rigid, too tightly wound to play. I leaned against the cage, putting myself up as bait, pretending to be dazed. Morales was so intent on finishing me he had no guard. I waited, calculating, measuring him with my left. The right followed and caught him on the point of the chin. He went down hard.

When he got to his feet, Morales rushed out to the center of the ring throwing punches. He was trying to show he wasn't hurt, but he was unbalanced. As he moved forward, my right leg swept his left leg out from under him. He hit the canvas. Sweeps such as these don't do damage, but they frustrate and disorientate a fighter. Morales got up slugging. I waded into the crucial zone, feeling the breeze from his desperate punches. They were still capable of damage, but I took the risk.

We were both swinging but I connected first with a hard left that sent Morales into the fence. He tried the overhand right, but this time I saw it coming. I blocked, bent his arm at the crook of the elbow, and spun him into a standing rear naked choke. In a split second he tapped out. It happened so quickly the crowd was stunned. For an instant, like the brief eye of a hurricane, there was dead silence. Then everything broke loose.

As I left the cage, Lena ran into me so hard she almost knocked me down. She kissed me on the lips for several seconds. I looked at her, and she smiled and dropped her eyes. It felt strange to taste Lena's mouth. I turned bright red, especially since Sensei was watching us. Even more surprising, he didn't seem upset.

I couldn't help but notice that Lena's lips were very soft.

A second later, a hand pounded my back. I turned around. Nick, his eyes shining.

"Not bad, Johnny!"

"That means a lot coming from you."

"Come to dinner on Sunday?"

"Can I bring something for your kids? What do they like?"

"They have too much stuff already, just show up."

"I'll be there."

Phantom strutted around like a proud father giving out cigars to anyone in reach.

"Lazio didn't even need his legs, he outboxed the boxer! I kept telling him he had it in him. It just took him a few fights to figure it out for himself."

Sensei was quietly ecstatic. He threw a party at a Chinese restaurant on Mulberry Street. The entire karate school turned out to honor my victory. Lena showed up, the only woman in attendance, sitting next to me. As was typical in these affairs, nearly everyone got drunk. As lavish toasts were made to my prowess as a fighter, Lena coughed and pretended something had gone down the wrong pipe. When Sensei lifted his glass and said. "John has proven himself as a warrior. He only has one more battle and then he will be champion," Lena pinched my thigh and winked for my eyes only. I'd never noticed how good-looking she was.

The evening ended and we all went our separate ways. On the drive out of the city I took stock of my situation. *Sure, I've proven myself.* I was a step away from the championship. It was everything I'd wanted. The sun was shining brightly but it didn't warm my skin.

For days afterward I distracted myself in every possible way. I worked out, saw friends, ate with Phantom and Sensei, tried to meditate. With some of the winnings from the fight I went to Jamaica, something I'd wanted to do for years. The coral sand and turquoise water were exquisite. But everywhere couples walked hand in hand, smiling into each other's eyes, touching and kissing. I watched them like a hungry dog.

I thought of Cindy. We'd had maybe ten visits, less than a day in a hotel room. My God! Was thirty hours all the time we'd spent together? So much had happened: massage, learning Thai, spirit houses, lost parts of the soul, gentle black eyes, bright spirit, sweet kisses. And the lovemaking—she was more than a memory, her essence lingered in my soul.

At night I strolled along the beaches alone, the softly breaking waves rolling onto shore, phosphorescence glowing like fireflies in the wet sand. Seemingly from inside the water came the sound of Cindy's sweet voice: "I have a surprise for you ... Tonight was best night of my life ... Tirak—I love you."

I kicked a bottle and it careened down the beach. Love? Finally, I had to admit it. Cindy had been my shaman, my horse whisperer, the one the diviner Shu had spoken about. Cindy touched me more deeply than anyone. Her intimacy cut to expose my most vulnerable core. She helped me to see myself, to remember something I'd once known but had forgotten. I knew, now, what I wanted. Love is the true path—the ultimate no mind. With love there's nothing to cling to. You must be naked.

I sat on the beach watching the sun burning like a ball of fire on the horizon. It hung for a while then suddenly dropped making the waves sparkle with orange and gold. *That night of the party,* Lena's joking and carrying on had been the same as always. But it wasn't the same. Even through her half-closed eyes I could feel the softness.

There was a strange flutter in my chest as I picked up my cell phone. Lena answered. "Johnny? What the! This is, well … the only time you've ever phoned me. I didn't think you even knew my number. What can I do for you?" she said flirtatiously.

"I'm coming home tomorrow afternoon. Can you pick me up at the airport?"

• • •

Ed promised he'd get me a title shot if I beat Morales, and Ed was a man of his word. But the fight wouldn't be until June of next year. It was a strange place to be: I'd beaten the worthy contenders of my division. I didn't need to fight. Didn't need the money, either. For the first time in my life I had a window of time to take it easy. Yet rest wasn't in the cards.

I'd talked about being a doctor with Cindy and joked about it with Mrs. Li. I didn't want to fight forever. *Perhaps it's time to stop moving my lips and start moving my feet, but what kind of doctor?* Everyone I spoke with was for allopathic medicine. The medical doctor had more prestige and commanded a better salary, but my experiences with Cindy and Mrs. Li showed me how powerful massage can be, and for years I'd played with Chinese herbs, made formulas for friends and to ease Ernesto's arthritis pain. Natural medicine was more my style.

But before naturopathy could even be considered, I had to first get a four-year science degree. And merely obtaining the piece of paper wouldn't cut it: naturopathic college was competitive, stellar grades were necessary. My forehead wrinkled in dismay. In length it was comparable to the many years I'd spent clawing my way through the martial arts. But karate had been a labor of love. I'd never been much of a student.

In September I enrolled in college and began the arduous courses. If it weren't for the discipline hammered into me by Sensei and Phantom, I'd never have made it past the first week. I spent so many hours in the math lab they threatened to charge rent. I left my house early and returned late in the evening. The college, two hours from my home, had become my new spot in the forest and my life revolved around it. By March of the following year, I knew it was time to leave the little cabin that had been my home since age eighteen.

As if to confirm my decision, Ernesto had to be put to sleep. His arthritis got so bad he couldn't get to his feet without assistance. He lost control of his bowels, and when I put him on his bed as I went off to school, he was down for the day and lying in his own feces when I returned. He was in a tremendous amount of pain, but it was still hard to let him go. Most people would have put him down long ago, but I had my own philosophy when it came to animals. If they were still enjoying life I kept them alive, convinced I could gauge their spirit through their eyes. Ernesto was a hard decision. Up till the very end he had a ravenous appetite. Once I lifted him to his feet he was game to walk down to the lake, and in the water his arthritis evaporated like a bad dream. He could swim for hours in the cold water. But the time came when hard days outnumbered the comfortable.

His was a body to hug, a heart into which I could pour my love. He loved me back without judgment. But now it seemed as if he'd done the job he came for and I had done mine. It was time to go. On his last day he ate the best steak money could buy and swam a couple of miles in the lake. I buried him in the forest behind our home. Within the week I'd found an apartment in the city.

• • •

The ringing of the phone jarred me awake. The clock showed 12:55. Lena muttered, "Who on earth has the nerve to call this late?"

"How should I know?"

I picked up the phone and said a harsh hello.

"Johnny?"

"Yes, who is this?" The connection was scratchy. I had to strain my ears to hear.

"Sawatdee ka. It's been a long time."

My adrenalin surged, instantly clearing my sleep-numbed brain.

"Cindy! How are you? Where are you?" I sat back down at the table, pressed my ear to the phone. I closed my eyes and focused all of my senses on hearing her voice.

"I'm in Thailand, and yes I'm good. How have you been?"

"Very busy." I caught her up on the major events of my life in the eight months since I'd seen her.

"You be a great doctor."

"Thanks, but it will be a very long time before anyone calls me doctor. Besides Mrs. Li."

"Oh," Cindy said. "Do you see Mrs. Li?"

"Not since last summer. I'd called for you and she told me you'd gone home. I went only to get your note, but she got another treatment out of me."

"I not surprise. Mrs. Li love you treatment. So do I."

"But you want to hear something far out? I moved to the city. My new apartment is on West Thirty-Second, not far from Asia House."

"That good, easy for you to go there."

"I don't go there. After you I have no desire to go."

"Kop khun ka."

"Did you start your business?"

"I have dress shop now, Johnny. Three girls sew for me, and one work behind the counter. But with money I bring back from the states I rich. I don't have to work."

"What do you do then?" I asked.

"I help my family, good to be home for that. I don't see them for so many year, so now we catch up."

"That's nice," I said. "What time is it in Thailand?"

"About noon, I just finish lunch."

"It's almost one in the morning here." I opened my eyes and watched a large moth fluttering around the light.

"Oh, I forget about time difference," she said. "Sorry to disturb."

"No, I'm happy to speak with you."

We were quiet for a minute, then she asked, "Did you find your woman yet?"

"As a matter of fact, you woke her up."

It was very faint, but I heard the long sigh that came from halfway around the world. There was a burning sensation in my gut that rose into my throat. I tried to make my voice smooth.

"What about you?"

"You don't believe, but I meet farang man. He teach English in my town. He speak Thai very good. The big news is we married and I with baby!"

"Wow! That was fast, Cindy. Congratulations."

There was a long pause I had no idea how to fill.

"Do you ever think about me?" she said finally.

"I've often thought about you, but there was no way to get in touch."

I strained to hear her voice.

"I get Mrs. Li's letter, tell me to call you. Now I married woman, I don't know if I should. But today I get massage, and memory of our time together so strong, I have to call."

Memories flooded my brain, details from my ten visits with Cindy.

"The reason I wanted to speak to you is ... I never told you how I felt."

"Mai pen rai, I with so many man—I can feel—I know you love me, Johnny, I always know. No need to say."

"I wanted to tell you that. And I wanted to tell you that you helped me, you ..."

"Mai pen rai," Cindy said.

Mai pen rai! The Thai words for *it's okay, you're welcome, it's all right, never mind*. No matter how great the debt it was always mai pen rai.

"No! Not mai pen rai. You healed me."

Cindy laughed. "I told you I good luck for you." And then she added, "And you good luck for me, too. Don't worry, Tirak, we do what we come together to do. Now you be doctor and I have what I always want."

"He's a lucky man."

"Kop khun ka."

• • •

For a minute I sat at the kitchen table, my face in my hands. Lena came out.

"That was an awfully friendly conversation," she said. "Who the hell is she?"

I took her in my arms and held her.

"A friend."

"A friend? Don't lay that bullshit. I heard you talking."

"We were lovers, but she's married now. Now she's just a friend—a very dear friend."

"Listen, you're not getting off the hook so easily. We've known each other for a long time, Johnny. When did you fit her in? You're going to tell me all about her, and who the fuck is Mrs. Li?"

"It's a long story. I *want* to tell you about it but it's going to take a while, and it's late. Let's go to sleep, okay?"

Lena snaked her arm around my waist and leaned her head against my shoulder. We walked the few steps into bed. She kissed me and snuggled against my side. In a few seconds she was asleep. I stayed awake savoring the warmth of her skin, her scent, and the rise and fall of her breath. Thoughts passed like fluffy clouds in a blue sky: an important test coming up in school, Nicky's daughter has a birthday next week. I stretched fully out. As sleep overtook my body my leg jerked slightly. A last thought flitted through my mind: the championship fight, just a few months away. My breath flowed easily. I'd take it as it came but—for now at least—I was home.

THE END

www.ingramcontent.com/pod-product-compliance
Lightning Source LLC
Chambersburg PA
CBHW021427110726
47901CB00008B/2329